Barry Dobey

A Burning Grudge

Contents

1

Differences With The Donaldsons.

April 2019

It was 6.00pm. Don Mason opened the front door and faced the mob that had gathered there. Ray Donaldson and his brothers, Mick and Jimmy were holding baseball bats and their friends Gary Blewitt, and Craig Thompson were holding large knives. Abe Gardener and Sammy Dodds were elsewhere.

The rest of the mob consisted of a number of Don's neighbours.

The Mcevoy brothers, Vince, Dean Joe and Alan were all half cousins of the Donaldsons, unbeknown to Don.

They had broken up an antique hardwood table from one of the empty houses and each held a table leg.

Mark and Amie Nesworth were a couple in their early thirties. Mark was scared of what might happen if they didn't support the Donaldsons, so they had picked up kitchen knives and joined the mob.

Zac and Moira Walker were both in their seventies. They had known Donaldson's father, Fred for many years before he died. They didn't have weapons, but had come along to support Ray, knowing that not supporting him could have consequences later.

Colin Markem was an old friend of the Donaldsons, again unbeknown to Don. Colin had been entrusted with keys to the gate. He had let the Donaldsons in.

Ray Donaldson's son Alec was standing behind his father holding a hunting knife. He was passing it from hand to hand, grinning at Don as he did it. Ray's wife Kylie was standing with him, holding a can of cider in one hand and a cigarette in the other.

Don gave a cold look towards the people before him and said nothing.

Ray Donaldson stepped forward. 'Come out here Mason, your time's up. We'll make it quick. You know you're not walking away from this.' Don said nothing. He felt sick looking around the neighbours who had betrayed him and let Donaldson and his thugs into the street, after all he had done to make their lives safer.

Ray stepped towards the gate at the end of Don's front garden. 'You see Mason, things have changed. If my son wants to hurt somebody, he hurts somebody, simple as that. It's ok now, you see. He can do what he wants out there, as long as he brings back what we need. Things were complicated back then, police, court, social services, there's no law now Mason, no law now. You can lock yourself away in there for as long as you like, but when you eventually come out, I finish it. You know you can't stay in there forever, might as well come out now.'

Don looked into Ray's eyes then he looked across at Alec Donaldson. 'It's the first time I've seen all your family together Alec, you don't half look like your uncle Jimmy.' He looked back into Ray Donaldson's eyes, 'you know, Ray I never figured you as a clever bloke, quite the opposite, but you have just made a very, very pertinent point. Your so right saying that there's no law now. It sums everything up in a nutshell. No fucking law now.' He looked around the group, Ray, his family, his hangers - on, the disloyal neighbours, then back at Ray, 'I've no intention of locking myself away, Ray. I accept your offer to come out now.'

As the others in Donaldson's group approached the front gate, Don stepped back into the doorway and reached into the house with his left hand.

* * *

November 1979.

There had been a bad incident in the alley, which was known as the cut, between Haig Road and Hollymount square, that morning. A gang led by Ray Donaldson had cornered Peter (Punter) Grayson and pushed him around before Donaldson had punched him to the ground. Punter was fifteen years old, blonde hair and average height for a boy his age, but quite thin. He was one of the very clever lads in Don's group of friends and he hated trouble.

Ray was sixteen years old and quite tall and well - built for his age. He was from the Donaldson family that lived in Cornwall Crescent. The Donaldsons all looked alike, spitting images of their dad. They were three brothers who looked identical, square headed, unusual round ears that stuck out and they all looked slightly cross eyed. They were quite disturbing, in that they always had the same facial expression, a kind of grin, where they curled up their top lip that made them look odd. They all had dark hair with buzz cut hairstyles, just like their dad. They were one of those families that your first instinct would be to have a laugh at if you saw them all together, but you would know it wasn't a good idea to do so. Brothers Mick and Jimmy were in the gang, surrounding Punter, with Sammy Dodds, Gary Blewitt, Craig Thompson and Abe Gardener.

Unfortunately, while Punter was being pushed around, he hadn't seen the punch coming so the blow had struck his right eye and, with no form of defence Punter had took the full force of the blow to his eye and dropped to the ground. He lay still, semi - conscious and unaware of what was going on around him.

Sammy Dodds rolled Punter over. 'Shit, look at his eye.' Punter's eye had swelled up and there was watery, red fluid running down his face. Ray pulled Sammy back. Sammy lived a few doors along from the Donaldsons, He was short and stocky, fair haired and freckled faced. He didn't mind pushing people around, but saw no sense in beating people up. 'Ray man, there was no need to punch him, we were just giving him a scare.' 'Fuck him.' Ray stepped towards Punter and kicked him in the ribs.

Mrs. Coates from nine Cornwall Crescent, just a few doors from the Graysons had seen the commotion and dropped her shopping bags and hurried to Punter's aid. As the gang scattered, she screamed at them, 'you bullies! I would tell your parents, but they're just as stupid as you idiots. Get away from here and don't come back.'

Mavis Coates was in her mid - fifties. She had never married, spending her adult life caring for her mother. It wasn't that she didn't want, or hadn't had past relationships, just none had worked out for her due to her commitment to others. She had never found a man that was happy to come second. She knew all of the kids in the neighborhood and was always knitting clothing for the new - born children. Mavis shopped and baked for the elderly residents in the street. Nothing was too much trouble for Mavis and she was returning from an errand for old Jack next door when she had come across this assault.

Mavis took Punter's hand. He had come around and started to cry with the pain and shock. 'Peter, I'm just going to the end of the cut and I'll ask Mrs. Allison to ring for an ambulance.'

An ambulance took Punter away, with both of his parents following in their white Vauxhall Viva.

At around four o'clock pm Mark Mijeson (Midgy) had come to the Masons' in Hollymount Square and told Don and his dad what had happened.

'Punter's got a detached retina in his left eye, Mace. Ray Donaldson and his gang beat him up in the cut. Kicked him on the ground and everything. They're operating tomorrow morning. He's in a really bad way. These arseholes are getting out of control. We can't walk past them without them starting something.'

Don Mason was furious. 'We need to do something about this bastard. He can't get away with what he's done. Every time we see the bloke, he's goading us and now he's hurt one of the lads. I'm going to get the lads together and arrange to give him a good hiding.'

Don Mason (Mace) was fifteen years old. He was very fit and took part in all the school sports, football team, rugby, cricket, he loved all sports. Don ran every day down the footpath through the woods, up the bank to the Bank Top pub and back from Stead lane, past the Terrier pub and up Dene View, towards home, about four miles. He had mousy brown hair and wore Reebok Tee shirt, jeans and Reebok trainers. He was wearing a navy Parka coat over the tee shirt, ready to go out with Midgy. Don was a good-looking young lad, only child of Jack and Lydia Mason.

Jack Mason knew the Donaldsons well. He had worked at Bates Colliery all his working life and Donaldson's father, Fred had worked the same shift for years. Fred was what the men called a neck - ender, an idiot who craved trouble every minute of the day. He would knock bait tins and drinks over at break time, throw coal at men when their backs were turned, the worst kind of idiot to be ten miles underground with. He knew that Ray Donaldson was just like his stupid father.

Jack shook his head, 'Don son, you and your friends need to learn that there's some people you can't knock sense into. You called Ray Donaldson a bastard and if he was a bastard a good hiding would teach to him to leave you all alone in the future, but that lad isn't a bastard, son. That lad is like his stupid father. He's a cunt.

Down the pit, one of the first things you learned was the difference between a bastard and a cunt. A bastard will push your buttons, provoke you, even take a punch at you, but even if you take a beating, if you go at the bastard and strike him back, he'll learn to leave you alone in future. Cunts are different, though. A cunt will provoke you, hit you spit on you, anything and no matter how you respond, even if you give him the beating of his life, he'll just do the same again the next time he sees you.

Down the pit, cunts were sent to Coventry. No one spoke to them or acknowledged their presence. Fred Donaldson had no friends at work, just brothers, all as stupid as him. When the Deputy put him on a final written warning he had to stop being such a cunt, or get the sack, but while he behaved himself at work, he was a cunt at the Market Place Club, knocking drinks over, insulting men in front of their wives, pushing people around, until the committee barred him. If you start a feud with these idiots, you need to consider that cunts have no boundaries. He'll just keep coming back like his stupid father. Let this pass. I don't want Fred Donaldson or his in - bred family putting our windows out, or worse.'

Don was still fuming. Midgy told him the others were all at Clarky's place so they left to meet up with the lads.

They got together in Clarky's dad's wash house in Hollymount square, just along the road from Don's house. Hollymount square was a double row of around fifty-five houses, built early 1900s in the form of a circuit. The centre circuit of houses all had original wash houses and were adjoined by high walls between the houses, so all the back gardens were in the middle of the complex. The outer row of houses started at one entrance on the front street of Bedlington and was built the same way, in a circuit around the interior row and the entrance road led all the way around to an exit back onto the front street. One way in, one way out, if you like. The back gardens, from entrance to exit overlooked the newly built Whitley memorial school, Welfare park, Bedlington Terriers football pitch then finally Hollymount Avenue, the next rows of housing down. An alley way half way down connected to Welfare Park and there was an alley further down again, where the incident had occurred, which adjoined Cornwall Crescent, leading to Haig Road and Beatty Road. Both Don and Clarky's parents lived in houses that overlooked Welfare Park and Bedlington Terriers football pitch on the exterior row.

Ian Clark (Clarky) was the brains of the group of friends. He had that dark ginger hair that looked like copper wire. He was tall and thin and was wearing jeans, sandshoes and a khaki tee shirt with the logo 'Don't push me.' He could work anything out and Don knew he'd already have a plan for singling Ray out for his beating.

Midgy spoke first, 'Mace's dad doesn't want us to wedge Ray Donaldson. He thinks it would be a bad mistake getting into a feud with them.'

Davy Dawson (Dowser) was sitting on a table beside the window. He was wearing black adidas samba trainers and adidas tee shirt with washed out jeans, dark haired and well - built for a fifteen-year-old. He had a khaki parker on. Dowser wasn't scared of the Donaldsons, 'what! why did you tell your dad, Mace?' 'He was there when Midgy told me.' 'So what? We just let this arsehole away scot free? Fuck that!'

Clarky spoke up, 'We may not need to bray him. How big is their bonfire on the wood head? Anyone fancy a look?'

Every bonfire night the Donaldsons, with the help of kids from Cornwall Crescent and Beatty Road built a massive bonfire at the top of the woods, behind Beatty Road. They spent the whole of October going around the neighborhoods asking for scrap wood, old doors, pallets, then set it all alight November fifth.

The lads left the wash house and headed for the woods, glancing at the massive wood pile as they passed. It was something to behold. Pallets round the outside enwrapping scrap timber, doors, fallen branches from the woods, anything that would burn. They had even got a telegraph pole that was the central support, standing tall through the centre of the pile. Clarky had a massive grin.

They all sat on the wall of the stone bridge at the bottom of the woods, about a mile on and Clarky spoke. 'It's Wednesday today and bonfire night is Saturday. Who's up for setting the Donaldsons' bonfire alight Friday night? Ray Donaldson will be gutted if his pride and joy goes up in flames a day early. Lighting that fire's his big moment. Let's wipe the stupid fucking grin off his face without a punch being thrown.'

Dowser and Midgy looked down. They didn't have to say anything. Clarky continued, 'It's ok lads, I know we'll be in deep shit if they find out it was us, I don't expect you to come, but I'm going to do it. All I ask is we tell no one. I'll go alone.' 'I'm coming with you.' Don had a massive smile on his face. 'Dad said not to get into a feud, but you can't get into a feud with someone who doesn't know who hit them. This will hurt Ray Donaldson far more than a beating. Clarky, you are a fucking genius.'

Friday turned out to be a real bad day for Ray Donaldson. He'd been in front of the head teacher for pulling pornographic magazines out of his school bag with his school books in his English lesson and he'd got detention, even though he had insisted they had been planted there.

Ray had also come in from games, his last session of the day, got dressed and put his hand into a pile of dog shit that someone had put into the pocket of his jacket. Ray spent the detention session, along with a few others, suffering the strong smell of shit that he was unable to get off his hands, as well as the smears left inside his school blazer, which was rolled up and on the floor.

It was Clarky. He'd gone into Ray's form class and planted the magazines in his bag at lunchtime and slipped out for a toilet break during the last session of the day and crept into the changing rooms with his surprise package for Ray's jacket pocket. Clarky was no tough guy, but he was not a guy to be fucked with and Ray had no idea of the magnitude of mistake he had made by punching Punter.

After school, the lads went into Ashington Hospital to visit Punter. He was in good spirits and he'd been told the surgery had been a success in reattaching the retina. He had a large dressing over the eye, which everyone found quite amusing. The conversation soon turned towards the Donaldsons and Punter wasn't keen on seeking revenge. He told Clarky he thought it was a bad idea to burn down the bonfire, 'If they find out it was you, they'll come after you,' but Clarky just laughed, 'well at least you've got a good alibi Punt. No, those fuckers are going to get some back, mark my words.'

At 7.00pm the ward cleared of visitors and the lads took the 401-bus home to Bedlington Market place and hung out till around 10.00. Don had told his dad he was sleeping over at Clarky's. Clarky's parents liked a drink and they landed home from the Market Place Club at around 11.30. After a few large spirits they were soon in bed and sound asleep.

Don and Clarky put their wool jumpers and parka coats on. Everyone had a parka in those days. They slipped out of the back door. Clarky had a paper bag full of dry straw and a small Panda Pop bottle filled with paraffin, which his dad used for a small greenhouse heater. There were dry kindling sticks in the bag with the straw, the kind his parents used to light the coal fire. Clarky looked at Don, 'got the matches?' 'I certainly have.' 'Ok Mace, this is how it goes down. We'll go down to the Picnic Field and double back along the river to the woods below Beatty Road. We slip up through the trees and up to the back of the wood pile. You keep watch and I get inside and light this lot. Then we leg it back to the Picnic Field' Don was shaking with fear and excitement, 'Sounds like a plan, let's do it.'

It was 1.00am when the two headed out. They left Hollymount Square onto the front street. It was dead quiet, no one around, not even a stray Friday night drunk. Lucy's night club at Bedlington Station closed at 2.00am, so it would likely be quiet until then. They quickly headed down the steep bank to Atlee Park, known to the locals as the Picnic Field.

The Picnic Field was a large grassed area, that got its name because of the annual Miners' picnic. Every year colliery bands paraded through Bedlington on Picnic Day and made their way to the Picnic Field. There was a large stone band stand on the level area of grass near the river Blyth and the grassed area led uphill towards Farmer's fields, that went on to Humford woodland picnic area. Humford had previously been an outdoor swimming pool, but closed down in recent years due to poor council funding. Humford was a popular spot for days out with the kids or dog walking, as it was a central access to the woods in all directions.

Don and Clarky took the Picnic Field footpath back towards what is now Bedlington Country Park and within five minutes they were at the bottom of the large grassed slope that led down from the rear of Beatty Road to the river. They took the path to the top and slipped along a small dirt track through the embankment of shrubs at the edge of the grassed area.

The wood pile was massive, possibly the biggest they had ever seen there. Don was a bit apprehensive. 'Are you sure you want to go through with this Clarky?' 'Fuck yes, look, there isn't a single light on down Beatty Road. In and out and we leg it back to the farmer's field at the top of the Picnic field to watch the fire.

Clarky put a pair of rubber gloves on that he'd taken from his mother's kitchen to prevent having the smell of paraffin on him if they were stopped by police. He opened the paraffin, poured it over the sticks and straw, dropped the empty bottle into the bag and took the matches from Don. 'Keep watch, whistle if you see anyone.'

Don kept look out as Clarky crawled into the centre of the pile. He laid the bag on its side struck a match and lit the straw. As he crawled back, he carefully removed the gloves and threw them in with the bag. Clarky slipped back across the field to Don and they sprinted down towards the Picnic field. They ran flat out along the riverside path, under the large stone bridge and past the band stand, eventually reaching the top of the grassed slope. It was pitch black dark, but from the vantage point they were at, they could make out the flickering of firelight coming out from the darkness in the direction of Beatty Road and the fire light grew and grew.

In about fifteen minutes there was a massive fire behind Beatty Road. It was blazing, a sight to behold and soon there were blue lights flashing and a huge commotion. They could see silhouettes of people running back and forward with buckets of water and police men and firemen trying to keep them a safe distance away. It was chaos, people were shouting and screaming. Clarky and Don watched for about twenty more minutes, then crossed the farmer's field and doubled back along Church lane to the front street. The street was quiet, but they waited until another fire engine and another police car had passed, before sprinting down the street and into Hollymount Square. They did a huge high five when they got back into Clarky's wash house. The mission had been a success.

The following morning around 10.00, Guy Fawkes Day, Midgy was at Dowser's door.

Midgy was excited, like he had something he was bursting to tell everyone, 'we need to get to Clarky's, you've got to hear this one.' The two lads ran all the way to Clarky's.

In the wash house 'war room' Midgy relished the news he was about to impart. 'I heard my mam talking to one of the neighbours about the fire last night. Firemen didn't put it out, they said it was best to let it burn out. It burned all night. The Donaldsons were trying to put it out with fucking buckets of water, man and Ray's welly went on fire, when he was stamping on some burning wood, he'd pulled out of the fire. The rubber sole on is boot melted, went up in flames and burnt his foot and leg. He couldn't get the boot off because it was on fire and he had molten rubber all over the bottoms of his feet, by the time somebody got there with a bucket of water. He's in the fucking Burns Unit at Newcastle General.' They all howled with laughter.

Clarky stood up from the seat he'd taken, 'We don't tell anyone about this mind, especially now we know the cunt got hurt. Looks like we won't be seeing Ray for a while.' Don stood up, 'I think we should go over and have a look at the fire. If anyone had seen us, they'd have been looking for us long before now. Everybody in the area will be having a look, we'll just go with the crowd. Try not to laugh, lads, were even for now.'

The lads walked through Cornwall Crescent and along the back of Beatty road, into the woods. A wide area of grass was scorched off and covered with ashes and there was burnt out debris, still glowing. There was a light breeze and every time the wind blew it picked up and scattered glowing embers. As they passed, there was still a lot of heat radiating from the remains of the fire. There were a lot of kids hanging about, so the lads made their way through the woods along to the top of the slope at the picnic field.

They never saw Ray Donaldson for some time after the fire, but when they did, he was his usual self, insulting, name calling, pushing people around, like the cunt Don's father had described. The bad news was that the stunt Clarky and Don had pulled that night hadn't taught Ray Donaldson a lesson at all.

Ray Donaldson never changed.

2

The Funeral.

Donald Mason left school in 1981, at sixteen years old, with average qualifications, four 'O' levels and five 'CSE's.' His father wasn't keen on Don working at the pit, so he'd arranged for Don to work at a friend's engineering business in Blyth and Don started his working life fetching and carrying for a tradesman and learning metalwork skills.

Don attended technical college and, over time became a skilled tradesman, making bespoke parts for engines, machines that were now obsolete. A lot of vintage car restorers came from all over the country and used the business for parts they were unable to obtain. If it had a spec. Don could make it.

Don's adult life started well, a decent paid job, good circle of friends, that had stayed together since childhood and he had married Lesley, the love of his life and bought a house on Bower Grange, one of the new estates in Bedlington at that time. Lesley had been in Nursing since leaving school and worked at Wansbeck General hospital.

Don and Lesley were happily married for thirty - five years and their Daughter, Melanie had married and given them two grand - children, Emma and Jamie.

Don enjoyed shooting and had a couple of .22 air rifles with good quality scopes. He would take Jamie to a shooting range at Dinnington, near Newcastle Airport, once a fortnight plinking targets.

Unfortunately, Don's life was to take a turn for the worst in 2018. It started in January, when Don's mother Lydia, now in her eighties was expressing concern about Dad. Jack had become forgetful over the last year, but this had worsened significantly at a quite rapid rate and a care manager From Northumberland NHS Trust was assigned. By March Jack was in a care home, diagnosed with Dementia and in rapid decline.

Don and Lesley supported Lydia to stay in her home in Hollymount Square, but she was never the same and Lesley had popped over to see Lydia, one afternoon and found her dead in bed. Cause of death was reported as a massive stroke.

This was devastating for Don, but worse was to come. In June of that year Lesley had become quite ill and after tests, they were told she was suffering Leukemia. She commenced treatment, but every intervention led to further complications and this was made even worse by what happened in August.

Emma, now fourteen and Jamie, twelve had stayed with Don and Lesley over the weekend, while Melanie and her husband Frank had gone away for a couple of days in York. They had booked a Spa hotel that had a golf course and the plan was for Frank to play golf and Melanie to use the spa during the day, then spend the evenings together, but they never arrived. Frank had made an error on the A1 southbound and overtook a tour bus, while being passed by a wagon. Both Melanie and Frank died in the accident.

Don and Lesley took custody of the grandchildren and supported them as best they could through the tragedy, the double funeral and the grief that followed, but Lesley never recovered from the blow of losing her daughter. She died on September 3rd peacefully in hospital with Don at her side.

Lesley's was the third family funeral in the space of a few months and Don had invited guests to the Northumberland Arms after the funeral, rather than back to the house. He just couldn't do it again. There were hundreds of people at the Crematorium. Lesley was very well known, both socially and through her nursing career.

Don stood outside Blyth Crematorium after the service and spoke with everyone who had attended as they came out. It was a Thursday afternoon, so a lot of people were returning to work or going home, but about thirty people were coming back to the pub for a drink. The friends kept together and stood back as Don shook hands and thanked people and as they filtered away,

Midgy came over with his wife Sandra.

Sandra had red hair and was attractive 55-year-old. The two had been married for 30 years and had purchased a property at Red House Farm, near Netherton. They had a grown-up daughter, Fiona, who worked for a sales company in Leeds. She hugged Don, 'We're coming back to the pub, Mace, Punter and Hope are here, hey, Dowser!' Dowser came across with his wife, Angie. Angie was 56 years old, dyed black short straight hair and very pretty. She had grown up in Hollymount square and had been friends with the group of lads since school and both her and Dowser had been together as far back as any of the group of friends could remember. They now lived at the Chesters estate at the top end of Bedlington, off Choppington Road.

Their two grown up children, Paul and Marie came over and consoled Don in turn. Dowser hugged Don, 'I'm so sorry mate, if there's anything I can do you know..' 'I know Dows, I know. Is Clarky coming?' 'Clarky's on duty Mace, but he said he's going to try to get away to join us for drinks in the North. Maeve's here though.'

Maeve Clarke was 50 years old, Clarky's second wife. He had split up with his first wife, Joan after he'd found she had cheated on him and he was so hurt by this he had sworn never to marry again. All this changed when Maeve came along though, she was very attractive, long brown hair, physically in very good shape. Maeve was a police officer and she'd met Clarky in Nottingham, during a training week and they had fallen head over heels for each other. Maeve had moved north to be with Clarky, after her two daughters Ruby and Simone had graduated and moved into careers. Clarky and Maeve lived at Dene View East, a way further down from Beatty Road, but their back garden overlooked the woods. It was the first home Clarky purchased many years back and he had done so much work to it over the years he couldn't bear to leave.

Maeve had taken a day off work to attend the funeral. Clarky had no kids of his own, but doted on Maeve's daughters. Maeve kissed Don on the cheek and hugged him. Maeve loved the group of friends and wives and felt she had to be there for Don. 'I'm sorry Ian couldn't be here, Don, he just couldn't get time off, but he said he'll definitely be at the pub later. We've both got tomorrow off though, to help you out.' 'It's ok Maeve, I know he has important stuff going on. I'll see him later.'

Punter and Hope came over, 'you ok Mace?' Punter put one arm around Don. 'We're here for you, Mace. Anything you need today, just ask.' Hope put her arms around Don and kissed his cheek. 'Lesley was a good friend, Don. We'll really miss her.' A tear rolled down her cheek. 'Thanks Hope, she was really fond of you.'

Hope Grayson was 45 years old, youngest of the group of friends. She had met Punter when she was nineteen, when the two of them had been working together at a factory on the Nelson Industrial Estate, Cramlington. There was an age gap, but they were inseparable and had married on Hope's twenty first birthday. Hope had long brown hair and was always smart in appearance, whether it be in a designer dress or just Jeans and top, she always looked well presented. Hope and Punter had a house at the Hartlands estate, at the top end of Bedlington, not far from the golf course.

The friends were all making a fuss of the kids as the last of the guests left and Don and the kids made their way to the limousine and travelled back to Bedlington.

The couples and guests had all got back to the pub first and when Don and the kids were dropped off at the market place Don could see Midgy standing outside. As Don got to the door Midgy stopped him and whispered, 'the Donaldsons are in the pub, Don, fucking Ray, Mick and Jimmy. Gary Blewitt and Craig Thompson are with them. They're making their mouths go from the back room, but everybody's just ignoring them. Looks like they've had a few, but you know the Donaldsons, they never could take their drink. Ray's got that fucking slapper, Kylie he married with him, what a boiler she is.' 'It's ok, Midgy, they'll disappear up to the Red Lion or the club for the cheaper drinks, soon, if they're not still barred. Just ignore the ignorant cunts.' 'I sent a text to Clarky, he said he's on his way.' 'Thanks, Midgy, now get the beers in man, I need a drink.'

Maeve had kept a table for Don and the kids and there was a pint and soft drinks ready for them. She knew Don had a taste for whiskey and there was a large Glenmorangie beside his pint. There was around 30 friends and family and Don gave the bar manager £300 and asked her to charge all the drinks to him, 'tell me when it runs out Lucy and I'll give you some more, but not those fuckers mind.' He glanced towards the Donaldsons. 'I know Don, they just rolled in a couple of hours ago, I couldn't do nothing about it.'

Don glanced over again. The back room was on the right side as you enter the pub and there was just a pool table inside and juke box on the wall. There was no dividing wall between rooms and Don could see all of the Donaldsons' company seated on bar stools in the pool table area.

As the afternoon went on most guests left and soon there were just the group of friends. The kids had gone with Franks parents to stay over, so Don could have a few drinks and he'd had a few pints and a couple of whiskies.

At about 4.00pm the Donaldsons group came through to the bar area and converged on the long table at the back behind Don's table. Don didn't acknowledge any of them. The usual crowd of aresholes were with Ray, with the exception of Abe and Sammy, who were down with that flu bug that was going around.

Ray was sniggering and spoke up from the group. 'What's the occasion Mason?' Don sat with his back to their group. He ignored Ray. He was still sitting with Maeve, seated on a bar stool at a small table and the couples were on tables they had pulled together around him.

Maeve looked over to Ray, 'It's his wife's funeral, Ray, as you well know.' Ray had that stupid grin on his face where he curls up his top lip. Everyone at his table were sniggering as he looked around them and he turned about on his stool, 'well I've always thought the only good Mason is a dead Mason.'

Don stood up, grabbing the hardwood stool he was sitting on and in one swoop smashed the stool full into Ray's face. Ray's stool went away from under him and he screamed in shock as he fell to the floor. Don grabbed him by the hair, lifted his head and in the space of a couple of seconds, he had viciously punched him in the mouth five times. Ray was so dazed by the first blow he was unable to raise his hands in defence and the blows to his mouth were extremely violent. Ray was laid out on the floor, blood pouring from his mouth. There were teeth on the carpet in front of his face.

Mick and Jimmy Donaldson quickly stood up and approached the table, but stopped when Midgy, Punter and Dowser stood up. Dowser pulled back his right fist ready to strike out, 'What the fuck are you going to do, Jimmy? Sit back down before I plant you, you fucking arsehole.' Don didn't speak to any of them. It was like he was in a daze. He took a few steps back, and looked at his right fist, that was still tightly clenched. He was unable to open his hand, but could see grazes on his knuckles. Don found himself standing at the bar. 'I'm so sorry, Lucy.' Lucy stepped forward, 'sorry for what? I never saw nothing.'

There was a commotion from Ray's table and Don turned around as Ray was being helped to his feet by his brothers. Midgy, Punter and Dowser were still stood up and Maeve addressed them all, 'I know all of you, Blewitt, Thompson, Kylie, Mick and Jimmy Donladson and I advise you all to go home. Get Ray to his feet and get out of here or I'm calling the station for back up. That was a bad thing you said, Ray, a very bad thing. You ought to be ashamed of yourself and you deserved what you just got. Help him out and go home, now, all of you.' Ray screamed, 'get off me!' and pushed away the brothers, 'I'm ok, I can manage.' He had an exaggerated speech impairment, due to the damage to his jaw and teeth. His wife, Kylie was crying hysterically and the company he was with were in shock.

Every confrontation they'd had in the past had led to Don and his friends backing down and walking away. Ray picked up a pint glass, smashed it on the table and lunged at Don.

As he pulled back his arm to strike Don with the glass, Ray went into a jerking motion, arched his back and fell to the floor. There was a loud crackling sound.

'Detective Clarke at your service sir, apprehending a Mister Burntfoot, who I believe is causing a disturbance.'

Plain clothes detective Ian Clarke was standing in the doorway holding a taser gun. 'Midgy, you are a fucking genius sir. You said these fuck heads would cause bother by tea time and you were exactly right.' He stood in front of Donaldson's company, 'now you lot can fuck off and if I see any one of you on the street again tonight you will be shot with one of these and spend the night in a cell.'

Ray's company, including his wife scuttled past everyone and out the door.

Clarky grabbed Ray's legs and asked Dowser to get the top half. Get this fucker into the back room, I want a word.' They carried Ray into the room, Dowser allowing Ray's head to catch the corner of the wall. He yelped. They dropped Ray onto the floor and Clarky sent Dowser out. Maeve came into the back room, 'Ian.' 'It's ok Maeve. We've all had bother with this fucker for years, including you, I'm finishing it tonight.'

Ray was spluttering blood from his facial injuries when Clarky put a heavy plastic bag in his hands. 'Hold this tight, Ray, I'm taking the tasers off. If you squeeze the plastic bag you won't get any further shocks.' Ray squeezed the bag and Clarky removed the tasers. He took the bag back off Ray and put it into his shoulder bag, along with the taser gun. Clarky then removed the rubber gloves he was wearing, right in front of Ray's face and knelt beside him.

'Listen up Ray, I've known you since we were kids and how old are you now? 57? And still the fucking cunt you were when you were 7, but it ends here. You've come here today and caused trouble at my friend's wife's funeral and that's crossed a line you didn't want to cross.

Now, you're going to get up in a minute and go through and apologize to Lucy, to my friends and to Don Mason.' 'Fuck you Clarky, fuck you! I'm making a charge for police brutality, look what you all did to me. I want the police, ring the police, Lucy!' Lucy looked away.

Clarky sighed. 'Well let's have it your way. Don't fucking apologize to anyone, get up and fuck off, go on. But one thing, Ray before you go. Ever since I got into the force I've been collecting. You know what I've been collecting, Ray? I've been collecting drugs and it's all for you. Every raid, every party, every dealer that I've confiscated coke from I've kept a bit and gradually filled a bag that I keep in a lock up. The bag I handed you when I took the taser off you was a kilo of cocaine. Your prints are all over it. Now, you fuck off without those apologies and assurances we will have no further trouble with you or your fucking in - bred family and you're going to get a visit from the drug squad. You fucker, I'll not only make you out to be the Bedlington drug Baron, but I'll put word around every dealer in the area, that you're making a take- over bid for their turf. I'll have you doing twenty years frightened to leave your cell or go for a shit or shower you fucking bastard.

And if I was you, I'd hurry back to Millfield, before Mick and Jimmy start spit roasting your missus, like they do when you're at work. Every time we bump into you in Bedlington you call our wives whores, but you married the Millfield bike. She gets fucked by every single one of your fucking neighbours, who tempt her into their house with a few cans of cider or a bottle of smart price vodka, when their wives are at work. She gets fucked by a different bloke every day of the week, including your own fucking brothers and you call our wives whores, you fucking mug. You start trouble every time you see us, you fucker and you couldn't even give it a break for a man's wife's funeral. You disrespectful fucking arsehole.'

Ray went quiet. 'OK I'll apologize, I don't want trouble with drug dealers, let me up.' He limped into the bar area, head down and apologized to Lucy, then he turned and apologized to Don and the friends. They all remained silent as he left.

Ray Donaldson had poor feeling in his right foot, due to the burns he suffered years back and he had a slight limp, made worse by the hurry he was in to get back home. He was furious. His own wife, friends and brothers had run off and left him. He was spitting blood from his mouth and his lower jaw was in unbearable pain. Even after the pounding his mouth had just endured, he still had that stupid semi grin, that just couldn't be wiped off his face. It wasn't a happy grin though.

When he got back home, Kylie wasn't there.

Mick and Jimmy Donaldson had never married and lived together two doors away, about half way along the left side of Millfield, looking from the front street. Ray knocked and, in a few minutes, Kylie stumbled out the front door, clumsily stamping her right foot into a high heel shoe. She had badly dyed long blonde hair and a bit too much badly applied make up.

Kylie was around five foot six, a size 18, but was wearing a size 14 short blue dress that appeared stretched to its limits and a navy velour track suit top over her top half, un zipped. She had mascara lines down either side of her face after her hysterical fit of crying at the pub and her lipstick was smudged. Kylie was struggling to keep he balance and, her shifting weight from one foot to the other, to avoid falling down made her look like she was dancing without music.

Ray stood at the front door and heard Jimmy call from where he was sat on the living room sofa, 'she was just having a drink with us till you got back, Ray, she was upset, poor lass.'

Neither brother had wanted to go to the door after abandoning Ray, particularly Jimmy, whose dick Kylie had just been sucking with Mick watching, on. Mick had the Donaldson curled top lip grin, eagerly waiting for his turn, when the knock came at the door.

Kylie had been drinking spirits with the brothers, on return home, about half a bottle of vodka in twenty minutes. She was drinking and they, as usual, were pretending to drink until she was blind drunk. Both brothers knew exactly how much alcohol opened Kylie's legs and her head was soon in Jimmy's lap and she had been sucking his dick, hungrily, just seconds after the third glass of vodka and coke she had downed.

Ray dragged Kylie back home.

After being slapped around the living room, punched and kicked a couple of times, Kylie called for a taxi and took Ray to Cramlington accident and emergency.

Back at the pub Clarky had some explaining to do. It seemed ok with Maeve that Don Mason had nearly taken Ray Donaldson's lower jaw off, but Clarky wasn't getting away with his part.

'What the fuck was that, Ian? Where did you get the taser,' 'Eileen?' 'Eileen? I thought she would be involved.' Eileen was a uniformed officer that had been a friend and colleague of Clarky since he joined the force. They were like two peas in a pod and even though Clarky had gone into detective work, they still spent any time they could together when he was at the station. To Clarky, Eileen was one of the lads, as good a friend as anyone he knew.

Maeve had her arms folded, 'So Eileen gave you a taser, that one's explained, so now what about a fucking kilo of cocaine, Eileen loaned you that as well?'

Clarky sat quiet with a huge grin. He put his hand into his shoulder bag and passed the package to Maeve. It was thick grey plastic, like what deliveries are often wrapped in, heavily taped around a dense, heavy pack. Maeve tore the tape back and opened one end of the pack. She turned it over and the pack dropped onto the table from inside. There were howls of laughter when the kilogram bag of Bero self - raising flour hit the table. Clarky grinned, 'I thought we might make a few scones Saturday?' 'For fuck's sake Ian.'

Lucy was crying with laughter behind the bar. She had pulled a round of drinks for everyone. 'These are on me, people and after that, does anyone want to see this CCTV footage before I delete it?'

Dowser stood up. 'Aye, the tooth removing stool incident and taser for me, can you burn it onto cd?'

Maeve wasn't laughing. 'I've known you a long time, Ian and these friends have known you even longer and this thing you have about Ray Donaldson isn't healthy. Every time he insults someone, causes trouble, you find a way of getting back at him and so it goes on. Just a month ago he insulted us and you bit back, then he threw a drink over us in the Red Lion. You went over to Millfield in the middle of the night and slashed his van tyres.'

'Well all he has to do is stop being such a cunt, you know? How do you feel walking into a pub and seeing him, knowing he's going to call me a pig, or call you a fucking whore, with that disturbing fucking grin? I just don't let him get away with it. If bad fortune comes his way, it's normally in response to his actions, what am I supposed to do?' 'Ian, this has been going on for forty - odd years. You know the kind of person Ray Donaldson is. You deal with worse versions of him all the time in the city. You know people like that don't stop being idiots. Some of the stunts you have pulled over the years have probably contributed to what happened today. It was awful, Ian. Ray Donaldson really hates you and your friends. You can't tell me he doesn't know that misfortunes that come his way aren't down to you lot. You're the only people around here not scared of him.' 'He's in his mid - fifties Maeve and still making as much trouble as he was when he was a kid and his idiot son is just as bad as he was.' 'All I'm saying, Ian is don't take it too far. Don't drop his name when your interviewing a drug dealer or say anything to get him worked over. I hope that was just an idle threat.' 'You know it was.'

All those years ago Don's dad had been right. Clarky and the lads had kept dialogue going with a cunt, who was attracted to them and the attraction was stronger and stronger each time he got knocked down.

This had been by far the worst incident yet, though.

Regulars were coming into the pub and the group of friends drank up, thanked Lucy and headed back to Don's parents' place in Hollymount square. They ordered a delivery banquet Indian meal from Bombay Nights takeaway.

Don had been doing some work on his parents' house in preparation to move in, so the place was a bit upside down, when they got there, but they were all happy.

Dowser got on the phone to make the order and Midgy was pouring drinks for everyone, from a drinks cabinet Don had stocked earlier with good vodka whiskey and gin.

Maeve followed Don into the kitchen when he went for ice. 'Let's have a look at that hand Don.' Don held out his right hand. There were grazes and cuts on his knuckles from Ray Donaldson's teeth.

Don reached up into a cabinet and passed Maeve an old first aid kit and a small bottle of Dettol. She put some warm water into a glass and added some antiseptic and mopped Don's fingers with damp cotton wool. 'I don't think you need a dressing, Don, just grazes, better letting the air get to them.' 'Thanks, Maeve. When it happened, I didn't even know what I was doing. I found myself stood over Ray, wondering what I had just done.' 'It was a bad thing he said, Don, you've been through a lot, maybe you were on the edge of something like this and it exploded with Ray's insult, no one knows.' 'I still feel empty, Maeve. I can't bring myself to care about how badly injured he is, I just don't care. I'm not happy I injured him, but then I'm not unhappy. If you told me he'd died I wouldn't care.' 'I'll speak to Ian, Don.

We'll stay over tonight and get a sharp start moving stuff from Bower Grange tomorrow morning. Let's have a good meal and a few drinks for Lesley. You know she wouldn't want you feeling like this. I'll pick the kids up first thing. If anyone needs you to bounce back, it's them.'

Don had decided to sell the house in Bower Grange and move to Hollymount Square with the two grandchildren. The house in Hollymount was a lot older, but it was in a good location for access into Bedlington and Don's dad had converted the old wash house into a really well-equipped workshop, which extended down the side of the garden.

Don had worked with his dad doing metal work projects for years and there was a small gas forge and a wide range of high-quality machinery.

Don had plans of selling the Bower grange house and taking a reduced pension retirement and making bespoke metalwork to earn a bit of cash as a side line.

By the end of the night all the friends had agreed to help him get moved at the weekend.

The following day Don, Clarky, Maeve and the kids moved the small stuff from Bower Grange to Hollymount Square. Don had hired a Luton van for the whole weekend and when the others got involved, on Saturday, everything was in place by Sunday. The all went down to the Shoes pub on the Horton Road and Don treat them to Sunday lunch to thank everyone for their help and support.

Bower Grange was a popular location and Don had an offer for the house within a few weeks. The kids were settling, happy to be living near schoolfriends and Don began setting up the home, workshop and garden the way he wanted it, with Jamie and Emma's help. His employer had agreed to Don's request of retiring early from work under his circumstances and within a month his pension was arranged, an offer had been accepted for the house and Don was getting enquiries about bespoke metal work from acquaintances in the trade, who had heard he'd retired. Finally, things were looking up.

3

The Assault

Alec Donaldson was the eldest child of Ray and Kylie Donaldson. He was coming up to sixteen years old, physically well built, a bit larger than most boys his age. He was the double of his father, dark hair, short cropped cut and he had the Donaldson permanent grin, a bit more exaggerated than his fathers. Alec, known to the family as Lec, was socially inept. He was unable to make eye contact with people and, if drawn into conversation his top lip would tremor, causing a slight speech impairment. Lec was a loner. Like his father had been before him, Lec was a violent bully. He was feared in the neighborhood, not just because of his violent nature and tendency to vandalize property, but because his father, Ray Donaldson would bring trouble to the door of anyone who challenged him, always taking his son's side. In Lec's case, though he didn't have a group of brothers or friends to accompany him, like his father had at his age. He was avoided by other children, mainly because no one was exempt from his violence.

Lec had a tendency to intrude into people's gardens and would stand and look through windows. He had scared many of the elderly residents of Millfield South, with this disturbing habit, a reaction he got a lot of satisfaction from and, if he caused someone to scream or jump back in shock, he would stand grinning at the person in distress.

Lec was coming up to school leaving age and would be officially left school in the Summer of 2019. He wasn't attending school anyway, though after being expelled for slashing a boy with a lock knife outside the Bedlington High School gates. Lec had served juvenile detention for this.

Ray Donaldson was a bricklayer and he had decided to employ Lec as a labourer when he left school. Whatever Lec's faults, he was a very strong kid and he did what his dad said, knowing he'd get a hard slap if he didn't. Ray would never relinquish the role of alpha male and he was probably the only person who could keep Lec in check.

Lec's sister, Maria was thirteen years old and did not live at the family home. Their mother, Kylie was an alcoholic and had neglected both children throughout their upbringing. She was drawn to anywhere she could get a drink, cider or vodka and from birth, Maria had been left with Lec, almost on a daily basis, while Ray Donaldson was at work.

Maria had been taken into care after she had told a school teacher her brother had been forcing her into 'sexual acts' and it had been reported on to social services. No one spoke of Maria around Ray Donaldson. He was in denial that his son would do such a thing and blamed Social Services for taking his daughter away from them. Ray was also in denial that his wife would show affection to other men, in exchange for alcohol, even though this is how he met her in the first place.

Kylie Donaldson was around fifteen years younger than Ray. Like his two brothers, Ray hadn't married and he had initially rented a house in Millfield a couple of doors from Jimmy and Mick, when he had got into employment. He had purchased the house in the eighties and had hooked up with Kylie at the time she was becoming known for her drinking around the street

Jimmy Donaldson was the first brother to associate with Kylie, though, but just like anything else they had over the years, such as toys, sweets, clothes, Jimmy's beloved Chopper bike, Ray had taken what he wanted from one of his brothers.

Kylie had been in many bust ups with wives and partners of men who had plied her with alcohol then fucked her, when she was younger. When Ray moved to Millfield, he regularly called her over for drinks, behind Jimmy's back, eventually forcing her to split with him and their relationship went on for years. She got pregnant in 2003, insisting the child was Ray's and they married at Morpeth Registry office. Old habits die hard, though and, although there was always drink in the Donaldson house Kylie craved male company and there were a number of men she frequently called on when Ray was at work, including Ray's brothers, Mick and Jimmy.

No one ever suspected Lec could be Mick or Jimmy's kid, though. He bore so much resemblance to Ray, but if anyone gave the matter a bit of thought they would probably conclude he bore a stark resemblance to Mick and Jimmy Donaldson, as well. Indeed, she had never stopped fucking the two brothers over all those years. They were both night shift workers at a local factory and they were home every afternoon, week days, while Ray was at work. Cider and vodka were ever presents in Mick and Jimmy's fridge. Top of the shopping list.

* * *

Don Mason's Granddaughter, Emma Jones was fourteen years old and attended St Benet Biscop Roman Catholic school. The family weren't Catholic, but the school had a good reputation for a very high level of education and successful exam outcomes. Frank Jones had attended an interview with the school headmaster in application for a place at the school and he was impressed with the headmaster's passion and enthusiasm towards the achievements of students.

Emma was a member of the school hockey and Netball teams and was very keen on sport and exercise. She had straight, light brown hair, medium length and, like her mother had brown eyes. She was very pretty and, like all girls of her age, gave a lot of time and effort to her appearance.

Emma had taken the loss of her parents really badly and was meeting a counsellor, weekly. Her mother had been her best friend, pillar of support, mentor, everything to her and her father was the sort of man who wanted the best of everything for his kids. She felt lucky she had such supportive grandparents.

Don was a wonderful grandfather, wholly committed to Emma and Jamie. Frank's parents, Mo and Bob were also, always there for them. The kids stayed over with them, every Friday night. Mo and Bob were older than Don and they had agreed, after the accident it was unlikely, they could manage having the grandchildren permanently.

Maeve Clarke had spent a lot of time with Emma, after the accident, as well. Emma had been drawn to Maeve since she was a toddler. Maeve always had a gift for Emma when she saw her and always gave her a lot of attention. Maeve would bring designer clothing, perfume or make up for Emma, while Ian would hand Jamie a tin of .22 pellets when they visited. Maeve would do Emma's hair while Ian caught up with Don and Jamie.

Maeve would take Emma out on a Sunday, when Don took Jamie to the shooting range and they would wander around the Metrocentre shops, trying on designer stuff, just like she used to do with her own girls at that age. They would have coffee at Starbucks and people - watch, pointing out good looking blokes.

Emma knew if there was anything, she needed advice about, that she couldn't discuss with grandad, she just had to text Maeve.

By February 2019 Emma was making progress. She was mixing and socializing with friends, as she had agreed she needed to, in her counselling. She was sleeping better and beginning to enjoy life again. She was a pillar of support to Jamie, who had also taken the loss of his parents badly. The two kids were an absolute delight to Don and, to be honest, it's highly likely Don would have been in a very bad place without them.

* * *

The class had been given a Geography project and asked to prepare a presentation on a European country of their choice. They were asked to work in pairs for the presentation date of 15th February and Emma had been meeting Kate Ashford after school each Wednesday to prepare. They would take turns to host and take snacks and drinks with them to their rooms to work.

With a week to go, they were nearly complete with the presentation, so the plan was to work at Kate's to finish it off, then do a few dummy runs, to make sure the power point and everything flowed.

Kate Ashford was the second daughter of Albert and Brenda Ashford. Kate had an eighteen-year-old sister, Lisa who lived at home with her baby daughter. They lived at Millfield, in a house half way along the right side, looking from Bedlington front street. Millfield was a spacious street of houses that surrounded a long oval shaped grassed area.

The grassed area had been a playing field over the years, but kids didn't play there now, because of the Donaldson's 'idiot' son.

Millfield was social housing that had been built many years ago, initially council housing, but a lot of people had bought the homes in the 1980's. The houses were large, semi - detached and had long back and front gardens. Every house had an out building, that had originally been a wash house, but most had been converted into garages.

Millfield South, behind the left side of Millfield had originally been prefabricated housing, build after the War, but in recent years all of these buildings had been converted to bungalows, specially equipped to house elderly residents.

Behind the opposite side of Millfield was Millfield North, further social housing and each area was entered from Millfield with exit onto Church lane that led to the front street at the far end.

When Emma and Kate got home there was a note on the mantlepiece. Something had come up and Kate's parents, sister and baby had gone to visit Kate's uncle in Morpeth. The note said they'd be back around 9pm.

Emma made some sandwiches and took some chocolate bars and two cans of Pepsi out of the fridge and they went to her room.

The two girls had tea and worked a while at the presentation. When they were happy with the completed work Kate put it all away and started up a playlist of songs she had on her iPod.

The two were listening to music and looking through you tube videos and Kate did a search for something she'd been told about. 'I forgot to tell you about this, Emma, it's from Brazil. People are saying there's a virus where people are dying, then coming back to life.'

A video loaded up, dated 21.10.2018, of an apparent lifeless body on what looked like a makeshift table. The body was covered with a white sheet and there were patches of blood - like stains soaked through. There were people around the table, some in white coats and there was a lot of people, all talking at once in Portuguese. Kate pointed to the screen, 'watch here, Emma.' Emma watched on as the sheet moved and the arm of the body stretched out. Fingers were moving and then feet and legs were moving under the sheet. The body sat up on the bed and looked around. As the sheet fell down the body it revealed round wounds, where chunks of flesh appeared to have been ripped from its arm and shoulder. The video continued, as pandemonium and panic broke out among the people watching and then the clip ended abruptly.

Kate did another search, 'There're a number of these, Emma. Rumour has it that it started with a flu bug, that has gone around the world this year. The bug was one of those that come and go in a few days, but a guy working in the rainforest got bit by a wild animal when he had the bug and it passed on another virus, something like Rabies, that's reacted with the flu thing and mutated into this. Apparently, he caused mayhem at the hospital he was taken to.

They're saying we're already having the same flu virus over here. But if this is the same, it could be a big problem. Here's another one.' Kate played a video of a man clumsily staggering around the ward of a hospital, stumbling into people. He appeared to be trying to bite patients and staff and Nurses and doctors were in a state of panic, trying to restrain him and evacuate patients away from him. The camera zoomed to the man's neck and there was a large wound. This time the bystanders were talking with American accents. Again, the footage ended abruptly.

Emma closed the laptop, 'It's got into America?' 'Seems so. It hasn't been on any news programs. Governments are covering it up, saying it's.' Kate pouted her lips and said, 'fake news,' in a very bad impersonation of Donald Trump. They both laughed and Kate went downstairs to get another two drinks out of the fridge.

Kate went into the freezer and pulled out an ice cube tray and as she was knocking ice cubes out and into glasses on the bench, she sensed a movement. As she looked up, she nearly fell back to the floor in fright. Alec Donaldson was standing in front of the kitchen window. He was grinning at Kate and passing a sheath knife from hand to hand. Kate darted to her left to lock the back door, but it was too late. Donaldson had got the door open and jammed his foot inside at the bottom. He crashed against the door and Kate fell. Donaldson kicked Kate and held the knife towards her face, 'give me the phone, give me it!' He snatched Kate's phone and put it in his pocket. 'Your friend's here isn't she? The pretty one with the brown hair.' 'No, I'm on my own.' Emma had heard the commotion and came to the top of the stairs. 'Is everything alright, Kate?' Donaldson grinned at Kate with his exaggerated top lip curl.

He set off up the stairs and looked back, 'say anything about this, Kate and I'll cut your throat.'

Alec Donaldson hadn't thought about the family having a land line telephone, though, so Kate quickly called emergency services, 'Police, I need police. There's an intruder in my house and he's attacking my friend with a knife, please come.' Kate ran upstairs but Donaldson had pushed the bed against the door. Inside Emma was standing, terrified, with a razor-sharp knife pressed against her chin. Donaldson was loosening his trousers and grinning at her.

PC's Eileen Moorhouse and Elliot Friend had been at a house in Choppington, doing a caution, when the call came. Kids had been congregating in numbers around Guidepost and causing anti - social behaviour. It was down to Eileen and PC Friend to go around the parents, in a futile effort to convince them that they needed to exercise a semblance of control over their out of control kids.

They had blue light and sirens going and got to the address in Bedlington in minutes. Elliot was a big guy and ran up the stairs. He banged on the door and called out at the top of his voice, 'Police! Open this door now! Alec Donaldson! I know you have a knife. Put the knife on the ground and lie face down on the floor.' Elliot was wearing an anti - stab vest and Eileen had a taser ready. Elliot forced full weight against the door, pushing back the bed enough to get a good hold on the door and he forced is way in. Emma was sat at the back of the room. She was undressed to the waist and had pulled a blanket off the bed to cover herself. She was sobbing and shaking with fear. Elliot pushed the bed aside so Eileen could get in.

Alec Donaldson was fastening his trousers. His belt was loose and his shoes were still lying on the floor, where he had kicked them off. He had thrown the knife out of the bedroom window. 'I haven't done anything! She's a slut. She wanted it, didn't you? I want my dad. You have to get my parents; I know the law.'

The taser hit Donaldson's chest and Eileen went straight to Emma. 'Cuff him now, Elliot.'

Elliot roughly dragged Donaldson across the floor, forced his hands behind his back and punched him four times in the ribcage. Donaldson was crying when Elliot handcuffed him. He removed the taser darts and very roughly dragged Donaldson out of the room. Donaldson was screaming. When they passed Kate he screamed, 'Your fucking dead, you! fucking dead!'

Eileen held Emma close. She was sobbing bitterly, 'please take me home, please.' 'Listen Emma, when things like this happen, there are a lot of things we need to do. You need to be examined by a doctor as soon as possible and we will do the same with him. We need the evidence so that he won't get away with what he's done.' 'I just want my grandad.' 'We're going to get your grandad for you Emma.' 'He had a knife. He was going to cut my face. He threw the knife out of the window.' 'I'll find the knife, Emma, please don't worry. I know you hadn't consented to this. I'm going to stay here with you as long as it takes for you to be able to come with me.' She was sat on the floor with Emma in her arms. Emma was crying bitterly and tears rolled down Eileen's face.

After a short while, more squad cars turned up. Ray Donaldson had seen the blue lights and come to the front gate. He was looking across when he saw Lec bundled into the police car.

He ran across the green and stopped as the car took Lec away. He ran to Mick's house and walked in, 'Lec's been lifted.'

The three brothers stood talking, as Eileen brought Emma and Kate out of the house. She had telephoned Kate's parents and informed them a crime had occurred on their premises and there would be police there on their return and that Kate was alright, but helping with enquiries. When Ray saw Emma being helped to the car, he knew what his son had done. He looked down and said, 'Mason.' Jimmy poured him a drink and they all sat down.

When Ray went back to the house, Kylie was sitting on the sofa with a glass of diamond white cider in her hand. She had topped up her glass with the last of a two litre bottle and the empty, plastic bottle was lying on its side on the floor.

Ray stood in front of Kylie. 'Lec's been lifted over the road. Coppers are all over the Ashfords' place. He's still a minor, so they should have informed me about it.' 'The phone was ringing Ray, when you were out there, maybe that was the police, what's he done?' Ray knocked the glass out of Kylie's hand and it bounced across the floor, contents going up the walls and over the carpet. 'They fucking called and you didn't answer?' 'No, you told me not to answer the phone when I've had a drink, incase it's Social Services ringing about Maria.'

Ray slapped Kylie's face so hard her head hit the arm of the sofa. She was screaming and crying as he stepped away. 'You fucking drunken slut! You can't even answer the fucking phone, fucking useless! I'm going to the fucking station. I'll find out why he's been lifted and what's going on.'

Ray set off walking towards the front street.

Mick Donaldson answered the knock at the door a few minutes later. Kylie was holding her face and sobbing. She'd put some lipstick on and sprayed herself with some perfume, she'd got last Christmas. 'What the hell's happened now, Kylie.' 'Ray hit me, Mick. Slapped me really hard. He called me a slut. I'm not a slut, Mick. Lec's been arrested and Ray's gone to the police station.'

Mick put his arms around Kylie. 'Come in, love, come in.' The door closed behind her and Mick continued to hold her.

The front door was at the bottom of the stairs and Mick kissed Kylie on the lips, putting his hands up the back of her velour top. 'No, you're not a slut, love, you just need to be loved. Tell you what, love, Jimmy will get you a stiff drink and we'll all go upstairs. You need affection, not violence. Ray doesn't know what you need.'

He called through to Jimmy, who was in the sitting room watching TV, 'Kylie's here, Jimmy, can you fetch a vodka and coke upstairs for her, nice large one, she's going to be here a couple of hours at least.' 'aye, on my way, Mick, I'll bring the bottle.'

A few minutes later, Jimmy entered the bedroom and put the drink and the bottle down on a set of drawers by the bedside. Mick was undressed from the waist down and he had removed Kylie's top and bra. He was pulling off her bottoms and panties as she looked across at the drink Jimmy had brought her. Jimmy smiled as he pulled down his trousers, 'first things first now Kylie, first things first.' Jimmy knelt on the side of the bed beside Kylie's head and as she turned her head and took his cock in her mouth, Jimmy looked down and saw the bright red hand print Ray had planted on her left cheek. He glanced and smirked at Mick, who was now pounding her hard. The two brothers had that smug, Donaldson curled top lip grin, they always have when they are fucking Ray's wife.

Ray Donaldson entered the police station and was greeted by PC Elliot Friend. 'I'm here for my son, Alec Donaldson, I need to know what's going on.' 'Have a seat, sir and I'll find the officer who is dealing with the case.'

Elliot Friend entered an office and spoke with Detective Ian Clarke. Clarky put his head round the door and glanced at Ray, who had his head in his hands, sat in the waiting area. 'Tell the cunt someone will be with him soon, Elliot. Tell him we rang his home, but he didn't answer. Someone will see him when they become available. Keep him here as long as you can. Give his fucking tramp missus time to run out of drink and go giving up her pussy for more. Then I'll fucking tell him what his son has done.'

Two hours later Ray Donaldson was accompanied into a room and Ian Clarke and Elliot Friend joined him. Clarky sat down beside Elliot at the opposite side of the table to Ray. 'Your son raped Emma Jones earlier today. He was caught red handed. Forensics are running tests to confirm, but we have enough to hold him in custody.' 'He wouldn't, he wouldn't do something like that. That Ashford kid is a fucking tease, have they not let him in their room to tease him and it's gone too far for them? That's what's happened, not fucking rape. You've got a fucking grudge against me. You and that fucking Don Mason. You know what he did to me.'

Clarky could see the dental repairs to Ray's face, when he was talking. The dentures were pretty obvious cheap looking false teeth, lowest grade.

Clarky sat quiet and let Ray finish. He looked across at Ray Donaldson. 'I'm speaking to you completely off fucking record, now Ray. Elliot, do you want to leave the room? You don't have to hear this.' 'I'm good, it goes no further, Detective.' Clarky continued, 'It's over, Ray. Whatever has gone on in the past is over. Your son's going to go down for rape, but you are going to fuck off completely. I want you out of Bedlington and I'm giving you a month. I don't give a fuck where you go, I just never want to see you, nor do I ever want my friends to see you again. I've been dealing with a family from Walker, the Franklins, you've probably heard of them, heavily into drugs and organized crime and a couple of them are in a lot of trouble after a failed armed robbery. They want to deal to soften some of the charges. In a month's time, if you are still in Bedlington, you are going to be part of that deal. I'll take anyone they inform on, off the streets, but in the course of discussions, your name will be dropped in as a threat to them. You know? Rival dealer, fucking drug baron of old Bedlington Town. Am I making myself clear, Ray? This is fucking over. If you're still living here in a month's time, sleep with a fucking gun under your pillow. Because these people don't leave loose ends. Leave and I say nothing to them. Your rapist son is in custody at the minute. You're welcome to wait in the waiting area until they ask you to join the rapist in interview.'

Clarky left the interview room and Elliot escorted Ray back to the waiting area.

4

The Virus

In November 2018 the World Health Organization were reassuring people all over the world that the flu virus that was affecting most countries in the world was a four-day illness with headache, nausea, cold symptoms and high temperature. Public health advertisements on television and radio were advising sufferers to only visit their hospital or GP if really necessary. It was nothing to worry about.

The advice would have been good if the flu had been an ordinary strain, but there was a complication to the virus that they had been unaware of.

Patient one had been a delivery driver in Brazil a month earlier. He'd been suffering a heavy cold, but had soldiered on that day, delivering goods to a scientific study centre near Manaus. He had stopped his wagon and was urinating at the side of the road, when he saw a small monkey lying still in the grass verge. It was alive, but looked sick, or injured. When he bent down to look at the animal it turned its head and bit the side of his right hand, breaking the skin. He had returned to the wagon and continued his journey, but his heavy cold symptoms grew worse and worse and he decided to divert to a medical centre in Manaus and seek attention. Patient one deteriorated rapidly and died shortly after admission to hospital.

What happened next consisted of two forms of virus transmission. Everyone that had been in contact with patient one had immediately contracted a flu - like virus, it was so contagious.

It was transmitted through touch, on breath, body fluids, indeed any form of person to person contact.

Patient one had been in contact with reception staff and an emergency doctor and nurses, who had then gone off shift. These people had gone home to families, out for a meal or a drink and within hours, the virus was spreading through the city. No one knew it was a serious condition until far too late. Within a few days a person would experience normal flu symptoms, mostly mild, then recover in about a week, at most.

People who had been infected went on with their lives, passing the virus person to person.

People travelled and holidayed, as normal and, within just a few days, hundreds of thousands of infected people were entering countries and cities, all over the world.

Unfortunately, there was a more fatal form of transmission and that was a bite.

After passing away from the virus patient one was covered and left in a side room for a few hours, until a porter could take his body to the morgue. The body never got to there, however.

Patient one started to move on the trolley on route to the morgue and the Porter diverted to a ward and pressed alarm call. He was bitten by patient one as he tried to help him to a bed and soon ten people, patients, doctors and nursing staff had been bitten, Patient one broke the skin of everyone he bit, but they had broken away from him in their panic. He had then bit a chunk of flesh off the forearm of a sleeping patient and he settled and sat down, eating the flesh.

Patient one was restrained and all the injured patients had wounds dressed and were admitted as patients, themselves.

Within hours monitors were alarming flat lines of the more seriously injured patients and even people who had suffered minor bite injuries were dying.

By 5am the following morning 150 dead bodies were stumbling out of the hospital and walking into the city.

The dead only had one purpose and that was to eat. If they had access to any form of food they would eat, then wander away, ignoring anything around them. If they did not have access to food, they would eat anything in their path, including animal or human flesh. It wasn't like you would see in a horror movie, though. The dead only took a chunk of flesh. It was enough to sustain them for a few hours. There were horrific injuries, however when a number of dead converged on a victim and they suffered multiple bites and, as the virus spread through Manaus and the dead multiplied, this was happening to many people.

Local police, medical centres and hospitals were soon overrun and the military were called in to contain the spread.

The military operation successfully contained the virus in Manaus. They soon learned the dead could not be taken down in a conventional manner. They continued to walk if shot anywhere except the head. In a coordinated raid special forces killed over a thousand reanimated dead, sealed off the city and every citizen was subsequently checked for bites.

A theory later forwarded to the WHO was that the mutated virus transmitted in a bite, had affected a dormant area of the brain, that was able to operate sight, hearing, digestive system and bowel movement and this, being the only part of the brain left alive needed to be damaged to make the kill.

World leaders were made aware of the virus and its potential and the WHO advised all countries to be on alert, in case there was recurrence. They passed the little information they had to world leaders and recommended prioritizing study of the virus and the formulation of vaccine to combat the disease and they flew experts to Brazil to join the study. They had secured a laboratory and kept a few of the dead restrained for experimentation.

There was a huge play down of the virus throughout the world, though. News media were branding social media telephone footage as hoax and conspiracy theory, but in reality, cases of the dead reanimating were happening all over the world. This was because the other form of transmission, person to person contact, had also left a dormant virus in the brain, but this virus only activated on death. There had been no travel restrictions to date, indeed, at first, people leaving Brazil were not even being checked for bites.

By February 2019 the British government had covered up countless cases of people rising from the dead, post mortem. They had issued guidelines to front line doctors to inject a toxin into the brain of everyone declared dead, to prevent the reanimation, but this was only being practiced in hospital setting. Where emergency services had arrived at a sudden death, accident or fatal incident, too late, there was cross infection happening through biting. Bite victims were panicking, overrunning hospitals, or trying to get home and in a few days the virus was out of control.

The timescale from bite to death and reanimation also varied greatly. Some people became seriously ill and died within an hour of infection, then raised within the next hour, but there were also people who lived up to a day and then didn't reanimate for hours. There was no explanation for the variance in timescales.

The Government issued a state of emergency on 1st March 2019. Everyone in the country was instructed to stay indoors and only leave for food and essential needs. By March 10th London was overrun. Cities were becoming no - go areas. Housing estates were emptying of residents, mostly through families ignoring lock down and going outside to search for food, or for relations who had not returned home, then not coming back, themselves.

People were in denial, ignoring the threat, some even taking selfie photographs beside the dead, but many people displaying flippancy towards personal safety soon turned a wrong corner and found themselves being the next meal for a group of dead.

All main roads were blocked by traffic trying to flee the virus. There were road traffic accidents on every main road, blocking all routes around the country. Bite victims that had tried to drive home had died and returned, while stuck in the traffic jams, then bit people who were trying to help them.

There was widespread ignorance that the dead were dangerous and this cost thousands and thousands of lives and created thousands and thousands more reanimated dead. and there were hordes of dead wandering motorways and main roads looking for food. Main roads were no - go areas, in the space of days.

In cities and towns, the dead were entering shops and supermarkets and there were crowds of dead gradually eating away all potential supplies, survivors would need. They would eat anything they saw as food.

The dead were digesting food to sustain the energy to exist and they excreted a stinking, watery dark black - red slime, which stained their clothing and ran down their legs and onto the ground. Where they had congregated in supermarkets, or anywhere there were vinyl floors, the ground was hazardous and the stumbling Dead were continually slipping and falling in the slimy surface. There was no safe way in and out of a supermarket or shop for the living. If a person fell to the ground in the vicinity of these things, they had no chance of survival.

The British military had tried at an early stage to cull the dead, but being attracted to any sight or sound that was out of the ordinary, masses of dead converged on them and, everywhere that a stand was made, it was overrun, when ammunition ran out. They had acted too late.

By March 15th there was no power. Power stations had shut down. It was now a global catastrophe. Communications were going down and TV and radio had ended broadcasting.

Vulnerable people were dying by the thousands and reanimating into flesh eating corpses and because of the genre of horror films, that had depicted such monsters, they were labelled 'zombies,' before media went down.

The last broadcast by the BBC and most media broadcasters, advised the public to avoid the dead and try to secure their premises. There were no government ministers making statements. By now politicians had abandoned the public and were trying to secure their own safety. Some had taken security forces away from defending the public, to ensure they got out of the cities.

The Media advice to stay indoors was sound advice on the short term, but no one had a supply of food, other than what they had shopped for prior to the catastrophe. By the end of March, people were going to have to leave their homes. Many already had.

Most housing estates were abandoned, with only a few families in each location keeping locked inside and these survivors soon made their way around their neighborhoods, scavenging for food from the abandoned houses.

Most people who had ventured out to find family, friends or a safer place hadn't made it. They had only added to the multiplying problem.

Survivors recognized the dead were attracted to towns and cities, so blocked ways in with cars, vans, or anything that would make a barrier.

There were thousands of dead wandering motorways and main roads, that had become blocked in the outbreak. They constantly wandered, seeking a way off these roads after food had ran out. The food that had ran out on the motorways,was living people.

5

Further tragedy

Don Mason was in the workshop working on a small job he'd been asked to do by the owner of a local fishing tackle and gun shop. He'd needed a silencer fitted to one of his own guns, for hunting, a twenty - two caliber rifle. He had also asked Don to make some good quality steel framed target catapults, that would fire ball bearings. Local shooting ranges were providing small target ranges for catapult enthusiasts and there had been a lot of requests at the shop for more professional standard slingshots.

Don had nine of the ten catapults packed in a box and was working on the rifle and Jamie was in the back garden testing the other, when Don heard the knock on the door.

Don took off his apron and went to the front door. Maeve Clarke was standing. 'Maeve, come in.' Maeve followed Don into the sitting room and sat on the armchair. 'Don, you're going to need to sit down. Ian's coming over to talk to you but you need to know there's been a serious incident involving Emma.' 'What's wrong, Maeve, has she been in an accident, what's happened?'

Don's heart was pounding. 'Don, Emma's been raped. She was doing homework with her friend, when the Donaldson boy, Alec forced entry to the Ashford's house in Millfield. The parents were out and he managed to block the bedroom door and force himself onto Emma at knifepoint. I'm so sorry, Don. The police were there in minutes, but too late. Alec Donaldson is in custody. He'd already confessed, but his father is making him deny the charges.'

Don was silent. It was like the bottom had fallen from his world. He couldn't talk. Tears rolled down his face and he put his head in his hands. He sat for a few moments then looked up at Maeve. 'I was going to take the kids for pizza at La Torre when Emma got back. I've been working all day and hadn't prepared anything. I need to see her. I need to see Emma.'

'Don, Eileen Moorehouse is outside in a squad car. She can take you to Emma. She's been continually asking for you. Emma is undergoing invasive examinations, she needs you, Don. Eileen will take you to Emma and I'll stay here with Jamie. If it's ok with you I'll tell Jamie.' Don nodded. 'When we get Emma home, Ian will come down and talk to you. I'll stay with Emma. Don, Ian's talking about setting Ray Donaldson up for a fall with an organized gang from Walker. Real nasties. If he does something like this and it gets out, it will cost him his career. These people have no loyalty, especially to police. If they come for Ray Donaldson and something goes wrong it could be traced back to Ian. He could end up in jail, Don. I know this is difficult and I'm here as long as you need me, but if Ian raises this with you later you have to know what it could lead to. We need to let the law deal with this, we have Alec Donaldson and conviction is a formality.'

Don stood up and walked towards the front door. 'I'll talk to Ian, Maeve, don't worry. I really appreciate everything you've done since I lost Lesley. Emma's going to need you more than ever, now. I need to get Emma home. I do appreciate you staying for her. I've never come across anything like this. All I feel is despair.' 'Don, it's going to be really difficult. Something like this can be life changing to a young girl. She needs everyone's support right now. We are arranging professional counselling for her, a specialist from Newcastle, she'll be in touch probably this evening. Don, you'll need to accompany Emma through her questioning. I know it's hard, but she needs to say everything that happened to her. I don't want there to be any doubt about this boy's guilt if it comes to trial. He confessed, but his father was absent, when he did it. He changed his story with his father there and that means going to Crown Court.' 'Maeve, do - gooders from Social Services got this kid released home early after he had scarred a young lad for life. Since he got home, he's terrorized his neighborhood. It's not safe for kids to play in the street when he's around, yet they think they can reform him and now this? Alec Donaldson is just like his fucking stupid father. He will never learn and, what if I bump into Ray Donaldson again and he says something about Emma? Ian isn't going to need a gang to bump the fucker off if that happens, mark my words.' 'Don, the detective interviewing Alec Donaldson will caution Ray Donaldson in regard to keeping away from your family.' 'He'd better keep out of my way, Maeve. He'd fucking better.'

Don left with Eileen.

Emma burst into tears on seeing her grandad. 'I'm sorry Grandad, I'm sorry, I was so scared. He..' Don held Emma in his arms. 'It's ok, flower, you did nothing wrong. That boy would have hurt you. You know he's slashed a boy before, he would have done the same to you. He's in custody now. You won't see him again. Maeve told me you need to be strong. You need to tell the police everything.' Emma held her Grandad close and sobbed. Don's heart felt like it was going to burst.

It was late when Don got home. Emma went straight to her room. Maeve followed and looked back, 'Jamie's in bed Don, he was upset, but he'll be ok.' Emma had burst into tears on seeing Maeve and Maeve went with her to her room and sat on the bed next to her. They both lay down and Emma cuddled tightly into Maeve. Nothing was said. They both just cried.

In the sitting room, Clarky was animated. Tears were running down his face. He could hardly talk with the emotion. 'He's fucking dead, that lad. I'm going to have him lit in any fucking institution he gets put in. Mark my words, cons will be told he's a bacon of the very worst kind, Mace. I know people in fucking jail, I put the fuckers there. You don't need to promise those fuckers much in return for a favour. The cunt's dead, fucking dead and as for his fucking stupid father, he a fucking goner as well.'

'Clarky, reel it in mate. You're talking about committing crime, here. You're the guys who put these people away, not the cons. Don't start getting involved in criminal stuff. Emma needs all of us to help her get through this. How do you think she'll feel if she sees you being led off in cuffs? What we need is the fucking rapist in jail. Emma needs no more and no less, mate. Just Alec Donaldson off the street for a long time.'

Clarky was still crying. 'The fucking arseholes, fucking in - bred arseholes.'

Don went into the drinks cabinet and took out a bottle of port wood finished Glenmorangie. He took two glasses into the kitchen and put two ice cubes in both, came back through and poured two very large drinks. 'Maeve will probably stay with Emma tonight, Clarky, I'll set up the couch for you and we can finish this bottle.'

He took the remote control and flicked through the TV channels. Sky news was doing a report on the flu epidemic that had gone around and they mentioned rumours about dead people being reanimated and walking around trying to bite people in London. They were showing telephone footage of incidents, then they showed an interview with a government minister, who was saying the current social media hoax footage was a widespread craze that was going too far. He emphasized that people were not getting up and walking post mortem.

Ray pressed auto rewind on the remote control and they watched the footage again of a man covered in bloodstained clothing trying to grab people in the street. There was panic and a woman he'd taken hold of broke free and retreated, screaming and bleeding through her blouse, from a wound on her left shoulder.

Clarky spoke up, 'Go out tomorrow and get groceries in, Mace. Get plenty to last a couple of weeks. I heard something like this happened in Brazil not long back and soon went out of control' 'You don't think it's real, do you? They can do anything with those photo shop things now, man. Just special effects. It's just a craze.' 'I'd get the shopping in anyway, Mace, you know what the public are like. They'll empty the supermarkets if they think there's a problem ahead. The one in Brazil caused a huge lock down. People were kept indoors for weeks until they got the virus under control. They said it was some tropical disease and denied everything about the dead rising. If the conspiracy theorists are right, there is a virus of some sort, that got out of a lab in the rainforest and it may be something that causes anger or violence. I'd be prepared for a few weeks lock down if there's something in all of this.' 'Ok, I'll take the car to Asda tomorrow and do a good shop.' 'I'm doing the same.'

The following morning Maeve and Clarky went home first thing and Don went to Blyth Asda. He filled a trolley with tinned foods, pasta, rice and anything that would store, as Clarky had advised.

Counselling was arranged for Emma and Don had been in contact with the school. He was retired, now, so had the time on his hands to be with Emma, when needed and kept occupied with some small jobs, when she wanted space.

Alec Donaldson was being held in custody and a date set for the 27th February for the case to be heard at Bedlington Magistrates Court. The case was expected to be referred to a Crown Court in Newcastle for prosecution.

As the court date neared there were further rumours of problems associated with a virus that was allegedly spreading around the country. The public were now being told to stay in their homes, and avoid unnecessary contact with others and there were now thousands of social media clips of 'undead' incidents. The government were in denial, but by now people were being asked to leave the side of recently deceased family members and, anywhere an ambulance was called for a serious incident, a heavy presence of police was accompanying the crews.

On the morning of the 27th February, Don Mason received a call from Bedlington Magistrates Court. The court had been suspended and all hearings cancelled until further notice.

Clarky's car pulled up outside and Don opened the front door to let him in. Emma had heard the car and come to the top of the stairs, but Maeve wasn't with him.

'Don, I heard the hearing had been cancelled.' 'I've just taken the call.' Emma had overheard and burst into tears. She went back into her room. Clarky continued, 'Listen Don, crazy stuff has been happening. I'm not supposed to tell anyone, to avoid panic, but I'm going around all the friends to warn them. This stuff with the dead walking around and biting people is happening. We've been called to incidents around the region. It's fucking horrific. Uniformed are accompanying ambulances to cases of sudden death. We've been issued fatal injections and trained to inject them into the brain of anyone who dies. We're all carrying the virus, we got it when that flu bug went around. It's dormant. We've been issued handguns. Ordered to shoot any of these things in the head if we see them, but I'm not firing a gun around them. It will just attract more. I've killed two of them by knifing them through the temple. If anyone dies, whatever the cause, they return in a matter of hours, some in less time. I've been told that Air cabin staff have been finding blood on the floors of aeroplanes, through people who have been bitten, travelling home and the same is happening with the rail and motorways. Don, don't approach one of these things. If they bite you it's fatal. I know they can be killed with head trauma, that's the only thing that stops them. Cities are affected now. The military are trying to get it under control in London. It's spreading there worse than anywhere. Don't travel, unless you have to, Don, traffic is bumper to bumper. Hospitals are overrun.

Places like Bedlington aren't badly affected yet, but if the rest of the country is anything to go by it will get here. Possibly in a couple of days. Get food in if you can, Don and lock down. These things wander around and they're attracted to noise and movement. I'm boarding up my downstairs when I get home. If they come anywhere near keep quiet and out of sight. They're looking for food and if they're hungry they will lose interest and look elsewhere if there's nothing to attract their attention. They don't just bite people, Don. In London they are emptying shops. They need food, small quantities, often, to keep them going. Shops are emptying there and there's so many of the things gathering where there's food, supermarkets are becoming the most dangerous of places. If the military don't get this under control, when the food runs out, they'll attack people and people will have to risk being out there among them to seek food. It'll be carnage, Don.'

'What about Donaldson?' Don knew what was coming and Clarky put his head down. 'We can't hold him under these circumstances, Don. We're expecting a state of emergency and all personnel will be in the field. He has to be released, along with a number of people we don't want on the streets. Alec Donaldson will be tagged and sent home and kept under house arrest. If he leaves the house, the station will be alerted and he'll be returned. If any of those fuckers turn up here, ring me and I'll be right over with this revolver. I won't hesitate to shoot anyone that's a threat to you and the grandkids.'

When Clarky left Don called in the two children. 'There's a serious problem developing throughout the country. I need you both to keep inside at all times. There are people walking around trying to bite others and if they do bite, the person bitten will die. If they come into the square we need to keep out of sight and dead quiet. Emma, I'm so sorry, but Alec Donaldson has been sent home. He'll be taken back in when there's officers available to keep him in custody, but all police personnel are being called to the crisis.'

Emma was mortified. Don held her cheek in his hand. 'Your safe with me Emma. No one will harm you. I need both of you to help me. We're going to board up all of the downstairs. I've got a few eight by fours of plywood in the shed. We're going to make a hatch in the fence at the bottom of the garden that we can use if we need a quick exit. The park hasn't opened for a few days, it's all locked up so it's a safe retreat. We can go around and make a few more escape hatches, so we can get in and out different parts of the park, quickly without being seen.

They went to work, working on the fences first, then returned and boarded all the downstairs back windows. Don measured up and pre - cut the plywood for the front window. Neighbours were asking him what he was doing and he told the truth. He was dismissed by most as overreacting, but later on he could see some neighbours starting to do the same. News reports were coming in on all channels about the impending crisis and the government requests for lock down had now become legislation forbidding anyone leaving their homes.

On 1st March 2019 the government announced a state of emergency. Police and armed forces were ordered to shoot on sight anyone showing aggressive behaviour and anyone looting shops. The military had a massive presence in the south, which was now being overrun and dead were multiplying in the north, through bitten people trying to travel home and contamination after natural fatalities. People were stuck in cars on all main roads. As conditions of drivers who had been bitten worsened, many of them left their cars and tried to make for hospitals on foot, but many died and crowds of dead were subsequently accumulating on main roads and motorways, all looking for food.

Police and the military had been underfunded by Tory cuts and austerity for years, now and there were no officers available to support the public living in towns and villages. By mid - March all efforts were being exhausted on futile attempts to regain cities and towns and villages had been abandoned by authority.

There was widespread panic in the north and Northumberland residents started to make desperate efforts to stockpile food, but the virus and the dead that came with it, was closing in fast, on them.

6

A Safe Place To Survive

Don was deeply concerned about Emma. He hadn't heard from Clarky and Maeve, other than text messages saying they were still alive, but they had been fighting a losing battle in Newcastle.

Clarky had rightly tipped Don off that electricity would go down in a few days and this would lead to widespread panic and lots of deaths, particularly of vulnerable and elderly people, causing further floods of the raised dead. The Police superintendent had tipped key staff off that they would shortly be sent home to protect their families.

At home Don knew time was running out.

The first 'zombie' seen in Hollymount square entered from the front street. Don had passed on everything he had been told about them, to neighbours and, as it wandered through Hollymount, people kept quiet and out of sight and it eventually made its way out of the opposite exit and back onto the street.

Don had watched it pass. He was deeply concerned that it could just have easily been twenty or more. Clarky had told him they congregate and walk in herds.

He walked around the Square, knocking on the doors of houses he knew were occupied and invited the neighbours to meet in his back garden after lunchtime.

There had been a lot of residents that had left the square. Some had attempted to get to family, such as parents, siblings and children. Some had left searching for people who had gone out and not returned and then not returned themselves. Some residents had panicked and driven north, hoping to distance themselves as far as possible from the south, that had dominated the news. Of the fifty-five houses, there was now only twenty-five occupied, around seventy people.

All the residents met in Don's back garden. Jamie kept lookout from the front bedroom window.

Don spoke, 'Listen, thanks for coming and meeting with me. I know you are all concerned about what is happening, but even with everything we're doing to avoid these things, we aren't secure. My friend has told us we're only a few days behind places like Newcastle and if this is so, we're very quickly going to be overrun and we don't have police support. I've been around the square and there's around thirty houses unoccupied. Some people have taken cars and tried to get elsewhere and I know there's a few people missing who have gone out to try to get food or find loved ones and not made it back. We can't just let the dead have a free access to the square. I'm planning to go out tomorrow and assess what's going on. I'm happy to do this alone, but we need to know what's out there.'

Hannah Rice spoke up. She was in long sweatshirt and sport leggings. She had short black hair and was very attractive. Hannah was married to Colleen, who was stood with her. Hannah had been a friend of Don's daughter, Maria since school and knew Don well. 'What do you propose we do Don? Everyone's concerned we are running out of food. It's obviously a death sentence going out there among them, but I can't see what else we can do. I don't mind coming with you' 'Your right about the shortage of food, Hannah, but I see the priority as securing the square. If we are safe in here, we can work out how we are going to manage together. I propose we get into the houses that have been left empty and put together a stock of food supplies. We can keep one empty house as a storage point and share out anything we find, on a daily basis, from the store house.'

Geordie Wells spoke up. He was late forties, greying black hair, medium build and was wearing jeans and a light blue un branded sweatshirt. He'd been working in the garden and still had wellies on. 'Don, if we get a few people together we can break into some of the cars that have been abandoned on the street. If we park a few up across the entrances, lie some on their sides beside them, so those things can't crawl under - and then another row, we can block off the ways in and out.'

Vera Sharp lived near the north entrance. Vera was in her sixties, with straight grey hair. She was thin and looked a lot older than her real age. Her husband Jackson Sharp had gone out to find her daughter, Maisy, minutes before Maisy had arrived home, but Jackson hadn't returned.

'Don, if we block the entrances there're two big metal gates behind the dog grooming shop on the end, that closes in their house and car park. The people who live there have disappeared as well, so if we can get chains and padlocks, we can secure the gates, then that will just leave the cut to Cornwall Crescent and the alley to the park.'

'The park alley is closed off. Park's been closed for weeks.' Neil Hipsburn stepped forward. Neil was mid - forties, a bit of a fitness enthusiast. He had light ginger hair and was wearing a white tee shirt under a grey tracksuit. Neil was a builder and had adapted his wash house to be a store for gear and there were pallets of bricks stacked up on his small wagon and six pallets on his drive. 'I can build a double wall between the two houses adjoining the cut. Give me a few days.' 'We'll labour for you,' Colin Markem raised his hand, 'I can mix cement and fetch and carry, Ben can help as well. Anything to make the place safe.'

Colin Markem and Ben Brown were living in Ben's father's house. They had managed to get to Bedlington, with the aim of seeking Ben's father, but when they got here, he was gone. Ben had cousins in Bedlington, that had said they would collect his father, but they hadn't turned up. Feeling fortunate to have reached Bedlington, they had agreed it was too dangerous to try to return and just stayed in Ben's dad's place. Colin was a salesman in Ben's double-glazing company. Colin was short, with fair hair and wearing light jeans and a black jacket. Ben was around five foot ten and a big lad, around eighteen stone.

Don looked around the group. 'Does anyone have anything they need to raise?' Ronnie Binns spoke. Ronnie was a greenkeeper at the local golf course. Ronnie was Short and stocky, around thirty years old. He and his wife Thelma had two daughters, Ashleigh and Katie, both under ten. 'Don, I know we have to secure the place, but I'm thinking long term, here. The gardens in the centre could make up a large allotment. I know quite a few people have greenhouses and stuff. I'm willing to go around all the gardens and look for seeds, onion sets, potatoes, anything we can grow. If anyone wants to help, we can make up a team and turn the gardens over, put them down to veg. It's walled in and safe. The kids can get involved.' There was a lot of enthusiasm from the kids to help with the garden and Don thanked Ronnie.

Don continued, 'The only weak point I can see is the rear garden area that sits against Hollymount Avenue. There's fencing, but if a lot of the dead go against it, it will go over. I suggest we board off all the back doors and windows of this line of houses.' Dawn Todd lived on her own in one of these houses. She had split up with her husband a few months back and she had kept the house.

Dawn was in her early forties, short brown hair and quite attractive. She was wearing a long denim dress and navy cardigan. 'I don't mind moving, if it's safer on the inside. I don't give a shit about the contents of my house either, I never had a say in what we bought with that bastard, anyway. Unhappy memories. I'll pack a few things move now. Can I have the Short's place?'

The Shorts were quite well-off residents of the square. Tommy ran a builder's yard at Cowpen Industrial Estate and his wife, Lou had the best version of everything. They were one of the first families to leave, Lou insisting they went to Gateshead to seek her mother. They had never reached Gateshead.

Don replied, 'aye, but one thing, mind, when Electricity goes down the sixty inch telly won't be much use.' 'I'll rough it then. Would it be too soon to wear Lou's designer clothes?' Don smiled. The other two families agreed to move and everyone went off to start work.

By early evening the entrances and exit to Hollymount square had been blocked off with cars. It had been a slow process, because dead were wandering around so the cars could only be moved one at a time before the men retreated out of sight. It was stop, start, until it was all in place. The pallets of bricks had been transferred and piled beside where Neil was going to build the wall. A foundation had been dug out and concreted in, ready for the bricklaying. The alley was closed off by the equipment.

The residents had allocated the house opposite Don's as store house and a number of neighbours had accessed the empty houses and collected a substantial amount of food, beverages, medicines and anything else that would be useful in the store.

Don had found thick chains and new heavy-duty padlocks and secured the pair of metal gates and Ronnie and the kids had found a huge quantity of gardening stuff, that they brought around to Ronnie's. There were two double wooden gates leading out to the street, either side of an abandoned dental practice and the men reinforced both.

With the place reasonably secure, Don went to check on Emma. Emma hadn't come to terms with Alec Donaldson being freed and she hadn't left her room since. She was deeply depressed and hardly communicating with Don or Jamie. She just appeared consumed by sadness.

Without Maeve's support, Don was really struggling. He took some tea and biscuits to Emma's room and found her asleep. He left them by her bed and went down to the workshop. He called Jamie in and pulled together some equipment.

Don hadn't heard from Meadow Park, the care home on Choppington Road, a road that leads out of Bedlington towards Choppington and Guidepost. He needed to know if his dad was alright, but communications were becoming unreliable and Clarky had told him electricity will go down any time and with that, so would phone networks. Don was really worried.

'I need some stuff pulled together, Jamie. See if you can find an old oak stair rail in the shed, son. I know your grandad was given one by one of the neighbours, last year to make something on the lathe.' Jamie went into the shed and Don went into the racking at the back of the workshop and pulled out a two metre length of ten-millimetre-thick stainless-steel rod. He started up a grinder and cut it down to five feet. He went through drawers and found some brass pins and laid them on the bench. Jamie came into the workshop with the oak handrail. 'Cut it down to three foot for me. Jamie.' Jamie laid the rail on a bench and went into the cupboard for a tenon saw and tape measure.

Don started a belt grinder and began sharpening one end of the rod. When finished It tapered from around six inches back from the end, to a needle-sharp point.

Jamie passed Don the rail and he clamped it into the lathe. He shaped the handle down to a thick dowel, then took it out and held it in two hands. 'Jamie, take the pencil and mark around my fingers on the grip.' Jamie marked the dowel and Don put it back into the lathe and sculpted indentations for grip. He gave Jamie coarse sandpaper and Jamie sanded the timber as it turned on the lathe.

Don found a long drill bit matching the size of the rod and marked it at two feet. He carefully drilled into the end of hardwood then mixed some epoxy resin. He coated the rod and inserted the blunt end into the handle, until it was in as far as it would go. Finally, Don took a drill that was equal to the width of the brass pins and drilled three holes at equal intervals, through handle and rod. He knocked the brass pins through against a metal forming block, then picked up the weapon and passed it to Jamie. 'What do you think?' 'It's brilliant, can I have it?' 'No, son, it's to keep me safe when I go to see my dad. Will you polish the handle for me? I need to pop and see Hannah.'

Jamie found some beeswax and a cotton rag and was proudly polishing the weapon he'd had a hand in making. It was a well - balanced, kind of harpoon – like weapon, but without a barb. Most importantly the blade was solid and had a three - foot reach. Don had no plans to get closer than that to any of those things.

Don Knocked at Hanna and Colleen's door around 8pm. They had made a pot of tea and Don Joined them. 'Do you really want to go out there Hannah?' Colleen rolled her eyes. It was obvious she didn't want Hannah to go and there and it had been discussions before Don arrived.

Colleen Rice was mid - thirties, shoulder length ginger hair and very attractive. The couple had been together for fifteen years and she was deeply concerned and rightly so.

Hanna answered, 'I have to help out, Don. We've got a lot of mouths to feed, here and we need medicines and all sorts, not just food. We need to know what we're doing.' She handed Don two rounders bats, that she's found in a cupboard, 'These are the only things I can find that might be used as a weapon.' Don took them. 'Leave them with me. They will be weapons by tomorrow. I'm going out eight o'clock tomorrow morning. Colleen, will you stay with my grandkids?' 'Of course, I will and Don, just don't let anything happen to her. She's all I have.'

The following morning Hannah and Colleen arrived and Don passed them both their rounders bats. He had inserted two spikes, that protruded six inches out of each bat around four inches from the end, they were needle sharp at the point. He had attached a leather wrist strap, designed to prevent the weapon from being dropped. He passed Hannah hers and she slipped the strap over her wrist and held it in front of her. Don held Hanna by her arm, 'Remember Hannah. If we encounter these things, they're not people anymore. Can you use this on one of those things?' Hannah looked at Colleen and kissed her on the lips. 'I have to Don. We have to learn to survive out there or die. That's the way I look at it.'

Don and Hanna exited the second metal gate and Don quietly replaced the lock. They made their way up the front street. There was a lot of cars, some parked, some sideways across the road and some abandoned, but there wasn't a clear path for any car to be able to travel up the front street.

There were two bodies lying on the ground about twenty yards further on and, as Don and Hannah approached, they rolled and faced them, arms stretched out. Both had multiple injuries, as if they had been knocked over and there was a car at the side of the road. Don neared the two dead and spiked the first, a young, fair haired woman. The spike went through the side of her head and she instantly died. As he pulled out the spike Hanna hit the other, a young man. He mustn't have died through the accident. There were bites that had been taken from his arms, legs and body. The spike on Hannah's bat went straight through the top of his skull and he was dead, instantly.

As they got to the market place, Don and Hannah saw a group of dead. A man was lying on the ground and was crying for help. There were four dead, all male and they were just sitting beside the crying man. 'Clarky told me they go docile when they have eaten.' Hannah nodded. Let's go over. They walked over to the scene and the dead showed no interest in them. One was still chewing, blood running down it's chin. They looked at the victim. There were bite shaped wounds to his neck, face and arms.

Don and Hannah took the weapons and killed the four dead. The man was crying, 'I shouldn't have gone out. I ran into a big group of these and got away. I thought I was going to make it home and ran straight into one of these ones. He had a hold of my clothing and I couldn't get him to let go. I dragged him from Church land to here, but I was exhausted. I went to ground and he bit me. I've been bit all over. I feel really cold.' Don held his hand.

'I'm so sorry, mate, there's nothing we can do.'

The victim went unconscious. Don looked at Hannah. 'We can't help him.' He un sheathed a hunting knife and stabbed the unconscious victim through the temple.

The two walked to the top roundabout and Don walked over the road and looked down the hill towards the golf course. There was a lot of movement down there. 'I think there's quite a few dead down there.' Hannah walked over, 'Don, let's have a look at the two supermarkets.'

Don had taken out his phone and was trying to ring Meadow Park to tell them he was coming, but there was nothing.

Don and Hannah walked between abandoned cars, down Choppington Road and stopped adjacent to Morrison's and Lidle supermarkets. The two supermarkets were either side of the road opposite Schalchsmule Road. They walked down to the mini roundabout that leads in and Don quickly beckoned Hannah to get down. There were hundreds of dead in the car parks and shops.

Don and Hannah quickly made their way down to Meadow park, at the bottom of the road and it was Don's worst fear. They looked through the windows and the residents and staff were reanimated dead. 'Is your dad there Don?' 'No. His room's around the back. Maybe he was inside when this started.'

They got to the rear of the building and Don tapped on his father's window. His dead father walked forward and stood in front of the window. He had one bite mark on his right arm. Don sat down on the ground and cried, head in hands. Hannah sat with him and put her arm around him. 'Give me the spike, Don.'

Hanna walked over to the garden and picked up a rock. She threw it through the window. As Don's father lent out Hannah put the spike through his head. She pulled out the spike and Don's father fell to the ground. She stuck the spike in long grass, that had once been a lawn and sat back down beside Don. Don looked at Hannah, tears running down his face. 'We can't risk burying him, Hannah, let's get back.'

Don and Hannah doubled back up Choppington road, but along the right side. Some houses had open front doors, so the two carefully entered and searched for food, medicines and anything of use. They put two dead to rest in the second house they looked in and after five houses they had all they could carry, in the back packs that they had taken.

Don and Hannah made their way back, carefully avoiding anything that moved and took the scavenged items to the store house.

Don took Hannah and embraced her, 'Thank you for what you did at Meadow Park, it was all too much for me.' 'I'm so sorry, Don, it must have been awful losing contact and being able to do nothing.' 'let's get you back to Colleen. I've got a few bottles of wine in the kitchen, that need to be drank, if you and Colleen want to pop over later.' Hannah smiled, 'Don't mind if I do.'

When they got to Don's house Colleen, Emma and Jamie were in the sitting room. Don could see Colleen had made friends with Emma and they had been chatting all morning.

Jamie asked about his great - grandad. Don shrugged his shoulders, 'I think they must have moved the residents to a safer place, son. He wasn't there.' Emma knew he was lying. She quietly stood up and went up to her bedroom. Hannah followed. She entered Emma's room with her and sat beside her on the bed.

Emma was crying, 'He's dead, isn't he?' 'Yes, Emma. I'm so sorry. Your grandad wanted to find him and bring him home, but Meadow Park was overrun.' Emma stood up and looked out of her bedroom window. It overlooked Welfare Park, Bedlington Terriers football ground. It was overgrown with knee length grass that had gone to seed. The goalposts were still there. 'I used to watch the Terriers from here on a Saturday. Kate would come over and we'd eat crisps and chocolate, drink coke and watch the footballers. Everything's gone now.

Everything's like this. Everybody's dying.' 'I'm helping your grandad make this place safe, Emma. You can help out. It's safe in the gardens over the road. They could use help digging and planting. Ronnie's a great bloke. Everybody's enjoying working with him.' 'When my grandad goes out, I'm terrified he won't come back. It's like everyone I love is dying.' Hannah stood beside Emma and looked out of the window. 'Tell me about the Terriers, who was your favorite player? – or should I say who was the best looking one?'

7

The Farm

Hannah and Don had become an effective team over the course of the week. Every other day they went out into Bedlington, breaking into houses and scavenging for food and supplies.

Electricity had gone down on the Wednesday and the priority was to find petrol - run generators and they checked garden sheds, garages and work vans, everywhere they went.

Neil Hipsburn and Geordie Wells had also ventured out and they were syphoning petrol from abandoned vehicles on the street, for the few generators they had picked up. They searched cars and vans for anything of use, particularly butane gas bottles that could fuel barbecues and stoves for cooking. Hannah and Don were searching gardens and sheds for the same.

Geordie would keep watch holding a cut - down piece of iron scaffolding bar, while Neil did the search. They avoided the dead, but Geordie had used the bar twice when he'd had to and, having caved the heads in of two dead, they were gaining in confidence towards venturing further afield.

Don and Hannah were working along abandoned houses, currently in Hollymount Terrace, adjacent to the square. They had found an abandoned house with an open door and Don had sprayed a black cross on the door, marked as a safe retreat. They scavenged the other houses, looking in vain for survivors, first. Don would spray a red cross on the door of any house they assessed as 'no – go,' either when there were too many dead inside to enable safe entry, or when they had cleared it of food and equipment, so they didn't go back to the same place.

They searched gardens and sheds for tools and equipment. Hannah found a sheathed machete in one garden shed, 'Don, do you want this? I prefer the bat.' Don took it and threaded his belt through the sheath. Hanna stood back, impressed, 'looks good on you Mr. Mason.'

If a number of dead appeared, they would spend time in the safe house until they passed. It was working well.

On the Friday after the electricity had gone down Don and Hannah were in between housing mid - way down Hollymount terrace, when they heard gunfire in the distance. Hannah held up her hand and Don lowered the crow bar, he was using to lever a door open. Hannah looked along the street, 'it sounds like it's coming from Millfield.' 'More like further over, Hannah, possibly by the golf course or Church Lane, let's take a look.'

Don and Hannah followed Hollymount Terrace to the front street. The street was clear, so Don guided her down to the Picnic Field and up a footpath that led to the farmer's field, behind Millfield South. There was repeated fire and single shots. Don stopped and listened, 'it sounds like an automatic rifle and a shotgun.' They crossed the field. The gunfire was clearly coming from the farm at the end of Church Lane, but suddenly the guns went silent. There were screams coming from near the farm house and Don and Hannah ran up to a conifer plantation about two hundred yards down the road to Humford and knelt down behind some trees. There were about thirty dead converged around two victims, who had been taken to the ground. A woman was running towards the house. She was holding her arm and screaming. 'Whoever was firing the guns are under all those bodies. I think she's been bitten. It looks like she'll get to the house. Look at the farm, Hannah.'

The farm was virtually surrounded by hay stacks, two high, that were wrapped in a tight, black polythene. They had surrounded the farm house and two large residential houses. A detached bungalow on the opposite side of the road was also within the enclosure. There were farm buildings inside the perimeter and the stacks made a large boundary between the farm and the other residential areas alongside. They walked along the edge of the tree line to get a better view and Hannah stopped for another look, 'It looks like they were putting a perimeter wall around the place. It goes all around the houses and half the field. The tractors still got one on the fork. They must have been working when the dead got in.' Don nodded, 'My friend told me noise attracts these things. That's where our emergency service has gone wrong. Firing guns attracts them in hordes. There's nothing we can do here, Hannah. The dead could be here hours, if they haven't all managed to eat. We'll come back this afternoon, hopefully they'll all have got hungry and wandered back towards the front street. We have to check this place out Hannah. This could be a contingency, if the square ever got overrun.'

Hannah and Don went back to Hollymount Terrace and continued the scavenging until their bags were full. They had found another petrol driven generator in the back of a builder's van.

People had been sharing houses in the Square, after the electric went down, so every generator was returning one family back to their house. It wasn't a lot, but it would run a heater, a light, boil a kettle or heat a water tank, so the generators provided some comfort.

Water was still coming out of the taps, with less pressure, but there was no gas supply.

At five o'clock Don and Hannah headed back down towards the Picnic Field. They hadn't told anyone about the farm. When they got to the conifer plantation, there was no movement. There were dozens of bodies laid on the field and they could see what was left of the two victims.

They walked over to the victims. It was horrific. There were two bodies, both men. There had been so many bites taken out of them it would be impossible to count. They had reanimated, but the tissue, muscle and tendon damage were too vast to enable them to stand and walk. They held out arms that had been bitten to the bone and they snarled.

'I'll end the one in the green jumper, you get the other one, Don.' They raised their spiked weapons and killed the two victims. There was a twelve bore shotgun on the ground and a

Browning automatic twenty caliber scoped rifle beside it. Don picked up the guns and passed the shotgun to Hannah, 'Let's not fire these.' Hannah nodded.

Don and Hannah carefully passed through the bodies that were laid out on the field. They had all been shot in the head, some of them chest, neck and stomach. Some bodies had heads missing where they had been shot from close range by the twelve bore.

They walked along the line of the black stacks, that were arranged two high along a perimeter. They looked like very effective walls. It also looked like the work had been going on for some time. The two approached the farm house from the gap in the stacks. It was obvious the farmers were nearing completing the boundary, when they had been overrun. The gate to the farm had been built up with timber and was wide open. Don closed and bolted the gate, 'This looks like it what was meant to keep the dead out while they worked.'

Don walked over to the tractor, 'the keys are still in this. House keys as well,' He shouted, 'Hannah!' A dead man was stumbling up behind Hannah from inside the boundary.

She turned to run, but it had taken hold of her back pack and was biting at it. Don Ran across, as Hanna desperately tried to get the bag off. She managed to slip her arms out of the straps and, as Don got to her, she bent down and he thrust the spike through the zombie's right eye. The spike burst out of the back of its skull. He turned to the side, lowering the spike and the body fell dead to the ground. 'Shit! Have you been bit, Hannah? are you alright?'

Hannah was patting herself all over. Don stood behind her, looked up and down and checked her body from the front. There was no blood on her clothing. Hannah was uninjured.

There were two more dead walking out of a barn beside the house. Don dispatched both with the spike, then checked the rest of the grounds. There were no more dead.

Don went back to the tractor and took the keys.

Don entered the house, holding the spike weapon ready. There was a faint voice, 'I'm in the living room.' Don and Hannah walked through. The farmer's wife was slumped in an armchair. She was holding her left arm tightly and there were bloodstains all over her right hand and clothing. 'I know what's going to happen to me, please sit down.' Don sat on a seat opposite and Hannah sat on the sofa. 'My name's Don and this is Hannah. We came earlier when we heard gunfire, but it was too late.' 'Marion.' Marion Heron was sixty years old, but looked nowhere near that age. She had dark hair and was quite well built. She was wearing jeans, walking boots and a floral patterned short sleeved blouse. 'My husband, Douglas. Did you see him? He's wearing a green jumper.' 'I'm so sorry Marion. They got overrun. The two men both died.'

Marion gasped with despair and cried 'My brother Keith was the other man. We were making a boundary for what was coming.' Don looked at Hannah. 'You knew this was coming?' 'Yes, my niece was in Brazil when the outbreak happened. She works for the World Health Organization. The authorities said they had contained the virus in Brazil. But they hadn't. The virus was transmitted by the flu, not just the biting. Everyone has this virus, you don't need to be bitten, but you'll know that by now, I suppose?' 'Yes, my friend is a policeman, a detective. How long have you been making the boundary?' 'Douglas didn't sell any hay last year. He stored it up in the large barn out there. My niece told us infected animals had been in transit between two labs in Manaus early last year and Animal Rights protesters had blocked a road. It had got out of control and protesters released the animals.

The incident on all the news, involving the man in Manaus hadn't been the first. That's why they went into Manaus with silenced weapons. The authorities knew they could not contain the dead with loud gunfire going on, but it seems this information wasn't shared. We haven't heard from my Niece for some time, now. My husband was shooting as a last resort. They had been trying to get the last few bails into the boundary and had under estimated the numbers of dead that the sound of the machines had attracted. Keith had heard someone outside screaming for help and opened the gate. It was a young woman, but the dead got to the gate before he could get it closed. She was badly bitten and fell, but Keith couldn't get the gate closed. They tried to clear the dead back to the gate with the guns. When they were running out of shells they were shouting for ammunition and I got bitten trying to get this to them. I walked right into a dead man and he grabbed my arm and bit. I got back into the house, but I couldn't help them. I hoped they had managed to run away.' The twelve bore shells and a box of 500 x .22 caliber bullets were on the coffee table.

Marion took her hand away from the bite. It was horrific, a deep wound with dark red inflammation that had covered her whole arm. 'We were careless, Don, The men normally only worked half an hour and went quiet, that's how it's taken so long, but when they got surrounded, the shooting only attracted more, I had to run back inside or I would have been eaten alive, but I didn't quite make it.'

Don went into the kitchen and filled a glass with water. He came back through and passed Marion the glass. Marion took a drink. 'Can you do something for me, Don? You can have this place when I'm gone. We stock piled tinned food, pasta, rice, even toilet rolls. The cellar is full. There's even spirits, wine and beer, it's fully stocked. Finish off Doug's work. Make this place safe. The animals are in fields about a mile inland, away from roads. Will you bury me with my husband and brother on this land? Please, Don.' 'Of course, Marion and we will finish this, I promise.'

Marion looked at Hannah, 'If you go into the fridge, there's a bottle of Champagne. It was a gift. The generator's running so it should be cold. In the cupboard above, there's a plastic tub with medication in. There are a few strips of sleeping tablets, zimovane, bring them through as well. Bring three glasses.' Hannah went through to the kitchen.

Marion smiled at Don. 'It's our fortieth anniversary this Sunday. We were going to have friends and family round if the virus hadn't reached us. Douglas spent a thousand pounds on fireworks. Four displays all set to go off one after the other. They're in the shed outside.

We'll never get to see them. You couldn't even set one off now. Is Hannah your Daughter?' 'No, she's a friend, I lost my daughter last year, accident.' 'I'm sorry, Don. She certainly looks at you, like a daughter would look at her dad.'

Hannah came back through with the champagne and pills. Marion popped all the pills from a blister pack into her hand and asked Don to open the champagne. Don poured three glasses of the Moet et Chandon and Marion took the tablets all at once. 'Cheers Don and Hannah. God bless you both. Don, you know what you need to do for me.' Hannah took a drink. Tears were running down her face. Don took a drink, sat on the arm of Marion's chair and put his arm around her. 'Happy anniversary, Marion.' He kissed her brow. In a few minutes, Marion was sound asleep and Don took his hunting knife and stabbed her through the temple.

There were no dead around when Don and Emma went back outside. Don carried Marion to the far end of her garden, then went over and one at a time, dragged what was left of the two men over. There was a JCB machine parked just along the road, where some works had been abandoned and Don walked over. The keys were in the ignition. 'We'll take it over and come back tomorrow to bury them. Marion said half hour shifts work, so we'll just work in those parameters. You can get up on top of the haystacks and keep watch and I'll finish the boundary. Let's keep this to ourselves for now, Hannah.' 'Ok, I wonder why the Donaldsons haven't been over here, Don. It's got to be safer than where they are living.' Don climbed into the JCB. 'They'll not move on a farm. They know the farmer will have a gun. Ray Donaldson is a coward. He wouldn't risk being shot. I reckon he's a big threat to people that aren't armed, though. I just count us lucky we haven't run into him.'

Don parked up the JCB and locked the farmhouse. He wrapped the guns and ammunition in a pile of blankets and the two headed back to the square. Don put his arm around Hannah as they were crossing the field, 'tell me about your parents, Hannah.' 'I lost them both when I was young, Don. Road traffic accident.' 'Oh, I'm so sorry, Hannah.' It's ok Don it was a long time ago.'

The following morning Don and Hannah left the square and spent two hours at the farm. Don dug a wide trench with the digger and carefully arranged the bodies side by side. Hannah kept watch as he covered them up and the two went inside to have a good look around the farmhouse.

Don found a gun cupboard and there was more ammunition. He had put the guns into his bedroom wardrobe, so he collected all the ammunition and put it into his back pack.

As they left the farm Don looked back at the makeshift grave, 'I don't know if Marion was religious, but she was wearing a cross. There's some oak left from when Jamie cut the handle for the spike. I'll ask him to make a cross.'

Don and Hannah returned every morning for the next three days and finished the boundary. They had found the animals, a dozen sheep, a cow, that was feeding a calf, two horses. There was a mesh covered pen with about a dozen chickens.

The farmer had erected a shed in the field and had stored bags of feed in it. There were two massive stacks of Hay in the middle of the field. There had been rain so the water troughs were still full, but there were also huge plastic water containers full with fresh water. The two agreed to feed and check on the farm and animals every time they left the Square.

8

Barry Miller

'Quick Daniel, open the door, open it!' Barry Miller had run from a house on the other side of the Hartlands. The Hartlands was a large housing estate, situated at the top end of Bedlington, off the main road, that leads past the golf course, out of Bedlington, towards Cramlington.

There were many different streets in the estate, but the area was known as the Hartlands.

Barry had gone out around abandoned houses in the Hartlands, looking for food, but this was a huge risk. There were thousands of dead wandering around the large housing estate. This had been caused by herds of the dead coming off the A1, near Gosforth and wandering along roads. One of the roads that a massive herd had followed, was the slip road that led to Seaton Burn and the Holiday Inn Hotel, near Cramlington. With all routes being blocked by traffic accidents and jams, the herd had followed the road along towards Bedlington.

The first housing estate they had come to was the Hartlands and they had quickly overrun this whole area.

Barry could only work one house at a time. There was no way of entering a property without attracting the dead and he always entered through a window and nailed it shut, so he was secure inside. Dead would wander around, looking for the source of the noise, but Barry knew, if he kept quiet, they would lose interest and wander off. He would bag food and anything of use from the house, wait for an opportunity, then make a break for home. This was a daily risk for Barry, since his wife had gone missing a week prior.

Daniel opened the door and Barry entered, grabbed the door and slammed it shut. As he turned the key to lock the door there were a number of sounds of thuds against it.

'Dad!' Daniel had seen the blood on Barry's tee shirt. It was a light blue Lambretta tee shirt, with a coloured target pattern and he was wearing jeans and black Nike running shoes. Barry had short ginger hair, that had grown out of cropped cut and he was freckle faced. Daniel was his double.

Barry fell into the sitting room and smashed a small coffee table in his fall. The shopping bag he was carrying spilled across the floor. There was a box of corn flakes, some digestive biscuits and various tins of food, beans, soup etc.

Daniel ran into the kitchen and filled a bowl with Water. He took a tea towel and brought them through. Barry pulled up his shirt, revealing two sets of tooth marks on his chest. They had broken the skin, but he had managed to break free.

Daniel started to cry. He was twelve years old, tight curled ginger hair and freckle covered face. He was quite small for a boy his age and he was wearing jeans, trainers and an Adidas tracksuit top. Daniel had lost his mother, just a week ago and, even though he was very young, he was well aware a bite was fatal.

Barry composed himself as Daniel cleaned the wounds. 'Dad, what will I do? I can't go out there and I can't stay here. How can I get help?' Barry took his son's hand, 'I can't be helped, son.'

Barry held Daniel's hand. 'You've got to be brave, son. We're going to wait till there's none of those things around and you're going to make for the farmer's fields, over there. The dead aren't wandering onto open space, because there isn't anything attracting them. There's a gap in the fence, I've seen it when I've been jogging in the past. Come to the window, you can see it from here. You need to try to find survivors, son. Keep off the streets.'

Daniel helped Barry up and Barry pointed to where there was a gap in the fence. There were two dead wandering around, but they had lost interest in the front door. They were just moving their heads from side to side, as if looking and listening for anything.

'There's somebody there, Dad. In the gap in the fence. It's a boy.' Barry looked across. He could just make out the figure of a boy, crouched behind the gap in the fence. The boy had thick, dark hair and was wearing black jeans and a dark grey jumper. He was watching the house.

The dead soon lost interest in the house and wandered off. Daniel was watching the boy, 'Dad, he's coming over here.'

Barry came across and watched the boy cross the road and pass through the front gate. There was a knock on the door. Barry stood behind the door, knife in hand. 'What do you want?' There was silence for a moment then the boy spoke, 'I know you've been bit. I saw you run into those zombies. I know your bleeding. I know your kid's there with you. You need to let me in, there's more dead coming, please.'

The door opened and the boy entered. He quickly sat down on an armchair in the sitting room, hands on the armrests. He knew from experience, if he appeared a threat to anyone who had bitten, things could get ugly quickly. He had dropped a bag on the floor, containing baby formula, rusks, tinned food and disposable nappies.

'I have no weapon, Mr. you don't need that knife. My name is Will Masters. I'm from a property that's set back off the road near Nedderton. I go around the estates looking for survivors. I move around by farmland where I can. I'm looking for kids who have lost their parents. I lost my parents two weeks ago. I know when something like this happens, the children have virtually no chance of survival. A lot of people turn, then end up biting their own kids, because they are scared to let them go out there. You have to let your son go. I'll take him.'

Will picked up the bag. 'The stuff in my bag is for my friend from school's niece. They're all terrified to go out. I'm trying to get them to come to the house. The adults could be a big help, but they're scared to go outside.'

Barry nodded. 'I know My son will have to get away from me. Is your place safe?' 'It's got fencing all the way around. Not perfect, but we keep quiet, that's our main rule. I've blocked the drive that leads in. There are less dead up there, than here. A few survivors are still in the houses, up Nedderton. They blocked Morpeth road with cars and also the road from Bedlington to Nedderton. Some of us help them out, there's some elderly residents who can't go out there amongst the dead. We scavenge and provide them with food. We scavenge mainly houses that adjoin open fields, so we don't have to walk among them. The Dead seem to be attracted to streets, shops and housing estates. They've no interest in open fields, unless they hear something.'

He looked at Daniel. 'My name's Will.' He held out his hand, 'Daniel.' They shook hands. 'Listen Daniel, the hard part is to get over to the field. There's a hole in the fence. We run as fast as we can. Don't look back. If we don't attract attention we head for the middle of the field. We can get to the house without ever going onto a road. Can Daniel come with me, Mr? It's now or never.' 'Barry, it's Barry.' He took Daniel in his arms. 'I want you to go with Will, son. Run as fast as you can. I love you so much.' 'Dad!' Daniel was sobbing.

Will stepped back, 'we've got a path, we've got to go. I'll keep your son safe, Barry, I promise. You're a very brave man. I'm sorry this has happened to you.' Barry stood at the front door and watched the two boys make for the gap in the fence. They both squeezed through. The boys stood inside the fence and waved, then they turned and ran.

Daniel was gone.

Barry was feeling cold and nauseous. He had a massive headache and as he went to close the door he passed out. The door was slightly ajar, but his feet were against it, preventing it from opening more than a couple of inches. He slept for four hours.

Barry woke abruptly. He felt excruciating pain in his chest. He felt physically ill throughout his body and he had lost so much energy, he couldn't move. All of his muscles were stiff and he was having major cramps in his legs, arms. fingers and toes. His jaw kept locking closed, so tightly there was blood coming from his gums. His eyesight was going from blur to dead sharp and his hearing from almost deaf to acute. His sense of smell heightened, to the extent he was overpowered by basic smells, then it just went away and he could smell nothing.

Barry looked down at his hands and arms. There was no skin tone, almost grey. He tried to roll onto his front so he could stand up, but he had massive cramps in his right hamstring and each calf muscle and he fell back down. He was starting to panic, but as he got agitated, he felt worse, like the illness was rushing through his veins.

Barry's breathing got shallower and shallower. He felt freezing cold, and the colder he felt, the harder it was to breathe and, as his breathing shallowed, Barry went to sleep and minutes later died.

Barry opened his eyes. It was slightly dark where he was and he looked around. He had tunnel vision and saw no colour. He looked around the room. He focused on everything he saw, but there was nothing processing what he was seeing. He looked at the window, nothing, a clock on the wall, nothing. There were no words in his mind, telling him what he was seeing. No thoughts. There was pain in his lower body and he put his hand there, but felt nothing.

Barry stood up. He had no feeling in his feet and as he took a step he fell back to the ground. He saw his right hand and held it in front of his face, nothing. He stood again and clumsily stumbled back into the sitting room. He saw a television, nothing, picture on the wall, nothing, but then something.

Among the things that had been spilled on the floor was a packet of digestive biscuits. Instinct made him see this as something and he could smell the contents of the packet. He knelt down and picked up the packet of biscuits. He held them in front of his face and bit the packet. It ripped open and broken biscuits fell to the floor. The smell was intense, irresistible. He picked up a handful and ate them. As he swallowed, the lower body pain started to subside.

Barry finished the something then looked at the box on the floor. Again, something attracted him. He tore open the box and passed handfuls of the something into his mouth. The pain was soon completely gone and Barry stood up.

Barry heard a noise outside. His eyes immediately focused towards that direction and he was drawn towards the sound. He lifted his head and inhaled through his nose to take a smell, but he didn't breathe the air, a waft just passed through the nose and out of his mouth. His windpipe had closed on death. He instinctively recognized the scent of those before him and had an urge to join others, that were like him.

Barry saw two, that were like himself and he walked towards them. They both had something running down their chin. He heard a loud noise and immediately looked at the source. Something was lying on the ground. It was making a lot of noise. He didn't have the pain, so he ignored the something and joined the two, that were like him. They all stood looking at each other, then they all knelt on the ground. They were content.

Barry closed his eyes and there was nothing.

The three that were the same suddenly stood up together. There were loud noises and they all turned their heads and looked the same way. They all had the pain again. They instinctively walked towards the sound, raising their heads to seek a scent of something.

They walked to the end of the Hartlands and across the main road, alongside what had been the golf course and followed the sounds over a large overgrown field.

There was a crowd that were all like themselves and they joined the crowd who were all walking towards the noise. As they got to the place the noise was coming from the noises changed and, as they got within sight, something was under a crowd. The two like himself walked towards the something and Barry heard another sound and instinctively turned and grabbed. He had a hold of something with both hands. He brought his hands up to his face and bit hard. Something was making a lot of noise, but he had something in his mouth and, as he chewed and swallowed the lower body pain eased.

The two like him had turned around and come back. They had both managed to bite something, just before the something had gone still and quiet and became nothing. Barry followed them towards the noise that the something he had bit, was making. It was gone and he stood, focusing on the surrounding area and raised his nose, trying to pick up a scent, nothing.

They continued down a yard into a large dark place. Barry stood still then knelt down. The two like himself did the same. The pain had gone. He closed his eyes. Nothing.

Barry opened his eyes when he heard a noise. He had that pain again in the lower body. It was a familiar noise and familiar smell. It was something. He walked out of the barn and saw something not far from him. He walked up to something and heard the same noise again, but from another something, that was across the yard, 'Hannah!'

He had something in his hands, like before, but when he bit it wasn't the same. It was attached to something but it wasn't what he needed to ease the pain. It was nothing, then he was holding the nothing in two hands. Something was breaking his hold and leaving him holding the nothing. He looked past that something and another something was approaching him. He dropped the nothing on the ground and opened his mouth to take a bite of the approaching something. The first something had bent forward, out of his reach and Barry looked up at what was moving towards him.

Barry felt nothing as his head slid off Don's spike and his body fell to the ground.

9

Orphans

Don and Hannah had gone to the farm at dawn, to check on the animals and go through the farmer's out buildings and tool stores, looking for equipment. The place was still secure and Don locked the gate behind him. They entered the house and started up the generator.

Hannah made tea and they sat and chatted. Don took a drink and looked at Hannah, 'we've got to tell the others about the farm, Hannah. I think, if we offer two or three families the chance to live here, we would have two very secure places, maybe secure enough to start rounding up survivors. A safe haven, of sorts.' 'I was going to ask, when I got the chance, Don, most people have friends and family out there. A lot of Hollymount, residents have died trying to reach theirs, at the early stages, but now we're finding food and managing not to lose people, we could get addresses and check out the nearest ones, at least. I'm disappointed we haven't found anyone alive, up to now.' 'It's like you said, Hannah, a lot of people panicked and ran. Others probably went to shops or supermarkets, looking for food.'

Don took a drink, 'Jamie and Emma have been asking me to check on some of their friends and I have friends around Bedlington that I haven't heard from since the phones went down. They will have been doing the same as us, I'm sure. Making their own homes safe, first.'

Emma went through the kitchen and turned off the small petrol run generator, that was stood outside the back door. She locked the door and returned through to the sitting room. 'We got a request for batteries from the kids. Their hand-held games and devices are losing charge and I know we're running out for the torches. We can keep an eye out for DVDS and games, make it a scavenge for kid's day. There's plenty food in the storehouse.' 'Yes, I noticed Jamie hadn't been playing with the Nintendo thing he has, lately. We've cleared Hollymount Terrace Hogarth Cottages. How about we start a new street? I don't want to venture anywhere around Millfield, in case the Donaldsons are still running around, so what about starting down Haig Road, on the other side of the park?' 'Ok, Don. We'll head there and see what we can pick up. We'll check for survivors first.'

Haig Road was one of four streets that were arranged in an oval shaped pattern, just off Welfare Park. It Adjoined Cornwall Crescent and Millbank Road and Beatty Road was on the opposite side, like a massive version of Hollymount Square. There were twenty-four houses down each side of Haig Road and Don and Emma knocked on doors. First priority was to find survivors and identify a safe house they could get quick access to, if needed.

They got no reply from any house in Haig Road. There were a lot of houses with dead inside. This was becoming a common sight to them. A family member who had been bitten early in the outbreak would be cared for by family, unaware of what the victim was going to become, until too late and this caused numbers of dead to be trapped in houses.

They got into 48 Haig Road through unlocked back door and found house keys inside.

Don sprayed a black x on the front door and put the keys under a ceramic pot beside the front door.

Don and Hannah found some sweets and medicines in number 48 and packed anything of use into Hanna's back pack. Don was dropping a packet of toffees into Hanna's pack, and he pulled at the side of the bag, 'There's tooth marks on the side of the pack, did you see them?' 'Yes, it was a close one, Don. Thank God you were there.' 'We need to be careful, Hannah, it takes some force to put as deep a mark into strong material like that. It would tear through skin. No wonder Marion was so badly injured.' 'My policy is just to avoid them, Don. We know if we sit tight, they lose interest, so we can retreat and hide. I don't want a fight. As long as we keep having a safe house nearby, I'm confident we're safe.'

They quickly cleared 48 and Don levered a side window of 46 and they entered. There was no one in the house, dead or alive. Don picked up a pile of Marvel comics and put them into

Hanna's bag, 'There's superhero stuff and kids DVD'S here. Dawn has been working in the gardens and gets on great with the kids. There're loads of films here, we can pass them on for the sixty inch telly, she so happily volunteered to inherit. I gave her a generator last week and the house has got some solar panels, so it should all work. Let's have a look upstairs. See if there's any games and batteries.' Don was looking through a boy's room at the top of the stairs when Hannah called from the main bedroom. 'Don, come quick.'

Don ran into the room and Hannah was looking out of the window. 'Don, two kids down the street are in trouble. One of them is hurt and the dead are catching them up.' Don had a look, 'They aren't going to make it to the top of the street, we've got to help.'

Don and Hannah ran outside. There were four dead just behind the two children. The injured boy looked in a really bad way. The other boy dragged him towards Don and Hannah.

Don and Hannah let the boys pass and stepped towards the four dead. In two blows from each, the dead were laid on the floor. More dead rounded the corner from Millbank Terrace and Don grabbed the injured child, He turned to the other boy. 'Number 48, son, the door is open.'

They all ran along Haig Road. Some dead were coming from the direction of Cornwall Crescent, but they managed to get to the front door. Hanna closed it behind them and ran upstairs, as the dead bumped against the door. Don laid the injured child on the sofa. The boy was around fourteen years old, thin, with dark hair. He was wearing a dark blue Adidas sweatshirt, jeans and Adidas trainers. 'Ellie! Ellie! We can't leave her like that.' He was crying hysterically, 'Oh God! Oh God Ellie.'

The other boy spoke, 'His name is Marty, Marty Lowes. I'm Will. Will Masters.' 'My name's Don, Will, my friend Hanna's looking for stuff to try to help you.' Hannah came into the sitting room with a dish of water and bed linen she had torn into strips. She knelt beside

Marty and gently took his hand away from his injury. She pulled up his top. 'It's not a bite, Don. The boy's been stabbed.'

Marty had a deep stab wound in his side. 'I don't know how bad it is, Don, I'm just going to try to stop the bleeding. We'll take him back to Colleen when the dead clear off.' She was holding a clump of rags tight against the wound.

Don led Will into the kitchen. 'Your friend has been stabbed, not bit, son. What's going on? How did this happen?' 'Don, kids round here are being hunted.' 'Hunted?' 'Yes, hunted.'

Will sat down at the kitchen table. 'I have a house near Nedderton, off the main road. I lost my parents a couple of weeks back. They went out and never came back. When I was looking for them, I found kids, like me. I took them in. A lot of kids have died after their parents got bitten. I'm going around looking for lost kids and taking them to safety. Marty is my friend from school. For the last few days, I've been going around all my friends.' 'Do you know my daughter, Emma Mason?' 'Yes, I know Emma and her friend, Kate Ashford. Kate's family live opposite the monster who is hunting us down. They're scared to leave the house and have barricaded themselves in. I take food for them and stuff for the baby.'

Don sat down beside Will. 'So, what happened to Marty, son?' 'I came to see if Marty was alright. He lives at Millbank place. I came all the way through the woods to avoid the streets. When I got to Marty's house, I saw Alec Donaldson coming out. I hid in a garden along the road, until he was gone. When I got inside, I found Marty like this, Don. He told me his parents are both dead. He put them to rest and buried them, himself in the garden after they died of bites.'

Will started to cry. 'Don, Alec Donaldson had stabbed Marty, then raped and strangled Ellie. She's only thirteen. He had told Marty he was leaving him alive to give her something to eat when she turns. Some of the kids staying with me have encountered him. We scavenge to provide food for our people and we pass food in for elderly survivors. He comes looking for us, stalking the kids, especially girls. We've lost four kids in the last week. He's more dangerous to us than the dead.'

'What about Alec Donaldson's parents, Will? Are they still alive?' 'I've seen them when I've been taking food to the Ashfords in Millfield. They've got a pallet wagon blocking one of the entrances and dozens of pallets, piled up, surrounding three houses and there's about nine people living there. They're getting into gardens from the woods. They have scavenged Beatty road, but they're looking for money and valuables, as well as food. They're out every morning. They don't help survivors. They all carry baseball bats. If they come across survivors, they beat them to death or Alec stabs them. They're making their way down towards Millbank. That's why I came to check on Marty. I would guess they'll be into Dean View by next week.'

Don ran his fingers through his hair, 'Clarky. I've got friends in Dean View, Will.' 'You need to warn them, Don. I followed the Donaldsons on Monday, when I saw them heading out of Millfield. They do about ten houses in a morning. There're about thirty houses in Millbank. The next area joining the woods is Dene View. It goes about a mile along the edge of the woods. It's ideal for them. How far down does your friend live?' 'About three streets down, Dene View East.' 'Don, I reckon they'll reach your friend by next week. Where is he scavenging for food? He may bump into them.' 'I don't know, Will.'

Hanna called for Don. 'I think the bleeding is stopped, I've got a lot of dressing packed on the wound, but we need to get Marty back to the square. The dead have wandered off, Don. Marty, do you think you could go piggy - back with us? We need to carry you about a quarter of a mile to Hollymount. The access is blocked down the cut.' 'Yes, anything, but my sister, Ellie?' 'I'm sorry, Marty, there's nothing we can do for her.'

They made their way back to Hollymount Square by cutting through Hollymount Terrace and onto the front street. Don managed to carry Marty all the way and they passed through the gate safe. Hannah locked the gates. She took Marty home, calling for Colleen on the way. Colleen came out and they took Marty inside.

Will stood with Don. He was shaking. 'Don, Alec Donaldson is very dangerous. Your gates look sturdy but they'll not keep him out. If he gets inside here your survivors could be in a lot of danger, especially kids.' Don looked around. 'I'll give it some thought. Come to my place. Emma will be pleased to see you. Will, please don't mention Kate's family. Emma has been really depressed since..' 'I know what Donaldson did to her, Don.' 'Hannah and I have been talking about rounding some survivors up. I need to talk with all the residents here first and I think you're right about the perimeter. When we're ready, we'll go for Kate's family first. You let her parents know that.' 'I will, Don.'

Will spent a half hour with Emma. She was pleased to see him and put on her bravest face.

He told her all about the orphans he had rescued. She knew quite a few people who had survived. Will didn't mention the murder victims, though. He could see why Don had asked him to keep this from Emma. Will was concerned at how low Emma was. He'd never seen her like this, but he'd recently seen others' suffering and Emma was suffering.

Will came downstairs from Emma's room and bid Don farewell. 'I have to get back, Don. We've got the place boarded up but if any of the kids have ventured outside and Donaldson is stalking around, I could lose another.'

Don handed Will a large sack. 'I made some professional standard catapults for a shop just before the outbreak. They're made to fire ball bearings, but I don't have any. Jamie says they fire steel nuts great though. I've got thousands of those. There're ten catapults in the bag, Will. The kids will learn fast with these, Jamie can hit a can from the full length of the garden. If twenty of you fire these at Alec Donaldson, it'll make him think twice about stalking your home. The bag's heavy because it's half full of ammo.' 'I'll manage, thanks Don and thanks for what you did for us out there.' 'Son, seeing you hanging onto your friend

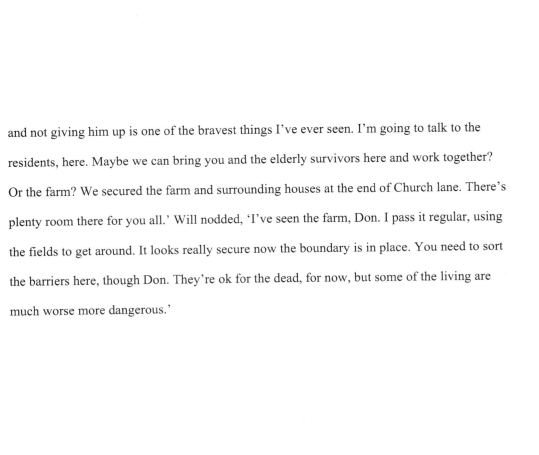

and not giving him up is one of the bravest things I've ever seen. I'm going to talk to the residents, here. Maybe we can bring you and the elderly survivors here and work together? Or the farm? We secured the farm and surrounding houses at the end of Church lane. There's plenty room there for you all.' Will nodded, 'I've seen the farm, Don. I pass it regular, using the fields to get around. It looks really secure now the boundary is in place. You need to sort the barriers here, though Don. They're ok for the dead, for now, but some of the living are much worse more dangerous.'

10

Securing the Square

The following morning Don went around all of the houses inviting the residents to meet with him at 1.00pm in the central gardens. After the previous day He'd agreed with Hannah to have a rest day. They were both exhausted.

At 1.00pm all the residents assembled in the garden. A group of college girls, Honour Reid, Julie Knight and Sam Lewis had found a couple of bread makers in the abandoned houses and taken some ingredients from the store. They had made bread, a few cakes and arranged jams and marmalade on a long table. Honour was nineteen years old, natural long blonde hair, quite tall and thin. She was wearing Adidas sport leggings, a long Adidas tee shirt and Adidas trainers, as if she had just come out of the gym. Julie and Sam wore variations of the same, Julie wearing matching Nike and Sam wearing Puma. Both Julie and Sam had dark hair and were very attractive girls. They had all returned from Northumbria University, Newcastle, when the decision had been made to send students home and just got out before the outbreak devastated Newcastle. They were staying in Honour's parents' home. Her parents had been stranded in Tenerife when the flights were halted. Honour had lost contact with them a couple of weeks back.

When everyone had taken a treat, Don spoke up.

'Thanks for all the work everyone has put in to keep us going. I've been out there with Hannah a number of times in the last few weeks and it certainly isn't safe. A few things have happened that you all need to know about and I still think there's a lot of work we need to do to make the place safe.'

Geordie Wells spoke up, 'The barriers are working, Don. No dead have got in, since we moved the cars and Neil put the wall up over the cut. It all looks safe enough to me.'

Don nodded, 'you're right Geordie, the barriers are excellent, but the biggest threat out there at the minute are alive, not dead. There's a family from Millfield, the Donaldsons, along with some friends, that are becoming dangerous. The boy, Marty we brought back here, had been stabbed by Alec Donaldson and Donaldson had raped and strangled the boy's thirteen-year-old sister. You all know what this boy did to my granddaughter. A young lad, Will Masters, who saved young Marty, has told me the Donaldsons are scavenging down Millbank place, accessing the streets from the woods. They are taking food and looting money and valuables.'

Dawn Todd spoke, 'I know the fuckers. What a bunch of fucking morons. What are they going to spend money on, for fuck's sake?'

Don continued, 'They're beating survivors to death with baseball bats and the boy, Alec is stalking children every afternoon. Will has been rescuing orphaned children and the kids are all living in a detached property off Nedderton Road. Colleen, how is young Marty, this morning?' Colleen stepped forward, 'We stopped the bleeding, but time will tell. If an organ is damaged, we haven't got anyone who can put it right. I cleaned the wound and stitched it up, but it's not ideal. If it gets infected it could be difficult. Hannah and I will keep Marty with us for now.'

Don spoke again. 'We're doing great here, but I'm really worried about being vulnerable to these people and possibly more like them. I propose we reinforce the entrances and gates with metal fencing. Neil, could you build brick pillars inside the boundary at two metre intervals that we can attach heavy fencing to.' Neil stepped forward, 'yes, it wouldn't be a problem, but we haven't got any fencing, Don.' 'You're right Neil, but I know where there's a lot. The rubbish tip at Bebside is surrounded by tall metal security fencing. If we can get enough of this fencing back here, I can build a fence across the gaps and we can put much heavier gates on the exit we use. There's burglar paint and grease in my garage, that would make the fencing hard to scale. Would you build the pillars, Neil?'

'Pillars would be no problem, Don but the rubbish tip is about two miles away. How are we going to get heavy fencing and bring it back here?'

'That's another matter we need to discuss. Hannah and I have secured the farm at the end of Church lane. The farmer and his wife were overrun and killed, while they were trying to make a perimeter and we have finished the work. The farm is secure and well stocked with food. I want to propose taking over the farm. We can occupy the farm and enclosed houses with some of our people. If anyone is interested, we can take you for a look. I think, along with the residential houses inside the perimeter, we could comfortably house five or six families safely, if not more. I think it would also be useful to have contingency. A place to retreat to, if we encounter others like the Donaldsons. If we secure this place and the farm we can start searching for your friends and families. Hannah and I are willing to visit any addresses you give us and bring back loved ones, if they have survived, but we need to secure the perimeter here first.'

Dawn spoke up again, 'so why haven't the Donaldsons taken the farm, Don?' 'I think it's probably down to farmers being renowned for having guns, Dawn. The Donaldsons may be beating people to death at the minute, but these are people who can't defend themselves. Ray Donaldson is a coward. He wouldn't stand in front of a man with a twelve bore shotgun. Whoever takes on residence at the farm will have the farmer's shotgun, though. It's still there.'

Neil spoke again, 'I'm with you Don, we can do this, but how are we going to get the fencing back here?' 'There's a big David Brown tractor and trailer at the farm. We can make it a three-day project. Day one, we head down to the picnic field and start moving cars to free up a lane. We need to clear a lane from the stone bridge along to the Horton Road, then around the Bebside Road corner. If we can get into the farm on that corner, we don't need to clear the Bebside road. We can get near the rubbish tip through fields. We'd come out just along the road from the tip. We continue clearing the road, till we get to the tip. If we encounter the dead in small numbers, Hannah and myself will put them down. If we encounter large numbers, we will use the woods and farm land to escape. Hannah and I will make safe houses on the way.

On day two, we'll take the tractor and trailer, with all the tools I need across the farmer's field and down the grass bank into the Picnic Field. Helpers can meet me there and we travel to the tip. We can break into one of the houses, to use as a safe house to retreat to, just in case. I'll take the fencing down in panels, with everyone else on lookout. If all goes well, we deliver it back and day three, I assemble. I can get the fencing with four helpers. Hannah said she'd come.'

Geordie Wells stepped forward, 'I'm in, Don.' 'Colin Markem put his hand up, 'count me and Ben in.'

'I'm in as well, Don.' Lance Smith stepped forward. Lance was 76 and lived with his wife, Dot just a couple of doors from Don. Dot had been gradually losing her memory over the last year and Lance cared for her at home, supported by the Northumberland Community Mental Health Trust. 'I'm coming to help with the fencing.' Don looked across at Lance, 'Listen Lance, I'm really grateful for your support, here, but you have Dot to care for, mate. It's really dangerous out there. Dot can't manage without you. Maybe if you help with the work inside the perimeter?' Lance looked around the group. His eyes had welled up with emotion. Geordie put his arm on Lance's shoulder, 'Don's right, Lance. We're doing this, so you and Dot never have to go out there. I was told you're working with Dot and Ronnie in the greenhouses, growing veg plants for the gardens. That's a huge contribution, here, Lance, huge. You don't have to risk your life to be appreciated.' Lance stepped back, 'thanks,

Geordie, I just need to know I'm helping in some way.' Don replied, 'you are contributing, Lance, we all see that.'

Don thanked the volunteers, 'I know it's a risk, but if we get this fencing up it will only leave the spaces above the wash houses of the outer houses. There are miles of barbed wire at the farm we can repurpose. I can sort the barrier above the wash houses with a bit of help.'

The following morning Don met with the group. Neil Hipsburn had already recruited four kids to help him with the pillars and they had carried a couple of hundred bricks to the first entry point. Neil passed the group with a bag of sand on his shoulder, 'come on you lot, we're already started, here.'

Don, Hannah, Geordie, Colin and Ben checked the road was clear and set off towards the Picnic field. There were no dead around and Ben went on lookout on the Bedlington end of the road and Colin went over the bridge that crosses the River Blyth and kept lookout up towards the Horton Road.

Don and Hannah knocked on the door of the large, detached house, just over the bridge. It had a plaque on the door, 'Bridge Cottage.' There were dead inside. Don took out a crowbar and forced the side door. They both stepped back. Four dead walked out of the house. There were more inside.

Hannah struck first and, in a few moments, the first four were dead. They could hear movement inside, but dead weren't coming out. Don went inside and found two children, both around twelve years old, that had died of horrendous injuries. They were both unable to get to their feet. 'Oh god,' Hannah had stepped into the room. Don spiked both of the children. The downstairs of the house was stinking, but they needed a safe retreat. Don dragged the dead children outside and around the back of the house, out of sight. 'Are you alright, Hannah?' 'Yes, Yes, sorry, Don. Poor souls.' They dragged the adults around the back. One adult had only one bite. The others had multiple injuries. 'Looks like the first one turned and bit the others. The children had most bites, because they were last to go. Probably hid, then tried to get out when they got desperate.'

Once they had a safe house, Don, Geordie and Hannah started moving the cars out of the left lane, working their way up the road. Ben and Colin moved along, as they progressed. As Colin got to the bend in the road leading to Horton, he waved at Don and Hannah. He held up two fingers, then slipped into the woods. Two dead rounded the corner and Don knocked his spike against an abandoned Ford Fiesta. The two dead walked straight into Don and Hannah's blows.

They gradually rounded the corner and made their way along the road. Most cars were unlocked and none had dead inside. Some car doors were wide open.

As they got onto Horton Road, Don signaled everyone over. 'We can allocate another safe house now. These are the old Doctor's houses.' There was a line of large houses overlooking the farmer's fields opposite. 'Hannah, we'll take one in the centre of the row.'

The others kept watch as Don and Hannah gained access to one of the houses. Don sprayed a black cross on the perimeter wall. 'If we need to retreat, look for the cross.'

They cleared to the beginning of Bebside Road. There were no dead in sight. There was a large block of flats, with the sign 'Bebside Hall' on the outer wall and the farm was about fifty metres ahead. Bebside Road was a route into Blyth and was blocked all the way back to the farm with abandoned cars.

The group were standing on the Horton Road looking towards the farm.

'They come by about every two hours.' Don looked up. The voice had come from a small close on the opposite side of the road, with three - storey houses, that overlooked the fields and woods. A man was sat at a small bistro table on a balcony. The close was surrounded with large vans and cars and there were bags of sand stacked between the wheels of all the vehicles. He had an air rifle propped against the glass balcony front.

Don looked along the Horton Road. In between cars he could see fallen dead. The man was dark haired, around forty years old and he was wearing a black Armani dressing gown over some pull - on grey joggers and a white tee shirt.

'I shoot the ones that are on their own, and I hide when there's a lot of them. A two - two pellet through the eye or temple does it. I figured, eventually I'd kill them all, but there's always more. They come off the Spine Road. Probably from all over. I'm running out of pellets. My name's Castle, Connor Castle.'

The group all looked at each other. 'Geordie Wells. I'm with Don, here, Colin, Hannah and Ben. Are you on your own? We're not looking for any trouble, Connor.' 'Yes, on my own. Everyone from the Close upped and left. The farm got overrun. The dead killed the animals as well.'

Don stepped forward, 'Listen Connor, you said they come every two hours, you mean the dead?' 'Yes, they walk back and forward along the Horton Road, like lost souls. About two hundred and fifty, then a few more every time they pass. More must be getting in all the time along there. There's no noise or stimuli to attract them, here, so when they get to the traffic jam on the Bebside Road, they just stand there, turn around and head back. Some wander off towards Bedlington, but the others seem to tread the same path.' He took a pair of binoculars and looked along the Horton Road. 'I'd say twenty minutes and they'll be back here.'

'Don continued, 'What about the farm, can we get through? we need to get to Bebside.' 'There were a lot of dead in the farm yard so I opened the gate and made a racket outside, then came back up here. When they wandered off, I closed the gate. The safest way to Bebside is through the fields. If you head into Blyth you'll get overrun. There's dead everywhere, there.' 'What about you, Connor. Have you got food?' 'Yes, I cleared out all the other houses and the farm house. I get rabbits in the hedges behind you there, every morning first thing. I pick one off when the coast's clear. I've got a gas stove and a load of gas bottles.

I'm running out of pellets, though. I'll probably have to stop shooting the dead, to get a few more weeks of meat.' Don stepped forward, 'Come with us, Connor. We've got a secure place at Hollymount Square, Bedlington. Your welcome to join us.' 'Maybe when I run out of everything, I'll come over, Don. I'm better on my own at the minute. A lot to deal with, as I reckon you all have as well.' 'You'll see us pass tomorrow, Connor. We need the fencing from the rubbish tip to secure our place.' 'Watch your step then Don, particularly the Blyth side. There's thousands of those things on the Spine Road.'

The Spine Road was a main stretch of road that was a route to Newcastle and the Tyne Tunnel, linking Ashington, Newbiggin, Sleekburn, Bedlington, Cramlington, Dudley, through Benton. It was also a route to the A1. When such main roads had become blocked, people had become trapped in traffic jams. The advice from police and military to stay in cars had led to infected drivers leaving cars in desperation. Anyone following police advice and staying in vehicles, soon had no escape, as the dead multiplied around them.

The group entered the farm and closed the gate behind them. There were no dead, so they passed through the farmyard and onto the fields. There was a clear route as far as they could see, they kept a good way from the roadside and made their way as far as the fields would take them. They could see the rubbish tip entrance. The fence was still there. They just had to move two cars and there was a path. Don scaled a wire fence, 'I'll cut a gap through this for the tractor and we'll fix it when we leave.'

They all crossed the road and walked down to the tip entrance. It was locked up. Don lifted the chain. 'The cutters will go straight through this. We can use the thermal lance to quickly cut the panels free. First job will be to take a safe house from one of those on the roadside. Geordie, we'll take down the fencing, while the others keep watch.'

After agreeing to the plan, the group decided to head back across the fields, home, so as to avoid bumping into the crowds of dead, that were due to pass Connor's house. They made their way across fields all the way to the ha'penny woods and came out by the stone bridge at the bottom of the Bedlington Country Park woodland path. In half an hour they had crossed through the woods, back to the front street and entered the gates to Hollymount Square.

Most of the kids were at Dawn Todd's place. She had the DVD player running and was handing out sweets and soft drinks to the kids, as they settled to watch Iron Man.

Don knocked on Emma's bedroom door and entered. 'Did you not want to join the others for the film?' Emma was looking out of her window over the Bedlington Terriers overgrown ground. She turned round, 'no Grandad, I'm ok. I'm just going to read and listen to music tonight.' 'Are you ok, sweetheart? I know you haven't seen Maeve for a while, but you seemed to hit it off with Colleen.' 'I'm worried about Kate, grandad. She lives right across the playing field from the Donaldsons. Alec Donaldson threatened to kill Kate, when..' 'I'm just securing our place first, Emma. If the Donaldsons get into here it could be very bad. We're not secure enough to keep out the living threat. The Ashfords are the first family I'm going to bring here. Will has been providing them with food and formula for the baby. Just another couple of days and I'll go over with Hannah. I'm going to look for Maeve and Clarky as well when we get the fences up. Listen, Emma, you know Jamie gets pellets for every birthday and Christmas? Where does he keep them?' 'In his bedroom wardrobe, with the rifle.'

Don walked into Jamie's room and opened the wardrobe. There were around thirty tins of pellets. He didn't just get them on special occasions, though. Don regularly looked on eBay before the outbreak and would buy a tin of pellets, if they were below £8.00 with free postage. He just didn't realise they had collected up to such an extent. He took six tins, each containing five hundred pellets and stepped back into Emma's room. 'I'm taking these for someone I met outside. I'll tell Jamie.' 'He won't even miss them grandad.'

Don found a small sack in the shed and put the tins of pellets inside. He tied the bag and put them into his back pack.

It was just starting to get dark and Don went into a kitchen cupboard. He grabbed a tin of hot dogs and started up a small butane gas stove, that was fueled by an aerosol tin of gas.

Honour and the girls had made enough bread to enable all of the residents to take some home and the smell of hot dogs heating up drew Emma downstairs. They had hot dog sandwiches and kept two hot dogs and some bread back for Jamie. Emma sat on the settee with Don and snuggled in. They both fell asleep.

At 9.00pm Jamie came in. He savoured every bite of his hot dog sandwich. Don took his plate when he was finished, 'I took some of your pellets for a man who is holed up on the Horton Road. He's been shooting rabbits for food and is starting to run out. I hope this is ok.' 'Of course, Grandad. I've got thousands.' 'The man told me the two – two will take one of the undead down if you hit through the eye or the temple, so if you ever have to, don't hesitate, an eye is a big target compared to what you hit at the range.' 'I'd shoot one if I thought we were in danger, Grandad. They aren't people anymore.'

The group met at eight in the morning. Neil was laying bricks on one of the pillars, 'I can get a few more courses on each pillar today. We should be ready by tonight.' Don looked at the brickwork, 'spot on, Neil, we're heading for the fencing, now. I'm just going to park the tractor up and get everyone inside on return, the noise will attract them. We can do the fencing tomorrow.'

The group left, for the Picnic Field. Don headed up the grass bank on foot and across the fields and opened up the farm gate. There were no dead around. He took the tractor and trailer outside the gate and locked up. A couple of dead were heading along from Church lane, as Don got back into the tractor and he drove off towards Humford, turning into the field that leads to the Picnic Field.

When Don reached the others, they all boarded the trailer and sat among the tools. He drove along the path they had made and stopped half way up the bank. Colin and Ben ran up the bank to check the road around the corner was clear and Hannah disembarked and kept watch behind. Colin and Ben walked around the corner and up the bank to the Horton Road. They were looking along the road towards Connor's place, when Ben went to the ground. A dead adult male had come out of the drive of the first property. They had made the fatal error of not checking the entrance drive. Ben was screaming and blood ran onto the road from under him. Colin stood for a moment, frozen stiff with fear.

Another dead man walked towards him. He took the hammer and smashed its skull. Colin turned and repeatedly hit the one who had taken Ben down. He dragged it off Ben, revealing horrific injuries. Ben was crying, 'help, Colin, help, I'm, help.' He had been bitten on the left cheek, but had pulled his face out of the bite. There were deep tooth wounds, though. There was blood pulsing out of a neck wound and Colin went to ground at his side. He started to cry, 'Ben, Ben, man.' Blood was gushing from Ben's neck uncontrollably.

Ben was reaching for Colin's hand and trying to speak, but went still.

'Something's wrong, Hannah, they just went for a look. They should be back' Don got out of the tractor and took his spike. When he and Hannah rounded the corner, they saw what had happened to Ben. They walked up to the scene.

Colin looked up. His hands were covered in blood, 'it's my fault Don. I just walked ahead and didn't check the drive to the first house.' Hannah helped Colin to his feet and embraced him, 'I'm so sorry, Colin. It's not your fault. You weren't to know.' Don took the spike and pierced it through the side of Ben's head. They lifted Ben onto the trailer and wrapped him in a tarpaulin.

The road was clear and there seemed to be no dead near Connor's house. Don took the tractor along and stopped beside Connor's place. The group moved a car that was stood against the stone wall, part of the road block, that was preventing the dead from heading into Bedlington. He drove the tractor through, then they returned the car. Connor was on the balcony holding the binoculars. 'I saw what happened, Don. I'm so sorry.' Don took off his back pack. 'When are the dead due back, Connor?' 'They went that way about twenty minutes ago, but I reckon they'll have heard the tractor and turned back. If you set off now you should be out of their earshot by the time they arrive.'

Don took the sack out of the bag and went up to the boundary of cars, that were arranged in front of the property. He stood on the bonnet of one of the cars and threw the sack up to the balcony. Connor caught the bag and opened it up. 'Shit, thanks Don, these will keep me going, no doubt. Wait a sec.' Connor went inside and came back out with something in his hand. 'I found these on my travels.' He threw a two-way radio down to Don and Don caught it. 'When you're ready to leave, Don call me on the channel I've set, there and I'll tell you when you have a window.'

They took the tractor and trailer and entered the farm. Hannah closed the gate behind them and got back on board. Don drove across the fields and stopped at the end. Hannah and Geordie got off the trailer and headed down the road to make a safe house. Within a few minutes the two returned. Hannah threw a black aerosol paint tin back onto the trailer, 'black cross on the safe house door.'

Don had cut the wires in the fence and he drove through the gap and out and onto the road. There were six dead walking towards them and Don drove past them up to the tip gates and turned off the engine. Colin was head down looking at the tarpaulin that covered Ben's body. He took the hammer and jumped down from the trailer. He walked towards the six dead, who had followed the tractor. Don and Hannah followed him. Don took down three of the dead, Hannah two. Colin was still hitting the one he had attacked, after all six were down, he was in a frenzy. The others stood back and waited till he tired out.

Geordie stepped forward, 'Colin, we need you focused here, mate. We can't change what's happened here. Don't get yourself hurt. We've all lost people. We all know how hard it is.' 'I loved him Geordie. I loved him. We were more than friends. We were in love. We've done everything together since we were kids. Inseparable, till now.' 'I'm so sorry, son.'

By the time Don had set up the cylinders for the cutting equipment, the group had to head for a safe house. They left everything as thirty dead waked across from the Bebside roundabout. They walked along the road the group had cleared and turned back when they reached the traffic jam.

The group waited until the dead were gone and then set a look out that covered the three directions, as Don started cutting fence panels free. After three stints, all interrupted by the need to spend time in the safe house, Don was freeing the large gates.

With all of the fencing they needed on board, Don and the group took the tractor into the field and Geordie took a roll of wire, hammer and staples and fixed the fence. They drove to the bottom of the field and switched off the engine.

They were safe and they had the metal fencing, they had come for.

Don got out of the tractor and joined the others. Geordie went into his back pack. 'Heather sends her love.' He pulled out two flasks of coffee that had been made with evaporated milk. He handed everyone a cup. They all savoured the smell of the coffee before they took a drink. He reached into the bag again and pulled out a king size bar of Cadbury fruit and nut chocolate. 'I found this in somebody's shopping, when we were doing the cars. Come on, let's have something nice, fuck, we've earned it.'

After their break Don went on the radio. 'Connor, what's the status?' 'Don, the crowd are outside my door as we speak. I'll call you when they've gone.'

Don kept watch from the trailer, as the others finished the chocolate. He knew he needed to get Colin back, in case he became un hinged and put them in danger, so he was hoping not to run into any more dead.

In around twenty minutes Connor spoke into the radio, 'They're away, Don, about twenty minutes along the road. You have your window. Make sure you shut the farm gate.'

Don reached Connor's place within five minutes and Hannah fastened the farm gate closed. The group made for the end car and moved it to let the tractor through. Don stood under Connor's balcony. 'Come on Connor, grab your stuff and come with us.' 'I'm ok, Don. I know where to come when I'm ready, I'm just not ready.'

The tractor drove through the barricade and Geordie and Colin returned the car. Connor sat down and topped up his glass of red wine. He watched the tractor all the way along the road, through the binoculars until it rounded the corner and went out of sight. He picked up a framed photograph that was on the small bistro table beside his drink and held it up in front of him. A beautiful woman and two beautiful teenage girls were smiling in the picture. Tears rolled down Connor's face. There was movement beside a car across the road, under Connor's balcony. Connor picked up the air rifle. A twenty something dead woman stumbled out from between the cars. She stood looking up at Connor. He took aim and shot her through the left eye. The woman fell dead to the ground and Connor stood the gun back against the balcony and picked up his drink.

The tractor followed the road around past the picnic field and up the steep bank to Bedlington Front Street. There were Dead around, as Don pulled up to the gates. Don handed Hannah the keys and stood in front of the others with his spike weapon. Hannah got the gate open and the others got inside, just as the dead were converging on Don. He spiked the first two through the heads as he retreated through the gate and Hannah secured the bolt. They all ran to the next gate and entered the square, locking it behind them.

The pillars were about three quarters complete. Neil was pointing the lower brickwork. 'It should be up tonight, Don. It needs a few hours before I lay any more bricks, but that should give the dead time to clear off.'

Don put his arm on Neil's shoulder. 'Thanks, son.'

The group headed back to their homes. Geordie put his arm around Colin. 'Stay with us for a few days, Colin, there's plenty room.' 'Thanks, Geordie, if you don't mind, I will.' Colin went inside with Geordie. They didn't have to say anything to Heather, she knew from Geordie's expression there had been tragedy.

The next day, Don was up early. He had called on Geordie and Colin and they had gone out to the trailer and brought Ben's body back to Ben's father's house. Colin was in tears. 'When we finish unloading the equipment, I'll bury him in the garden.' Geordie put his arm around him, 'we all will, Colin.'

The three unloaded all of the metal fencing and Don locked up behind them. It was safe to work.

In two hours, the first fence was up. It was attached between brick walls and the pillars, Neil had made. They had taken breaks after each use of machinery, so as not to attract too many Dead. By lunchtime, the second fence was up and Don and the others were working on the gates.

They left the outer gate until last and managed to get this installed, just before Dead appeared. The college girls had come out with overalls they had found in a shed, that were far too big for them and Don gave them a step ladder, paint brushes and grease and burglar paint. They started painting grease on the lower half of the fencing and burglar paint on the top. When the route down the front street was clear, Don and Hannah took the tractor back to the farm, via the Picnic Field. The farm was secure. Don went into the storage shed out back and took six large rolls of barbed wire, fencing wire and staples. Hannah helped him to load them onto the trailer.

After securing the gate, Hannah got into the cab with Don for the ride back. There was no seat, but plenty room to sit by his side.

Don started up the tractor, 'after we bury Colin, I need to get barbed wire across the wash houses, then we're done.'

All the residents attended a small funeral in Ben's father's garden. Geordie and Ben dug the hole and had wrapped Ben in a sheet. They carefully put him into the hole and filled it in. The place was silent.

Ralph Tindale, an elderly resident carried a tray into the garden. It was covered in small spirit glasses. He had a bottle of Haig Whiskey on the tray and he served the adults with a drink and toasted Ben.

The resident filtered away and Geordie caught Don up to fit the barbed wire above all the wash houses. An hour later Colin climbed up the ladder. 'Need a hand?'

The three spent all day fitting barbed wire across the gaps and after a long hard shift they stood in the middle of the road and looked around. Don shook hands with both men, 'I think that's the safest we can make the place.' Geordie put his hand on Don's shoulder, 'You were right, Don. Looking at what we've done here, it was worth the effort. I wish Ben had seen it, though, Colin.'

The three men walked across to Ben's dad's garden and stood by the grave. Don put an arm around Colin, 'Jamie is making an oak cross for the farm family. I'll ask him to do another.'

Colin was crying. 'Thanks, Don, I'd appreciate that. I hope this is the last grave we dig, Don.'

'Me too, Colin.'

11

Alec Donaldson

Alec Donaldson was scared. He'd always managed to avoid the dead and never got himself into a situation like this. He was sat in the front seat of a dark red Nissan Juke with around fifteen dead pushing against the doors and windows, all around the car.

He'd taken a big risk entering the Hartlands, but the girl he was chasing was beautiful. She was about fifteen years old, long, thick black hair, wearing tight navy leggings and red tee shirt. She had good sized breasts; she was perfect. He really wanted her. She had reached the end of the houses, adjacent to the large playing fields, next to the cemetery, when she stopped and started screaming and banging the crowbar she was carrying against a car. As Alec got closer, she turned and ran over the fields. It was too late when Alec realised what she was doing. He ran headlong into a crowd of dead. Alec diverted right and ended up running along a street, towards another large group.

They were walking in his direction and there was no way past. He about turned and the other way was the same. He had no exit and time to try to get into a house, so he tried car doors. The Juke was unlocked and he quickly got inside and shut the door.

Alec sat for two hours, head down against the steering wheel, terrified. Some dead had wandered off, but others could see him and they circled the car, continually pushing against it, looking for a way to get to their food.

After two hours of this terror, Alec heard the sound of a car horn, coming from the end of the street. The dead surrounding the car, turned and walked towards the sound. The car horn was continual.

As the last of the dead cleared the car, Alec saw a man approach from a house across the road. He was around Alec's dad's age, late fifties, grey hair, grey beard and was wearing combat trousers, olive jumper and army issue type black boots. Some of the dead had seen him and were making their way back to the car, as he opened the door.

'I'm Jack, son, come with me, we don't have much time.' He held out his hand and pulled Alec out of the car. As Alec got to his feet, he thrust his hunting knife into Jack's lower abdomen. Jack screamed and fell to the ground. 'What! God, what have you done, I was helping you!' Jack was screaming with the pain.

Alec Donaldson stood over Jack as the large group of dead approached. He grinned at Jack, with a disturbing expression, curling his top lip, as if in total satisfaction 'I'm Lec, Lec Donaldson. I've got loads of time, Jack, loads of time.'

Alec Donaldson ignored the screams from behind him as he walked towards the overgrown fields. He looked across the field she had crossed and whispered to himself, 'I'll get her next time.'

* * *

Alec Donaldson had never fit in with others for as long as he could remember. As an infant he would take toys off other kids in his classroom. He'd hit, scratch and bite children to make them cry. His parents were constantly being called to school following incidents, involving Alec.

For as long as he could remember his mother never showed him affection. It was as if, because he was a boy, Alec was the property of his father and his mother, Kylie Donaldson would leave him alone and spend all her time with his uncles and neighbours, when Dad was at work. He had to regularly swear to his mother he wouldn't tell Dad, and believed her when she frequently told him something bad would happen to him, if he did.

Alec Donaldson looked like his father, Ray and his two uncles, Jimmy and Mick. The family had striking facial features, square headed, curled up top lip, slightly cross eyed, large round ears that stuck out. They all looked the same.

From a very young age Alec had realised his father was feared around Bedlington. Alec enjoyed hurting and upsetting others and, with people being afraid to challenge his father, he felt he had a free hand to do anything.

Knowing the neighbors were scared of his dad, Alec invented fun games. He liked to follow younger kids and corner them and scare them until they cried. He'd take his knife out and threaten to cut them and he frequently slapped or punched younger boys.

Alec's favorite game was 'window scare,' though. He'd get into gardens and look for someone working in their kitchen then stand in front of the window until they looked up. He was thrilled with the responses, screaming, dropping plates, falling back, it was all funny.

Over the years there were incidents almost every day, where Alec had approached younger kids and beaten them up for no reason. The police had issued warning after warning and, by the age of thirteen Alec Donaldson was a known menace to Northumbria Police.

Alec had no real friends, growing up. Maria was born when he was two and a half years old and, by the time he was five, he was being left to attend to her, while his mother visited friends and neighbours.

He loved Maria. She was the only child he didn't want to hurt. Maria didn't have the Donaldson features, nor did she resemble Mam. Maria was special.

Alec was devastated when Maria was taken into care. Mam was blaming Alec, but Dad wouldn't hear any of it. Alec would never do such things to his sister. It was social services lying, trying to take his kids off him, but while Dad defended his son, Kylie never forgave Alec. The blame she directed at him compensated for the guilt she felt about neglecting Maria from birth.

Alec underachieved at school. He wasn't interested in school work of any kind. All that interested him, was status in the playground. He wanted the reputation of hardest kid in the school, but Kelvin Andrews wore that badge. Kelvin was the school rugby captain, scared of no one, but unlike Alec, Kelvin never picked on weaker kids, more like he defended them and Kelvin had warned Alec Donaldson off, a number of times through high school. Alec always backed down to Kelvin. He didn't ever want to be in a fight where he may be hit back.

Alec Donaldson was fifteen years old when the incident occurred, involving Kelvin Andrews. He had approached a middle school boy on his way to school, punched him to the ground and taken his lunch money. Unfortunately, the child was Kelvin Andrews' younger brother.

As Alec left the school gates that afternoon for home, Kelvin confronted him and punched him in the face. It was a one punch fight. Alec Donaldson cowered as Kelvin stood over him.

Alec had never been in this position. To him, fights were always Alec throwing all the punches and the victim being injured and upset. As he got back to his feet and while Kelvin was warning him never to go near his brother again, Alec Donaldson pulled a lock knife out of his blazer pocket and slashed Kelvin's face.

Alec Donaldson was elated walking home from Bedlington High School that afternoon. He had taken down the toughest guy in the school and he was now top dog.

He was arrested on arrival home.

Alec Donaldson was convicted of aggravated assault and spent six months in a detention centre. His family never visited.

Detention was alright, though. Alec Donaldson quickly learned who was strong and who was weak. It was simple. Avoid the strong and hurt the weak. There were people in detention just like himself and he managed to avoid conflict with the wrong people.

Alec Donaldson returned home from detention, just before the first cases of the virus were being reported. He was delighted when he was told he had been expelled from school and didn't have to go back. It meant Kelvin Andrews couldn't get back at him.

Dad had told Alec he'd be working for him after his sixteenth birthday and Alec was excited. One thing he'd never had was money. His parents spent most of what they earned on tobacco and alcohol.

It was on an afternoon during his expulsion from school when he saw Kate Ashman's parents and sister go off in the car. He knew Kate was due back in from school and he'd been watching her for a while. She had a friend, Emma Jones who was beautiful. With everyone out of the house he decided to pay Kate a visit.

He hid behind the back garden shed as Kate got home and unlocked the back door. Emma was with her. After a while he could hear music from the direction of the upstairs window.

He walked up to the kitchen window and stood looking inside. As he glanced across at the back-door Kate entered the Kitchen and went into the fridge. He stood looking at her, passing his hunting knife from hand to hand and smiled as she dropped the cans of coke. He quickly grabbed for the back door and forced his way inside, took Kate's phone and went up to be with pretty Emma Jones.

* * *

'There you go Lec.' Jimmy Donaldson put down the wire cutters and pulled away the electronic tag that Alec had been wearing on his leg since the court hearing was cancelled. He'd been out lots of times in the last week and no police had shown up at the door.

For Alec Donaldson, life couldn't be better, now. Everything he was good at had become important.

His days were simple. In the morning he joined the men seeking supplies and the afternoon was free to do anything he wanted.

The supply run was currently at the end of Millbank place. They always worked with six people. Alec and Ray went every day. Alec was always first to enter a property and make the way safe for Ray. Ray was there to manage the money and valuables. The others were either Jimmy or Mick Donaldson and three of the friends. Abe was unmarried, but Sammy was married to Cynthia, Gary was married to Amanda and Craig was married to Sharon. They all had grown up children they had recently lost contact with.

Kylie was in constant conflict with the friends' wives, though, so when the men went out, one friend stayed with the wives and Mick and Jimmy took turns to stay with Kylie, an arrangement they all seemed very happy with.

The family dynamic had changed when Ray had moved the friends into Millfield, though. Uncle Jimmy and Uncle Mick lived with them now and Sammy, Gary, Craig and Abe had moved into two adjoining houses. They had sealed off all around the houses with tall stacks of pallets form an abandoned pallet wagon that Craig had found and somehow managed to get to Millfield.

The rules were simple. Everyone had back packs. One pack was for money and valuables, another for cigarettes and alcohol, one for clothing and the rest for food, medicines and drugs. They always had a safe house to retreat to if they encountered too many dead and any living, they found were led into the rear garden killed with baseball bats. The men weren't in the business of helping others.

Alec Donaldson had urges and he could follow those urges every afternoon. When Mam and Dad started drinking, he would slip out and head for the back streets, looking for survivors. If he found a girl, she was his and, now there were no police, he could leave no one to tell the tale. He could seek out and chase down kids for real now. Not just to threaten and make them cry. Now he could finish the hunt with a kill and there was plenty prey for a predator of his

stature.

This was Alec's world now. He was powerful and feared around Bedlington. No one was

safe from him. He felt no pity or remorse for his actions, just pleasure.

Yes, this was Alec's world.

* * *

'Howay Alec, Man!' Dad was angry. Alec had overslept and everyone was ready to go out

for supplies except him. He quickly pulled on jeans and a grey sweatshirt and squeezed his

feet into trainers, without loosening the laces. 'Ready Dad.'

Ray pushed him to the front of the group and Alec slid a pallet sideward and crawled

through into the front garden. There were no Dead in sight so they all left. Kylie had come to

the door. She was wearing a long burgundy dressing gown and she was in her bare feet. Her

hair was bleached blonde, but the bleached hair was growing out, revealing dark ginger

coloured hair underneath. 'Ray, see if you can get more vodka and I need a dye for my hair.'

He didn't reply.

The group headed down the back of Millfield south and down a footpath towards the Picnic

Field.

Kylie closed the hatch and walked back into the house. Jimmy was standing in living room

doorway at the bottom of the stairs. 'I thought they would never fucking leave.' Kylie smiled

and stepped towards him. She loosened the bow of the dressing gown strap and it fell open.

Kylie let the dressing gown drop to the floor, brushed past Jimmy and walked over to the

settee. She went onto all fours on the settee and Jimmy dropped his trousers and stepped onto

the settee behind her. Kylie looked back, 'it's been a week since our last chance, Jimmy I need this, fuck me, now.' 'Oh, I'm going to fuck you alright, Kylie. Ray's taken me with him every day this last week, the bastard. I'm going to fuck you, nice and hard. I fucking need this.'

The group made their way along from the Picnic Field along to the woods behind Beatty road and followed the path into the woods. Ray stopped. 'The first of the new houses is up there. We'll climb up the bank, through the trees and get in through the back garden.'
The six were soon at the bottom of the first garden.
Alec Donaldson entered the garden and walked up to the house. There was a small top window open and he could hear voices.

Alec looked through the window from the side. He could make out an old woman and a younger man and woman. He recognized the voice of the man. It was the copper who roughed him up when he was arrested.

'Keep the doors locked, Iris, we'll be back in a couple of days.' 'Thank you so much, Ian.'
The couple left and Alec climbed onto the garage roof and crossed to the front. The couple had encountered dead as they left and they had been split up, the man, running towards Millbank Place, called out, 'get to number fifteen Maeve, I'll meet you when they clear off.'

Alec waved the group over, as he got down from the garage roof. The group moved into the garden. Ray looked through the window, 'a fucking old woman, that's what's taking you so fucking long?' 'They were here, dad, the coppers, the one that pushed me around.' 'The Clarkes?' 'They got split up after they left. They didn't see a group of dead coming out from behind a van, between them. She's at number fifteen and he ran up to Millbank place to draw them away.'

Ray took a crowbar out of the bag and forced the kitchen window. Alec climbed through. The old lady was screaming with fright. Alec stood and grinned at her. He grabbed her by the arm and led her into the garden. Ray Donaldson took a baseball bat and struck Iris across the head. She fell dead to the ground.

There wasn't much in the house, a little money, the food Maeve and Clarky had left Iris and a little jewelry. There was forty pounds in her purse.

There was a safe path to number fifteen when the gang left out the front door. When they got there the men hid behind cars and Alec Donaldson tapped on the door. He heard a voice inside, 'That didn't take long.' The door opened and Alec stepped forward and thrust his knife into Maeve Clarke's left ribcage. She fell back, grabbing her side with her right hand. Alec Donaldson stepped back, as the others approached the door.

Ray Donaldson stood in front of Maeve holding a baseball bat. 'You fucking pig bitch, I'm going to cave your bitch head in!' Maeve was coughing and blood was running into her hand from the stab wound. Ray stepped forward and as he raised the bat, two shots rang out. Abe Gardener fell to the ground. He lay still. The others ducked down as two more shots rang out, just missing Alec.

Sammy Dodds looked along the road from behind a car. 'Ray we need to get back to the first house let's move now.' They ran for Iris's house as Clarky rounded the corner. He held the gun in two hands and fired four times. Two shots hit Sammy Dodds, who was at the back and he fell, but the others had run between cars. Clarky emptied the chamber, each round hitting cars right beside the fleeing group. Ray Donaldson stopped when he realised Clarky had ran out of ammo. He turned just outside Iris's front door. 'We'll be back for you Clarke! We know where you live now. You'll be as dead as her soon, fucker!'

He turned and ran inside.

Maeve had bled out. Clarky knelt beside Maeve and cried. What was he going to do without Maeve? He sat holding her in his arms, 'I'm sorry, I'm sorry I ran, Maeve, I'm sorry.'

He heard a voice outside, 'I need help, please, dead are coming.' Abe gardener had been shot twice in the middle of the back. He couldn't move his arms and legs. 'Please, it wasn't me. I didn't know the boy would do that.' Clarky walked to the front door, 'It wasn't you?' Clarky walked past Abe and over to Sammy Dodds.

Sammy had been shot in the lower back and under the right shoulder. He was trying to get to his feet. Clarky grabbed him by the hair and dragged him down the street towards Abe. He threw him to the ground. 'Look mate, I never take part in killing. I don't carry a weapon. I just look for food, that's all. It wasn't me that did this.' Clarky kicked him in the face. Blood was pouring out of Sammy's mouth. 'It wasn't you either, then?' Clarky took the revolver, loaded a new magazine and shot Sammy's left kneecap off. Sammy was screaming in agony.

He looked along the road. There were dead coming from both directions. Clarky went into the house and looked into Sammy Dodds' pleading eyes as he shut the front door. He sat back down beside Maeve.

Clarky could hear Sammy and Abe screaming for help as the dead got nearer, then screaming for mercy, as they started eating them.

After a few minutes it went quiet outside. Clarky took a knife out of a sheath that was hanging from his belt and pierced through the side of Maeve's head. After an hour he opened the safe house door and carried Maeve past the two un recognizable bodies on the road outside and along to their own house. He put Maeve down on the armchair and sat with the revolver on his knee. Clarky cried his heart out.

Alec Donaldson walked ahead of the group all the way back. It was only ten o'clock and they were finished for the day. They didn't have much to take back and Dad was pretty angry

It looked like Sammy and Abe were dead, so there would be a lot of upset at home. He decided he was going straight out. Maybe he'd get another chance with that dark - haired girl with the red top.

He grinned as he thought of her tight red top and large breasts. He was the only one in the group smiling.

As they neared Millfield Ray Donaldson was in a foul mood. No one took the chance of talking to him. He wasn't accustomed to things going wrong and he certainly wasn't going to be the one to face Cynthia. He went into the house.

Kylie was sitting, red faced on the settee in her dressing gown. 'Where's Jimmy?' 'Oh, upstairs, I think, he's been up there all morning.' Jimmy had heard the group sliding open the pallet and he'd dashed upstairs. Jimmy finished fastening his trousers in his room, then walked downstairs. 'What the fuck's happened., Ray?'

Alec left the house, while the adults were talking. He could hear crying from the next house, probably Cynthia.

Dad was really unhappy. Alec decided he needed to think of something that would please dad.

First things first, though. Alec planned to head for The Riggs, the large houses on the left, on the road out of Bedlington towards the golf course. That's where he'd seen the beautiful dark-haired girl with the impressive tits.

The hunt was on.

Alec Donaldson was pulling back the exit pallet, when Ray Donaldson came to the front door. 'Where you going Lec?' 'Just out and about.' 'Not today, you're not. Go get Gary and Craig.'

* * *

12

The Ashfords.

Albert Ashford's number one priority was ensuring the safety of his family. He had a wife, two young daughters and a baby granddaughter to protect.

When news broke of the outbreak reaching Newcastle, he started to pack the car. The family were originally from Morpeth and Albert had friends and family over there. He had contacted his brother and they were making space at their house in Morpeth, for the family to join them.

Albert had to be careful and avoid the Donaldsons, though. Alec Donaldson had been arrested for a serious crime, that had happened in their house and Ray Donaldson had been outside his house a number of times asking him to come outside and discuss the matter. The whole family were being intimidated by the Donaldsons. His youngest daughter Kate was the chief witness in the case.

Albert carried the phone at all times and Detective Clarke had given him a number to call on speed dial, if he had concerns about their safety.

Unfortunately, Albert had acted too late. Thousands of people were trying to head north, through all routes and word had got to Albert, that there was no way out of Bedlington, that would avoid traffic jams. His brother advised him to stay home.

When Albert called Detective Clarke that afternoon, Ian Clarke couldn't help. 'I'm sorry Mr Ashford, all units are outside the Newcastle and Gosforth area. The situation here is critical. You need to stay in your home. Keep quiet, the dead are attracted to sound. Get plenty food in for your family, now. Use the time you have to board up your house. Use anything. The dead are heading your way. We cannot stop them.'

The family had walked to the nearest Supermarket and joined the hordes of panic buyers. With as much as they could carry, they made for home. Their eldest daughter Lisa wasn't producing enough milk for the baby, so they had bought as much formula as they could.

With his wife, Brenda looking out from the upstairs windows for the Donaldsons, Albert took floorboards he had lifted from a spare bedroom, one by one and boarded up the downstairs of the property and reinforced the doors. A few others in the street were doing the same.

The Ashfords sat tight as the virus arrived at Bedlington. Albert knew the main threat to his family from the Donaldsons would be if communications went down.

Many cars left Millfield in a desperate attempt to escape the trouble ahead. and soon there were very few residents left.

It wasn't much more than a week before they saw the first dead man walk past. He wandered in from the direction of Church lane and clumsily limped past. Throughout that day more passed, some horrifically injured, bite marks all over them.

The Donaldsons had been busy. They had taken a wagon, laden with wooden pallets and pushed through the now abandoned cars and they had parked it along the road from their house.

Ray Donaldson had claimed the abandoned houses, alongside his and moved a group of friends there.

Over a few days the Donaldsons had built up a boundary of wooden pallets around the three houses.

Albert and Brenda kept watch from the upstairs windows every day. They saw the Donaldsons leave every morning, normally in a group of six and they would return by midday, carrying heavy back packs.

The Donaldsons gang had all obtained baseball bats, on their travels and Albert feared Ray would soon come over and take retribution for his daughter's part in his son's arrest.

At first, this never happened, though. The Donaldsons had quickly realised the dead were attracted to towns and buildings, so they had begun entering housing estates from the woods.

Unbeknown to Albert, Ray Donaldson had become obsessed with accumulating money, tobacco and expensive alcoholic drink. The group were looting houses and Ray would spend his afternoons drinking expensive whiskey, smoking cigars and going through valuables and money they had looted.

The Ashfords lived in constant fear, though.

When Bedlington had become overrun, Albert was desperate. Food was running low and they were running out of baby formula for Amelia.

It was chance that gave them a lifeline, though. One Morning there was a knock at the door. Albert stood behind the door, 'Who is it?' 'Will, Will Masters. I'm a friend of Kate. I'm checking she's alright. I have food. I have stuff for the baby.'

Will Masters knew when the Donaldsons were likely to be out looting. He had seen them a number of times, when checking on friends. He knew the danger Alec Donaldson was. He knew he could get in and out of Millfield, avoiding Alec Donaldson in the morning.

Albert let Will in and he sat with Kate and her family. 'I know your situation, Mr Ashford. I can bring food down to you, every other day, but it's a big risk. Alec Donaldson is murdering children all around Bedlington and I have survivors at my house near Nedderton, all children aged between four and fifteen. I know it's a risk, but if you come with me you can all stay with us. We're more secure at my place than you are here. We really could use adult support at our place'

Albert gave the matter thought then made the worst decision of his life. 'It's too risky to make a run for Nedderton, especially with the baby.' Will stood up and walked to the back door. 'I'll be back then, but if you come, we only have to make it to the woods, over there. We can use farmers' fields to get most of the way. The dead aren't attracted to open spaces, unless there's noise.'

Albert thanked Will and locked the door behind him.

And this went on. True to his word, every other morning, Will arrived with food, drinks and baby stuff.

* * *

As they neared Millfield Ray Donaldson was in a foul mood. No one took the chance of talking to him. He wasn't accustomed to things going wrong and he certainly wasn't going to be the one to face Cynthia. He went into the house, leaving Mick, Gary and Craig to break the news about Sammy and Abe, to Cynthia and the others.

Kylie was sitting on the settee in her dressing gown. 'Where's Jimmy?' 'Oh, upstairs, I think, he's been up there all morning.' Jimmy had heard the group sliding open the pallet and dashed upstairs. He finished fastening his trousers in his room, then walked downstairs. 'What the fuck's happened., Ray?'

'We ran into that fucking copper, Maeve Clarke. Lec stabbed the bitch and her fucking husband turned up with a gun. He shot Abe and Sammy. They're dead, Jimmy. We just got away through a garden and into the woods.'

Ray carried his backpack upstairs and threw it, angrily on the bed. He had a collection of around thirty bottles of spirits, of all kinds, on a set of drawers, that were below the bedroom window and he poured a large Glenfiddich onto a crystal whiskey glass.

He took a drink and looked out of the window. On the opposite side of the playing field he saw the bedroom curtain move in the Ashford's house. It was Brenda Ashford. She was looking out of the window. His top lip curled and quivered. Ray had a lot of anger to vent and he had come upstairs to have a drink and compose himself. He walked down the stairs.

'Change of plan. Jimmy, get your bat.' Ray picked up his baseball bat and headed for the front door.

Alec Donaldson was pulling back the exit pallet, when Ray Donaldson came to the front door. 'Where you going Lec?' 'Just out and about.' Not today, you're not. Go get Gary, Mick and Craig.'

Gary Blewitt, Mick Donaldson and Craig Blewitt came out to the next-door house with Alec. Ray was standing at the exit. 'We're going to pay the Ashfords a visit.'

Alec's face lit up. He grinned and slid open the exit panel.

There were no dead in sight. The gang crossed the overgrown playing field and Ray stood in front of the Ashfords' house, holding a baseball bat and a crowbar.

There was panic inside the house. Albert addressed the family in the front bedroom. 'I'm going to open the window and try to keep him talking. I want you all to go out the back and get to church lane. Do what Will said, head for the fields and follow them along past the Hartlands. You'll only need to cross one road, so look for a safe place to cross when you get to the golf course, go now.'

Albert opened the window as Lisa and Kate made for the back door. Brenda had the Baby. She kissed Albert, 'We'll wait at the golf course,' 'no, Brenda, keep going, I got it wrong, we should have left with Will.'

Albert opened the window.

Ray Donaldson was stood on the road. 'We can do this the easy way, or the hard way, Ashford, all the same to me.' 'Leave us alone, Ray, we haven't done anything wrong.'

'Nothing wrong, that lying little fucker of a daughter of yours was going to put my son away, because her and her friend's cock teasing went too far. No, Ashford, you and me need to talk. Get yourself out here, don't make me come in and get you.'

Kate was first down the stairs. She unlocked the back door and stepped outside. She was struck with a blow to the side of the head and she fell to the ground. Lisa was right behind her and Alec Donaldson thrust a hunting knife into her left side. She screamed and fell.

Alec Donaldson stepped past her and made towards Brenda and the baby. Brenda retreated into the bedroom and put the baby into the cot. 'Please don't harm the baby.' Alec Donaldson grinned. His top lip was curled and quivering with satisfaction.

Albert walked in front of his wife and the baby, as Ray and the others entered the room.

Ray and Jimmy dragged the couple downstairs and onto the playing field. Alec dragged Kate.

At the Ashford's back door Lisa Ashford's breathing was shallowing. She was cold and felt really sick and the pain was intense. Lisa held her side, where she had been stabbed, tight, but blood was just running out of her. She could hear Amelia. Amelia was starting to cry.

Lisa felt sleepy. She was trying to drag herself back into the house, but her strength was draining out of her. She passed out in the doorway.

Ray lined the three up on their knees in front of the gang.

Brenda Ashford was crying hysterically, 'the baby, the baby.' Ray smiled at her, 'don't worry, your daughter will soon take care of the baby.' He smashed the bat across Brenda's head and Jimmy hit her three more times.

Albert said nothing. He sat head down, sobbing, resigned to what was going to happen. Kate was silent. She was in a state of terror. Every inch of her body was trembling. It felt as if everything had gone into slow motion and she watched as Craig Thompson and Gary Blewitt beat her father to death.

Ray stepped towards Kate. 'So just you, then, you little whore. Teasing my fucking son then getting the coppers. You deserve this.' Ray raised the bat and Alec stepped forward, 'she's mine, dad, she's mine. Let me take her.'

Ray lowered the bat, 'Ok Lec, but she doesn't live to tell the tale.' Lec grinned.

Kylie Donaldson had come to the bedroom window. She screamed at the gang, 'the baby, the fucking baby! You can't just leave it there.' Ray looked up at her. 'Come and get it then. You bring it up.' Kylie closed the window. Ray looked at the others. 'Any of you going to adopt this fucking baby?' They all looked down. 'I thought not. The mother will turn soon. She'll find it.'

The gang headed inside the Donaldson place and Ray poured them all a drink. 'This is for Abe and Sammy. We're going to have a good drink for them today. Fucking Clarke is going to pay for what he did.'

Outside, Alec Donaldson was dragging Kate towards an empty house at the end of the street. She was resisting so he stopped and slapped her face, hard. He dragged her the rest of the way, then took a key out of his pocket and took her inside. This was Alec's safe house. No one bothered him here. He dragged Kate to the main bedroom, closed the door behind him then started to undress. He pointed his knife in Kate's direction. 'I'd undress too if I was you.'

* * *

Don Mason had promised Emma he would call on the Ashfords when he had secured the square. Hannah called in at 10.00am. Emma was downstairs having a cup of tea with Don.

Emma had been really down and Don was hoping he could get the Ashfords back to Hollymount Square, for Emma's sake. 'I promised we would call on Kate and her parents, today, Emma. Im heading off with Hannah and we'll go through Millfield North out of sight of the Donaldson house and seek them by their back door. All being well we'll have them back here soon.' Emma smiled. She couldn't wait to see Kate. She had been depressed so long; Kate would be a huge lift for her.

Don bid Emma and Jamie farewell and left through the front door. Hannah hung back. 'Look, Emma, it's really dangerous out there. You know they might not be there, now. Lots of people have left trying to get to safer places. Don't build your hopes up too high.' 'I know, Hannah, I know and, be careful. The family Grandad spoke of are dangerous. They'll kill you if they see you.'

As they left Don and Hannah knocked at a few doors. They had agreed to give keys out for the gates. There were four sets.

Don gave a set to Colin Markem. Colin was housed next to four brothers, Vince, Dean, Joe and Alan Mcevoy. These men were all in their thirties, but had kept themselves to themselves from the start, self - sufficient, if you like. They had been climbing the fence and crossing the park for exit and entry to the square. Colin had indicated to Don he would join the brothers and Don and Hannah thought it best to give them all a key.

Geordie Wells was given a key. He scavenged for petrol, tools, anything he could get from vehicles. He would take any willing volunteer with him.

No one else wanted a key, so Don carried one and a spare was hung in the store house.

The Front street was quiet, when Don and Hannah left. They set off towards Church lane. They took down a group of four dead, that were wandering ahead of them, down Church Lane and entered Millfield North. There were six more dead ahead of them and Don and Emma quickly dispatched them with clean punctures to the heads.

Don held back as they got to the entrance to Millfield. 'Wait here a minute.' Don crossed the road and looked over the playing field, towards the Donaldsons' place. He could see the

Ashford couple lying dead in the long grass. He returned to Hannah. 'Something's wrong, Hannah.'

Don and Hannah entered the Ashfords' back garden, over the fence from a Millfield North garden. The back door was open and Lisa Ashford lay dead in the doorway. Don crept over. Lisa had a stab wound her left side and there was a stab wound through her temple. Don heard a noise coming from upstairs. He lifted the spike and crept up the stairs. As he got to the top, he heard a voice. 'I've got a knife. I'm only here for the baby. Give me a path out. You won't see me again.'

Don took the spike and pushed open the door. Will Masters was distraught. He was holding baby Amelia in one arm and a hunting knife in the other.

'Don! Hannah!' Don took the baby and passed her to Hannah. Don put his hand on Will's shoulder, 'We've got to get out of here fast. Where's Kate! Will, where's Kate?' 'I don't know, Don. She wasn't here.'

The three left through the back door and headed along Millfield North. Hannah had given her spiked bat to Will, so she could carry the baby and he and Don led the way to church lane. There were more dead than before, but Don and Will managed to forge a path through.

They ran down the front street and made it safely to the gates. Don was shaking as he tried to fit the key into the lock. Hannah passed him the baby. 'Let me, Don, there's more dead coming.' Hannah quickly unlocked the gate, got them all inside and locked it behind them. They made their way to Don's house.

They all sat down in Don's sitting room and Don poured a large whiskey for himself and Hannah. Will was crying and couldn't stop shaking, can, 'can I have some of that.' Don poured another.

Emma sat beside Will and put her arm around him. He was sobbing, 'I got there too late. I took them food and baby milk. I always go in the morning to avoid the Donaldsons, but they'd been. I saw them walking away from the bodies on the field.'

Emma started to cry, 'Kate's dead?' 'Kate was the only one I didn't see, Emma. I got there and found Lisa on the step, she was still alive, unconscious, but bleeding heavy. I couldn't help her. I held her hand as she died, then I heard the baby. I heard Mrs. Donaldson calling to them from the bedroom window, so I knew they were still outside, but I kept down in case they spotted me. I sat for half an hour, scared to look out the window in case I was spotted. When I decided to look everyone was gone. I'd put the knife through Lisa's head. She'd be in my path out if she turned. Don, they had left the baby to be eaten by her mother. What kind of people could do something like that?' He was crying again. Emma pulled him closer and they both cried.

Hannah picked up the bag that Will had been carrying. 'Will, is there baby stuff in the bag?' 'Yes. I don't know what I'm going to do, Hanna. We can't rear a baby. I don't even think I could even get her home safely. The dead will hear her from way off if she cries.'

Hannah sat down beside Will and held his hand. 'Will, Colleen and I were going to go in for IVF just before this outbreak. We wanted a baby. We can keep Amelia, if that's ok?' Will looked up. 'Would you do this for me, Hannah?' 'Will, this is the most wonderful gift I could imagine anyone ever giving us, especially in such awful circumstances. You've risked your life and rescued this baby from the most horrific fate. I'm so sorry for what happened to your friend's family, but Colleen and I will do what's best for the baby, I promise.'

Hannah left. And headed for home. She entered through the back door. Colleen was sitting with Marty, who was laid on the settee. She stood up as Hannah entered the room. Hannah passed Amelia to Colleen. 'We'll talk later, it's a long story.' Tears ran down Colleen's face. She knew Hannah was deeply disturbed. Colleen knew Hannah would explain in her own time and she instinctively knew that something very bad had happened to lead to Hannah bringing a baby home. This wasn't the happy family story Colleen and Hannah had been planning before the outbreak. Colleen held the baby and pulled the blanket she was wrapped in aside, revealing her face. She kissed baby Amelia and held her close.

Don got up to leave the room. Emma was comforting Will, who had witnessed an awful atrocity. There wasn't much Don could do. Jamie had gone to his room. As Don left Emma spoke, 'Grandad, none of you saw Kate, she may have run.' 'That's what I'm hoping, sweetheart. Hannah and I are going out tomorrow, we'll be on the lookout for her. There are too many dead on the streets to go out now and I'm exhausted. The others may see her as well. Let's not give up hope.'

Will stayed another hour then called up to Don to let him out the gates.

As they walked through the Square Will looked around. 'Not bad, Don, not bad.' Don unlocked the inner gate, 'the offer's still on for you and your friends to join us, or move into the farm. Bring the survivors you provide for; they'll be safe with us.' 'I'll talk to them, Don. Give me a little time. I don't think we've seen the last of each other. I'll be down with stuff for the baby, anyway, no doubt. Oh, those catapults, you gave us. Some of the kids are becoming pretty good with them. They use them for a distraction, putting out windows, or hitting cars to divert Dead off their track, but a few have made kill shots. Eye, temple or back of the head. If Alec Donaldson runs into them he may get a shock.'

Don opened the outer gate and Will made off towards the entrance towards the farmers' fields above the Picnic Field. 'Be careful out there, son.' Will looked back, God bless, Don.'

When Don returned Emma was in tears, on the settee. He poured himself another whiskey and held her close. Don knew this was another huge blow for Emma. He was deeply concerned about her state of mind. 'I'm going to look for Clarky and Maeve, tomorrow, Emma. I need Clarky and Maeve, here. We'll look out for Kate, as well.'

A tear ran down Don's face as he held his granddaughter. He was putting everyone's needs before his own, but he knew deep down, things weren't right. The events of the last year were starting to take their toll on Don Mason.

13

The Last Straw

Don made his way to the bathroom at 7.00am. He looked in the mirror. He hadn't shaved for two weeks and his beard was white, matching his hair. He used to wear his hair short and combed back, but it was about three months overgrown, covering his ears and neck length at the back.

He turned on the tap. The pressure was low, but he half filled the sink and washed down. His hair was all over the place so he cupped some water in his hands and wet his hair. He took a hair brush and brushed it back. 'God, I look old.'

Don went into the wardrobe and pulled out a pair of clean jeans. He took socks and underpants out of the top drawer and got dressed. He put a black tee shirt on, then a navy Reebock sweatshirt, he had bought just before the outbreak. It was still in the JD Sports carrier bag.

Don put a pair of brown Merrell trainer - type walking shoes on and went downstairs.

It was quiet around the square. Don walked over and checked the boundary, as he did every morning and all was well.

He had arranged to meet with Hannah and Geordie, around 1.00pm to look for Clarky and Maeve. The Donaldsons were renowned for looting in the morning and they didn't want to chance running into them, especially when they would be taking the same route to Dene View.

Don opened a tin of spam and cut into six slices. He opened a tin of chopped tomatoes and started up a small butane gas stove. He poured some hot tomato over two pieces of spam on his plate and boiled some water in a small pan and made tea.

After breakfast, Don started tidying downstairs. When Jamie came down around 8.30, he served some spam and tomatoes and took the rest to Emma's room. Emma was still in bed. 'Are you getting up, Emma?' She didn't answer.

Don put the food on her bedside table and left the room.

Don spoke with Jamie downstairs. 'We're going out looking for Clarky and Maeve today and we know Kate is out there somewhere, so while I'm away, I'm going to ask Dawn to pop in from time to time. Emma isn't well, so keep an eye out for her.' 'I'll just stay in my room today, Grandad. I've started a new Super Mario game.'

Don met up with Hannah and Geordie and they left for Dene view. They entered the woods by the Picnic Field and headed through Bedlington Country Park, until they reached the woods adjacent to Knox Road and Millbank place.

Don saw a track through the grass, heading up the slope, 'that's where the Donaldsons must have been accessing Millbank and Knox Road.' They followed the woodland path and found another track, 'they've been accessing Dean View West from here.' The group walked a further hundred yards and Don stopped them. 'They haven't accessed any further down, by the look of it. There're three streets down Dene View, Dene View West, beside Millbank Place, Dene View, in the middle and Dene View East at the bottom. Clarky lives half way down Dene View East. It looks like the Donaldsons haven't reached there. Follow me.'

The group followed the woodland path and Don pointed to an area that looked reasonably easy to ascend. 'We'll go in here. I'll know Clarky's house from the street.'
They climbed to the top of a steep fern covered bank, that led into tree line and eventually reached the back gardens of Dene View East. Hannah climbed over a garden fence and the others followed.

Don tapped on the kitchen window of the house. Doors were open inside, leading to the living room and there was no activity inside. He took a crowbar out of his back pack and levered open the window. He banged the crowbar on the kitchen bench and there was nothing.

Hannah climbed inside. The key was in the back door and she unlocked it and Geordie and Don entered. Don held up the spike as he ascended the stairs and he checked the whole upstairs.

Don entered the sitting room and Hannah passed him a key chain, 'this was hanging beside the front door.' Don opened the front door and looked along the road. It was quiet. He lifted a potted plant, that was beside the front door and put the keys underneath. 'This is the safe house.' Geordie closed the door and it latched shut. Don took a can of black paint out of the bag and painted a large x on the door.

The three walked into the road. There was still no signs of living, or dead, but Don knew where they had come out. 'Just a bit further down.'

Don, Hannah and Geordie reached Clarky's house and Don stepped up to the front door. He tapped on the door. There was no answer. The curtains were closed, so they couldn't look in. 'Let's try the back.'

There was a wash house, now workshop at the side of Clarky's house. The door at the side led to the back door of the house. Don tried the door and it opened. He did the same with the back door. It was unlocked. Don entered the house and passed through the kitchen. He could see the first armchair, through the open living room door, from the angle he was entering. Maeve was slumped in the chair. Her head was to the side and Don could see a puncture wound on her right temple. He stepped into the doorway and Clarky was sitting at the opposite side of the room, two hands on his police issue handgun. The gun was pointed at Don. 'Clarky, It's me, Don.'

Clarky lowered the weapon and put it on the arm of the chair.

Don called in the others and they entered. Emma turned away in tears at the sight of Maeve. She didn't know the Clarkes, but seeing this was heartbreaking. Geordie put an arm around her. 'We'll be in the kitchen.' Geordie took Hannah into the kitchen and closed the door.

Don knelt down beside Clarky, 'God, Clarky, I'm so sorry. What happened to Maeve?'

Clarky sat head down. 'Donaldson.' Don stood up and picked up a half full bottle of Famous Grouse, that was on the coffee table. He took a drink and passed it to Clarky, 'tell me what happened.'

Clarky took a drink, 'We had popped up to Dene View West with some food for a survivor, Iris, an old lady. One of the only fuckers round here who took my advice to stay indoors. We had number 15 marked as a safe house, in case we ran into trouble and we were making our way back. I got distracted, when I thought I heard something, but Maeve had kept walking, then a group of dead, that we hadn't spotted, came out from behind a white van. Maeve had a clear path to the safe house, so I called out for her to head there and I ran towards Millbank Place and hid in a garden till they passed. When I set off back, I saw a group of men outside number 15 and I ran along Hudson Avenue and down Poplar Grove, to come in round the back of them.

I saw Abe Gardener and I could hear Ray Donaldson threatening Maeve, so I stopped and shot Abe twice. When I rounded the corner, I could see them all running between cars. They had hurt Maeve, I could see her lying in the doorway, covered in blood. Sammy Dodds was at the back and I had a clear shot so I took the bastard down, but the others got into Iris's house.

I had to go back for Maeve. When I got back, she was.' Clarky started to cry, 'She was fucking dead, Mace.' Don took Clarky in his arms and Clarky sobbed. 'I didn't get to say goodbye, she was just gone.'

Don knelt in front of Clarky, 'Dodds and Gardener, were they dead?' 'No, they were both alive. Abe Gardener couldn't move his hands and legs and I dragged Sammy Dodds down beside him and shot off his kneecap. The gunfire had attracted a lot of dead, so I closed the door while they were eaten. Donaldson said he's coming for me, so here I am.'

Don shook his head. 'Ray Donaldson will be full of hell, now, but he'll not come here, Clarky. He knows you've got a gun. Clarky, you need to come with us. We've secured Hollymount Square. Tall fencing, barbed wire. It's about as secure as you could get a place. We've got a good number of people living there and space for more. We've got the farm at the end of Church Lane, as well. It's stocked for a long-term survival situation and has a good perimeter.'

Clarky went through the kitchen to the workshop. He took a spade and walked to the bottom of the garden. The others followed. There was another spade hanging from a hook. Geordie took it. Clarky had started digging and Geordie stepped beside him. 'My Name's Geordie, I'm a friend of Dons' let me help you there.'

The two men dug a deep trench and Don and Emma brought Maeve's body to the garden, wrapped in a bed sheet.

They stood over the grave, after the men had buried Maeve. Geordie stuck the spade in the ground. Clarky picked it up and passed it back to him, 'I don't think we're finished with these.'

The group made their way towards Dene View West. As they neared number 15 Don held up a hand. 'Are those two Sammy and Abe?' Clarky nodded, 'What's left of the fuckers.'

The two dead were laid face down on the ground, there was huge chunks of flesh missing from all over their bodies and muscles and tendons were eaten off their legs. They were unable to stand, so scratched at the ground with what was left of their hands to try to pull themselves towards the group.

Don stepped forward with the spike and Clarky stepped in front of him. 'Leave them like that, Mace.' Don lowered the spike and they walked past.

As they arrived at Iris's house, Hannah stopped and looked towards Millbank Place, 'Oh God!' A young, dead girl was stumbling down the incline into Dene View West. She was wearing a vest top, but had no clothing on the lower part of her body. There was purple bruising around the young girl's throat.

Hannah walked towards her, 'It must be Marty's sister.' She walked over and struck the girl with her spiked bat. The point entered the girl's temple and she fell dead to the ground. Hannah rolled the body over. There was a gold necklace around her bruise covered neck and '*Ellie*,' in gold letters, hanging from the chain. Hannah took the chain from the child's neck and put it into her pocket. She turned away in tears. Geordie opened the front door, 'I'll get a sheet, we cannot carry her like that.'

The girl's face was covered in dried blood. She had bitten someone, at some point. There was dark red slime down the backs of her legs, which stank. Geordie came out of the house with a bed sheet and wrapped the child in it.

Iris lay still in her back garden. She'd suffered major head trauma and had died instantly. The only blessing was that this had prevented her from turning.

Clarky knelt beside her. 'She couldn't have resisted against anybody. Why hurt her, when they could have just taken what they wanted?'

Don took Clarky's spade and he and Geordie started digging. Hannah knelt beside Clarky. His tight dark ginger hair was now thick and mostly white. He was quite a large man. The outbreak had provided him with a much-needed diet, but he was still well built.

Hannah put her hand on his shoulder. 'I'm Hannah, I've seen first - hand what these people are doing, Clarky.' 'These aren't people, Hannah, they never have been.'

Don and Geordie stepped out of the hole. Hannah had found another sheet and Clarky picked Iris up and laid her down. Geordie took the child and laid her beside Iris. They lowered Iris and the child into the hole, one by one and Don and Geordie buried them.

Don looked over the garden fence, down the track to the woodland path. He turned to the group, 'Emma's in a bad way and hearing about Maeve is going to hit her hard. She didn't even get out of bed this morning.' Hannah put an arm around Don, 'I'll tell Marty about his sister and I'll ask Collen to come over, maybe stay with Emma a while.' 'I'd appreciate that, Hannah, I'm beginning to feel way out of my depth with this.' 'We're all here for you Don and your family, let's get back.'

* * *

A line of houses in Millfield Court, overlooked the front street. They overlooked the gates to Hollymount Square, as well. Alec Donaldson stood back from the bedroom window, as the gate opened. He watched Don Mason, Geordie Wells and Hanna Rice exit the gate and lock it behind them. He turned and faced Kate Ashford, who was lying on the bed, hands tied behind her back. 'Time to go.'

Alec had put duct tape across Kate's mouth and he'd tied a rope around Kate's neck and held it as they left through the back door and made their way along the inside of the Millfield Court estate and out at the top of the Picnic Field Bank. He guided Kate across the road and headed down Hollymount Terrace, towards Beatty Road.

At the top of Beatty Road, Alec led Kate left, through Cornwall Crescent, then pulled her into a garden. They hid behind bins, as a large group of dead walked past, then, when they were out of sight, Alec led Kate through the rest of Cornwall Crescent and half way down Haig Road. There was an alley leading from Haig Road into Park Road, alongside Welfare Park, at the opposite side of the football field to Hollymount Square.

Alec knew Emma's house. He'd been here before, looking at her bedroom window through binoculars. He had a car on the path alongside the fence and he helped Kate up to the top onto its roof.

Alec jumped down and pulled his hunting knife from its sheath. He stabbed a dead middle - aged woman through the temple, who had wandered out of a back yard, nearby.

Alec climbed back up and pushed Kate against the fence. He lifted her up and dropped her into the park. Kate fell onto her front. She was unable to put her hands out to break her fall and was winded on impact with the ground. Blood ran down from her nose.

Alec dropped into the field, alongside Kate and dragged her past the football clubhouse and into the park. They crossed the park towards the fence surrounding Hollymount Square back gardens and Alec dragged Kate along the fence - line, up to where Emma's house was.

Emma had been in bed all morning. Her mood was so low, she had no motivation. She was sure something bad had happened to Kate and couldn't stop thinking about this.

There was a crack against her bedroom window.

Emma covered herself in her blanket and ignored it. Jamie didn't, though. He'd heard it from his room and he peered between his curtains. He saw Alec Donaldson stood in the field with Kate in front of him. Alec was holding a knife.

Jamie ran to the wardrobe and fitted the oxygen bottle connector to his air rifle and turned it on, to pressurize the gun. He fumbled for a tin of pellets, opened the lid and quickly poured pellets onto the window sill. He opened the window, from behind the curtain and went to get the gun. It seemed like an eternity waiting for the gun to get up to pressure but it got there.

Alec Donaldson had thrown another stone and hit Emma's window. This time she got out of bed and walked over to the window. She opened the curtain and was horrified to see Alec Donaldson standing on the other side of the fence to her garden. Kate was stood in front of him, hands tied behind her back and tape over her mouth. Her eyes were bulging with horror and she was crying and shaking her head

Alec Donaldson smiled when he saw Emma. He took the hunting knife from the sheath and held it to Kate's throat.

Jamie was quickly disconnecting the gun from the oxygen bottle when he heard Emma screaming. He ran to the window and rested the gun on the window sill, between the curtains. He saw Alec Donaldson through the scope standing, knife in hand grinning up at Emma's window.

Emma was screaming hysterically as Alec cut Kate's throat and let her drop to the ground. He lifted the knife and pointed it at Emma.

As Jamie took aim for his eye and flicked off the safety, Alec glanced to his window, saw the gun and turned to run. The pellet went through his right cheek, smashing top and bottom molar teeth.

Alec spun and fell to ground holding his face. Jamie quickly reloaded again and this time aimed at Alec's temple. He fired as Alec turned to run and the pellet went through the back of Alec's right ear, leaving a bleeding hole. Alec was screaming as he ran. He was out of range before Jamie could reload.

Jamie ran into Emma's room, she was screaming, 'No! No! Kate! Not Kate!'

Jamie ran to Dawn's house. He was franticly knocking at the door, 'Help! Dawn, help!'

Dawn ran into the house and upstairs into Emma's room. Jamie followed, 'Alec Donaldson was there, Dawn, he killed Kate on the field. Emma saw it happen. I tried to shoot him, but he moved each time I shot. I shot him through the face and I think I hit the side of his head, but he ran away.'

Dawn looked out of the window. Kate was lying dead in a pool of blood. She closed the curtains and sat on the bed beside Emma. 'I'm so sorry, Emma, but he's gone. Jamie shot him from his window. Sounds like he hurt him bad. I'm so sorry, your friend is dead. She couldn't have survived what he did.'

Emma couldn't talk. It was like she was choking and she gasped for air. She couldn't stop shaking and she fell against Dawn. Dawn held her for over an hour. Nothing was said.

Eventually Emma spoke. 'It's me he wants. He won't stop killing until I'm dead, Dawn. Everybody in my life dies. I can't bear it any more, Mum, Dad, my great grandparents. I haven't heard from my grandma and Grandad Jones. Will says he's stalking kids for fun.

Grandad is in danger every day. What if something happens to Jamie? I can't live like this. He'll do that to me, what he did to Kate, he'll do that to me and others. People will die because of me.'

Dawn pulled Emma close, 'what bad people do is not your fault, Emma. That boy has an evil streak. If anyone is to blame for that, it's his parents. This place is as safe as we can get it and that's down to your grandad. That boy knows if he comes in here, he won't get back out, that's why he didn't try to get over the fence. He knows there's a gun here now, as well. He'll think twice before doing something like this again.'

Along at Beech Grove, over the street, at the end of Park Road, Alec Donaldson broke into an empty house. He ran upstairs, into the bathroom. His mouth was full of blood and his face was in extreme pain. He took a mouthful of water and spat it into the sink. The bottom of the sink quickly covered with blood and bits of broken tooth. A flattened lead pellet lay among the debris. He felt the broken teeth with his tongue, they were sharp and scratched. He looked in the mirror. His Right cheek was covered in blood, which had run down his neck. He mopped the blood away with a face cloth and saw the hole.

Alec turned his head to the side. His left ear was torn from top to middle. The pellet had gone right through taking the attached tissue with it. There was a v shaped part of the ear missing. He winced, as he dabbed it with the face cloth. His top lip was curled up, but not with satisfaction, this time.

* * *

As they got to the Picnic field, on the way back, Don stopped. 'Hannah, I'm going to take Clarky over to see the farm. You two go back, get some rest.' Clarky hugged Hannah, then Geordie, 'Thanks for everything, you two. If you hadn't come, I'd have probably died down there. I was lost.'

Don and Clarky headed for the farm.

Don opened up and showed Clarky the farm building and the houses. 'There's a young lad going round saving orphans, Clarky. Fifteen years old. Fucking bravest person, I've ever seen. He's looking after thirty kids and some elderly. I want them to have the farm, with a few adults.'

Clarky walked down to the food store, 'fucking hell, they were prepared,' Don joined him, 'yes, they really were, they had a niece working at the World Health Organization, who had tipped them off that things would be this bad. The only thing they got wrong was that they got bitten.'

They spent another hour or so at the farm and headed back to Hollymount square.

When Don entered the house, Hannah, Geordie, Dawn and Colleen were waiting. Don looked around the room, 'What's going on? is everything alright? Emma, Jamie.' Hannah stepped forward, there's been a bad incident, Don, Emma and Jamie aren't hurt, but Kate Ashford's dead.' 'Dead?' 'Don, Alec Donaldson brought Kate to the field outside. He threw stones at Emma's window to get her attention, then cut Kate's throat. Don put his head down.

Has anyone told Emma about Maeve?' Geordie replied, 'no, Don. We thought she'd need

you here for that.' Hannah put her hand on Don's shoulder. 'I'll come with you to tell her.'

Don stood silent for a moment. 'Where's Emma now?' Dawn replied, 'she fell asleep, Don,

I think it's all too much for her.' 'And Jamie?'

Jamie was at the top of the stairs. He was crying. He'd heard everything. Maeve was dead.

Clarky ran up the stairs, picked him up and cuddled him in.

Don walked to the door. 'Let Emma rest, Dawn. Can you stay a while longer?' Dawn

nodded. 'Clarky will you stay with Jamie?' 'Sure thing, Mace.' 'Hannah, Geordie, we need to

pull some people together. We need to go over to Millfield and end this threat.'

Geordie knocked on Colin Markem's door. 'Colin, we've had a really bad incident, that

affects the safety of the square. The Donaldsons are becoming too much of a threat to us.

We're meeting in the centre garden in a few minutes time.' 'Ok, I'll be there.'

Geordie knocked on Neil and Ronnie. They also agreed to meet.

A few minutes later Don, Hannah, Colleen, Neil, Geordie, Ronnie and Colin met in the veg

garden.

Don spoke first, 'I'm putting a group together to go over and take the Donaldsons down,

tomorrow. They're becoming too much of a threat. This afternoon, Alec Donaldson killed a

young girl under my granddaughter's window. These people will destroy us, if they get one

chance. They murdered my friend's wife. Two of them were killed down Dene View, the

other day, so there's Ray, Alec, Jimmy and Mick Donaldson, Craig Gardener and Gary

Blewitt, left. They carry baseball bats, all of them. The plan is hide in houses nearby and

surround them, as they return home. My friend, Clarky has two handguns. He will carry a gun

and I'll carry the other. We'll shoot as many of them as we can, then the rest of you take

down the others with your weapons. Is everyone in?'

Everyone agreed to the raid. 'We leave midday tomorrow.'

Don made his way home, with Hannah. They knocked on Emma's bedroom door and went inside. Don broke the news about Maeve. Emma was broken hearted, she sobbed, as Hannah sat down on the bed and held her.

Don looked on, helpless. He went downstairs and sat beside Dawn on the settee. 'Kate? Did anyone deal with the body?' Dawn nodded, 'Jamie, showed Colleen the hatch in the fence. Colleen did it. Emma's body is in the shed. I thought we'd bury her tomorrow morning.' Clarky came downstairs. 'Jamie's ok Mace, he's just worried about his sister.' He walked to Don's front door. 'Listen Don can you let me out of the gates, there's something I need to do?' Don stood up, 'I've put a group together to take out the Donaldsons tomorrow, Clarky, please don't go over Millfield after Ray.' Clarky, shook his head. 'No, it's something else. What time are you leaving for the Donaldsons?' 'Twelve. Clarky, they go out most mornings. I'm hoping to catch them coming back. We need your guns, though.' 'I know, Mace, I'll be here.'

Don walked to the gate with Clarky. Clarky handed him the two handguns. 'Just incase I don't make it back, Mace. Put one between Ray Donaldson's eyes for me, man.' 'You'll be back. You wouldn't miss this for the world, you?'

When everyone had left, Don opened two tins of beans and sausages, heated them on the stove and shared them out. He took a plate to Emma's room, but she was in bed. Don left the plate by her bed. He didn't know what to say to her. Tears ran down his face and he felt despair of not being able to help his granddaughter.

Jamie came downstairs and they ate together. Jamie was disturbed. 'Grandad, it was awful, what he did to Kate.' Don looked across the table, 'He's a very bad person, son, but we're going to put a stop to this tomorrow.' 'I shot him, Grandad, just like you said, aiming at the eye, but he moved both times as I fired. I think I really hurt him with the first shot.' 'That's alright, Jamie, this boy had killed Emma's friend. You couldn't do any more than you did, son. Don't ever be frightened to shoot at a threat. Things are different, now.'

Jamie took the plates away and Don went into a cupboard and took out a packet of Kit Kats. He poured himself a whiskey and passed two Kit Kats over to Jamie. 'Put one on Emma's table when you go up.'

Jamie played Super Mario on a hand held device until Don was ready for bed. They both went upstairs to bed around ten thirty.

Don awoke to a noise, coming from inside the house. There was a knocking coming from somewhere upstairs. Don looked at his watch, it was four twenty am. He quickly got out of bed and carefully opened his bedroom door. He heard the sound again and picked up the spike, by the oak handle. He stepped out of his room onto the landing. Jamie's door opened and he held his hand up and waved Jamie back into his room. The sound was coming from Emma's room. He opened the bedroom door, then sunk to his knees. Emma was hanging from a walk-in cupboard door. She had connected three belts together and attached them to the inside door handle, and hung herself on the other side.

Emma had turned a few hours later and the banging was her trying to move away from the door and the belt bouncing the door back and forth. Emma was looking at her granddad, holding out a hand, as if to reach him. Jamie screamed from behind Don, 'Emma, no!' Don led him downstairs, then made his way back up. Don was heartbroken as he entered Emma's room. He took the spike and pierced it through her temple. She was gone.

Don took Emma's body down, unwrapping the belt from around her neck, then dropped to the bedroom floor and held Emma close. He remembered being at the hospital when she was born, her first steps, how he felt the first time she called him Granddad. He sobbed.

Don took Emma's body and laid it on the bed. He called for Jamie and Jamie stood beside the bed, crying.

Don picked up a note that was beside the beans and sausages and Kit Kat, that had been left for Emma. It read;

Dear Granddad / Jamie

I am so sorry, that you will find me this way, but it is clear to me I have no more time on this Earth. Everyone I love is dying and I just can't take any more loss. It is clear to me that this is the answer. The world today is misery to me, a torture and, even when we have made our home safe, the danger is coming to us. Alec Donaldson will eventually get to me, Granddad, he will kill everyone I love, and I cannot die, the way Kate did. I cannot continue to see my loved ones taken by him.

I love you all, Jamie, Granddad, Clarky, Hannah, Dawn. Thank you for trying to help me, but I must go now. I have chosen this way to die, so I cannot harm anyone when I return. Grandad, please bury me with Kate.

Love forever

Emma.

Don held Jamie and they both cried. Jamie eventually fell asleep and Don carried him to bed. He wrapped Emma in a sheet and carried her downstairs.

Don carried Emma to the shed and laid her beside Kate. The others had wrapped Kate in a blanket earlier and Don took a spade from the shed and started digging. His head was spinning, but he didn't have time for grief. There was no way this was going to stop him from taking down the Donaldsons. He repeatedly told himself he would deal with this later.

The following morning Hannah came around at ten o'clock. She knew something was wrong, immediately on Don answering the door, 'Don?' 'Emma's dead Hannah, she took her own life last night.' 'No, no, no, Don please, no.' Hannah started to cry.

Don embraced Hannah. 'I've dug two graves at the bottom of the garden, Hannah. will you ask people to come around?' 'We can't go after the Donaldsons, now mind, Don. This is too much for you. I'll talk to the others.' 'Hannah, how many more survivors are going to die out there if we put this back. They're killing children and vulnerable people. We have to finish this, Hannah. We have to.'

There was a large gathering in Don's garden and he laid Emma and Kate in the grave. Don picked up the spade and Geordie took it out of is hand. 'Let me, Don.'

At five to twelve the group assembled at the first gate. Don looked around, 'Where's Colin?' Geordie replied, 'I gave him a knock, no answer.' Don looked back down the square. 'We can't wait. We said twelve, he'll have to catch us up if he's slept in.'

They made their way to the outer gate and Don opened up. He was locking the gate, when he heard a call from over the road.

Clarky was walking across the road. Midgy and Sandra were with him. Dowser and Angie were there with their son, Paul and daughter, Marie. Don embraced all of the friends. 'Punter?' Clarky put his head down, 'Punter didn't make it, Mace. Hartlands is overrun. I saw Punter and Hope through their front window. Hope had been bit and Punter had put her to rest. He'd taken his own life, cut his wrists. I went in and put him to rest. I'm sorry, Mace.' Don was silent for a moment, then turned to the group.

Don introduced the friends to the group and Hannah stepped forward. 'Colleen, can you take the new friends down to Dawn's? We have enough people now. The baby needs you. Go join Amelia at Dawn's.' Colleen was holding her spiked bat, 'but,' Don took the bat and passed it to Midgy. 'Colleen, you need to be with the baby.' Don opened the gate and took Colleen through to the inner gate. As he unlocked the gate he looked up at Colleen, 'Hannah's right Colleen, you're needed here.' Colleen nodded, 'I know, Don.' Colleen made her way to Dawn's house with Sandra, Angie and Marie.

Don returned, locking the gates behind him. He passed his spike to Dowser and took two hand guns out of his back pack. He passed one to Clarky. Don took his machete from the sheath and passed it to Paul. Everyone else had something to fight with, Ronnie was carrying

a garden fork, Geordie, his piece of scaffold bar and Neil had a bricklayer's hammer.

Don Stepped onto the road, 'Let's go.'

14

The Betrayal

The group made their way to Church lane and were met by small group of dead, coming down past St Cuthbert's Church. Dowser, Midgy and Paul stepped forward, quickly taking down six dead.

Paul's machete had cut the top off a dead man's head. The body lay looking up at him and the top of the head and brain were laid in the road, 'Jesus, this is a sharp piece of equipment, Don.'

Dowser had spiked three of the group, 'I'm keeping this when it's over, mind. This is some weapon, Don.' Don nodded and set off down Church Lane. The group followed. As they entered Millfield North, Don stopped the group. 'We'll hole up in houses either side of the street, so when they return, we can quickly surround them. No fucking survivors here, mind. When they get to their entrance, that's when we move, all together.'

Dowser and Paul took the house that the Donaldsons would pass first. Ronnie and Geordie took the house just past the Donaldsons. Don, Neil and Hanna watched from the Ashfords' house and Midgy and Clarky were two doors from them. The bodies of Albert and Brenda Ashford were still lying in the grass out front and they'd moved Lisa's body to the side to get into the house.

They sat tight.

In the first hour, there was nothing. The place was quiet. Dead, wandered past, now and then, but no sign of the Donaldsons. They sat all afternoon. It got to four o'clock and Don went over and joined Clarky and Midgy. 'There's no sign of them. They only go out mornings, this is late for them.' Clarky looked over at the Donaldsons' houses. 'Let's go take a look. We'll take them in their houses, if they haven't gone out today.'

Don and the others crossed the field and the members of the group on the other side joined them. Don slid the pallet to the side, by a crude handle that had been fitted and they entered.

Don took a crowbar to the first front door and they rushed in. There was no one there. There were drink glasses and plates that had been used, but no people.

They tried the other houses, but no one was there, either.

The group went outside and looked around. Hannah stepped forward, 'Don, maybe something has happened when they were out, there's no one here. Do we wait?' 'No, they would have been back by now, something's not right. A few of them have wives, where are the women? We need to get back to the square and have a rethink. Maybe Ray Donaldson expected Clarky to come after him with the gun and they relocated?'

Clarky responded, 'Mace, they wouldn't just up and leave. Rays wife is an alcoholic. You saw all the bottles of spirits. The house is stocked with tons of food, money and valuables. They've just left that? I don't think so. I say we head back. Have a rethink, maybe hide out down Dene View, tomorrow? We know they're scavenging there. They may have food, but Donaldson wants valuables. Look at the stuff lying around here.'

Don set off towards Millfield North, 'we'll head back, talk about it back at my place. We can't sit here all day.'

As the group were approaching Church lane, they saw a young boy running towards them. There were dead following him and he tripped and fell. Midgy, Hannah, Geordie and Paul set off towards him and got there as he was scrambling to his feet. Four dead were just a few feet away from him. Hanna recognized him as he got to his feet. 'Jamie! Run this way.' Jamie ran towards Hannah, just as a dead woman grabbed for him. Her fingers brushed his back as he just avoided her grip. Hannah ran past Jamie and took down the woman with one blow.

Midgy pierced the heads of two teenage dead boys, with Don's spike and Geordie and Paul took a dead elderly man down with scaffold bar and machete.

Jamie ran to Don. He was terrified. He was crying and the front of his trousers were dark where he'd wet himself. He couldn't talk and was shaking, uncontrollably. Don knelt down and hugged Jamie. 'Jamie, son. You know you're not allowed out of the square for any reason. It's really dangerous. What are you doing? You could have been killed.'

Jamie composed himself enough to talk. 'Grandad, the Donaldsons are in the Square. An hour after you left, they just walked in. Alec Donaldson's dad was shouting to everyone in the square, threatening to kill everyone.' 'They walked in, Jamie?' 'Yes, Grandad. Colin Markem was with them and the Mcevoy brothers. Colin let them in with his key. Grandad, they're waiting in the yard behind the gates for you to come back. A whole lot of them with baseball bats, table legs and knives. They're going to kill you all. Grandad, I don't think they know your friends are with you, just Clarky. I heard Mr Donaldson say they're waiting for four of you. They're going to go for Clarky first because he's got a gun. Grandad, I was terrified they would come into the house after me, but they wanted to be in the store house. I watched them from the bedroom window.'

Hannah knelt down beside Don, 'Jamie, what about Colleen and the other residents? Amelia?' 'Everyone stayed indoors, except for a few. Mr Donaldson was calling them to come out. He said he's going to deal with everyone that didn't come out and join with them, after he's dealt with you. They're all hiding in the house beside the gates, watching for you coming. The women who were with them are in the store house. Colin gave Mr Donaldson the key.' Don looked at Hannah, 'There's a gate key in there as well. Who joined them, Jamie?'

Jamie thought for a moment, 'the Mcevoy brothers and Colin came in with them. When the shouting started Mark and Amie Nesworth came out. Old Zac and Moira Walker joined them, as well. I think everyone else locked their doors.'

Don spoke again, 'what about you Jamie, how did you get here?' 'I sneaked out the back when I saw Ray Donaldson walking down the street about half an hour ago. I thought he might come to our house, but he went into the store to talk to the women. He looked over here a couple of times. I was scared. I went out the back, got through the fence hatch and ran to the end of the park. When I got out, I ran into a crowd of dead, but I managed to get around them and run off. I left the dead behind at Beech Grove, but when I ran into these four, I was tired. I couldn't run much more. I just made it to here. I knew you were at Millfield. I had to warn you.'

Don looked around. There were more dead coming down Church lane. 'Let's get into a safe house and put our heads together.'

They entered an abandoned bungalow on Church lane and sat in the back room around a dining table to formulate a plan, as a large group of dead passed.

* * *

At 5.30pm nine people passed quietly through the fence and into Don Mason's back garden. Don, Hannah and Jamie quietly entered the back door. The others climbed fences, either way and made their way along the street and into empty houses. They all knew the plan and by 5.40pm they were all in place. At 5.45pm Don Mason crossed the street and knocked on the store house door and walked back to his doorway. Kylie Donaldson came to the door and saw him standing. She ran out of the house and made her way around the square towards the outer gates. Don could hear her shouting 'Ray! Ray, he's here, Mason's here.'

Don climbed the stairs and opened Jamie's bedroom door. 'If anyone comes through this door shoot them in the face.' Jamie was sat on the bed with his .22 air rifle.

Don walked across to his own room and opened the wardrobe door. He checked the twenty –

two caliber Browning. It had a full magazine, around twenty rounds. He tucked Maeve's

pistol in his belt and picked up his spike.

Don stood in his sitting room and watched through the window as Ray Donaldson and his

gang converged outside. He watched as Ray went around everyone giving out instructions.

He looked closely at the people that were gathering. They were all armed, but no one had

guns of any kind.

A brick came through Don's upstairs front window and Ray Donaldson stepped forward,

'Come out here, Mason I want a word with you. This place is ours now. Anyone with him, I

want Mason and Clarke. Give them up and you live.' Hannah kept low, watching out the

window, through net curtain that was flapping in the breeze, from the back of the bedroom, as

Don stood watching. Hannah whispered, 'It's time, Don.'

Don made his way downstairs to the front door. He stood for a moment composing himself.

He looked down and stood the rifle against the wall to the left of the door. It would be out of

sight to Ray Donaldson as he opened the door. Safety was off and it was ready to fire.

Don looked back, 'are they still on the road, Hannah' 'yes, Don Ray's nearest. He's in the

middle of the road. The others are on the path opposite and either side of Ray. Ray's son and

mother are outside the store house. His son's got a large knife in his hand.'

It was 6.00pm. Don Mason opened the front door and faced the mob that had gathered

there. Ray Donaldson and his brothers, Mick and Jimmy were holding baseball bats and their

friends Gary Blewitt, and Craig Thompson were holding large knives. Abe Gardener and

Sammy Dodds were elsewhere.

The rest of the mob consisted of a number of Don's neighbours.

The Mcevoy brothers, Vince, Dean Joe and Alan were all half cousins of the Donaldsons, unbeknown to Don. They had broken up an antique hardwood table from one of the empty houses and each held a table leg.

Mark and Amie Nesworth were a couple in their early thirties. Mark was scared of what might happen if they didn't support the Donaldsons, so they had picked up kitchen knives and joined the mob.

Zac and Moira Walker were both in their seventies. They had known Donaldson's father, Fred for many years before he died. They didn't have weapons, but had come along to support Ray, knowing that not supporting him could have consequences later.

Colin Markem was an old friend of the Donaldsons, again unbeknown to Don. Colin had been entrusted with keys to the gate. He had let the Donaldsons in.

Ray Donaldson's son Alec was standing behind his father holding a hunting knife. He was passing it from hand to hand, grinning at Don as he did it. Ray's wife Kylie was standing with him holding a can of cider in one hand and a cigarette in the other.

Don gave a cold look towards the people before him and said nothing.

Ray Donaldson stepped forward. 'Come out here Mason, your time's up. We'll make it quick. You know you're not walking away from this. Don said nothing. He felt sick looking around the neighbours who had betrayed him and let Donaldson and his thugs into the street, after all he had done to make their lives safer.

Ray stepped towards the gate at the end of Don's front garden. 'You see Mason, things have changed. If my son wants to hurt somebody, he hurts somebody, simple as that. It's ok now, you see. He can do what he wants out there, as long as he brings back what we need. Things were complicated back then, police, court, social services, there's no law now Mason, no law now. You can lock yourself away in there for as long as you like, but when you eventually come out, I finish it. You know you can't stay in there forever, might as well come out now.'

Don looked into Ray's eyes then he looked across at Alec Donaldson. 'It's the first time I've seen all your family together Alec, you don't half look like your uncle Jimmy.'

He looked back into Ray Donaldson's eyes, 'you know, Ray I never figured you as a clever bloke, quite the opposite, but you have just made a very, very pertinent point. Your so right saying that there's no law now. It sums everything up in a nutshell. No fucking law now.' He looked around the group, Ray, his family, his hangers - on, the disloyal neighbours, then back at Ray, 'I've no intention of locking myself away, Ray. I accept your offer to come out now.'

As the others in Donaldson's group approached the front gate, Don stepped back into the doorway and reached into the house with his left hand.

Don lifted the Browning, aimed and fired twice into Gary Blewitt's chest. Gary fell to the ground and lay still, on his back. He had dropped his knife and blood was running between his fingers, as he held his chest with both hands. Don fired two more shots into Jimmy Donaldson's upper body. He heard Kylie Donaldson scream, 'Jimmy! Jimmy!' as Jimmy Donaldson fell dead to the ground.

As Don lifted the gun to aim at another, Mick Donaldson jumped the garden wall and grabbed the gun. The two went to ground, wrestling for the weapon. Mick Donaldson's head suddenly went back and he arched his body backwards. Hannah was standing over him. Her spiked Bat was still stuck in the back of Mick's head. She yanked the bat back and he fell, dead to the ground.

In the panic, the Mcevoy brothers ran towards Don and Hannah. Clarky emerged from a house adjacent to them and shot each brother in the upper body, from the side. They all dropped the table legs they were yielding and went to ground, screaming.

Craig Thompson was stood beside Ray Donaldson. He was frozen with fear. He didn't know what to do and just stood, hands by his side with the knife pointed to the ground, 'Ray! Ray!' Paul leapt a wall from opposite the store house and swung the machete. It nearly decapitated Craig Thompson. He fell to the ground. His head lay to the side at ninety degrees to his body.

Ray lifted the baseball bat to hit Paul, as he was removing the machete from the skin that was attached to what was left of Craig's neck, but Don had pulled the revolver and he shot Ray through the left kneecap. Ray dropped the bat and hit the ground. He was screaming on the ground, rocking back and forth, holding his knee.

Colin Markem was sitting on his knees in the middle of the road, hands in the air, 'please, please don't hurt me, please.'

Don took Ray Donaldson's baseball bat. He swung it at Colin's head. Colin lifted his hands in defence and the bat broke his right arm. He was screaming and crying. Colin's right forearm hung, limply and he held it with his other hand. He was begging Don not to hit him again.

Don stood over Colin, 'you fucking treacherous bastard! All the work I did to make this place safe for you, for these people and this is how you thank me? We built this place up to keep danger out and you give the key to this murdering bastard and his psychopath, rapist son and they just fucking walk in. What did you think these people were going to do with the residents here? Rape? Murder?' He pointed the bat at Ray Donaldson. 'This man here left a baby to be eaten by its mother after his son had murdered her. His son murdered a fifteen-year-old girl on the playing field, just there, yesterday. We put down a thirteen-year-old girl this morning, who this fucker's son had fucking raped and strangled. He raped my granddaughter and he caused her to..' Don turned away, then turned back, 'He's fucking hunting, raping and murdering children out there, you fucker. What were you thinking?' Don looked away. 'I can't even look at you, Colin.'

Mark and Aimee Nesworth dropped their knives, as Clarky approached them, revolver in both hands. They knelt on the ground. Clarky looked into Mark's eyes, 'How long before they'd be fucking your wife, mate? Or worse? You wanted to put these monsters in charge of your future? This place? you must be the stupidest man alive.'

Clarky walked over to over the Mcevoy brothers. They had all taken gun shots to the upper body, but were still alive. He took the revolver and put a head shot through each brother.

Geordie came forward and gathered the Nesworths, Colin Markem and Zac and Moira Walker, together in the middle of the road. Midgy stepped forward, 'Mace, the boy went into the store house with his mother and they shut the door behind them.'

The group surrounded the enemies, that were sat on the road, as Don approached the store house with Hannah and Clarky. Paul stood over Ray Donaldson, holding the machete, 'Please make a move, Donaldson, let's see if I can remove your fucking head completely.'

Don took his key and opened the front door. 'Don't hurt us!' Cynthia Dodds was standing in the middle of the living room. Amanda Blewitt and Sharon Thompson were sitting on the settee, crying. Don stood back and beckoned them out. They joined the others in the road.

As they passed Ray Donaldson shouted to them, 'tell him nothing, Lec will get help.'

Cynthia spoke to Don, 'Alec and Kylie ran out the back door and through the gardens.'

Don turned to go back through the house and then saw Will walking down the road. 'Don, the gates were wide open, what's going on? I heard gunfire. There'll be dead everywhere, soon. I've tied the outer gate closed with my belt, but it needs to be locked.' Will looked around, 'God almighty, what's happened, Don?'

Hannah ran to Will and took him to the side. 'Listen Will, something awful has happened. Alec Donaldson murdered Kate yesterday on the field below Emma's window. Emma took her own life last night. We went to raid the Donaldsons this afternoon, to end this, but we'd been betrayed and the Donaldsons got in here. We've just taken the place back.'

Will stepped back and slumped against a wall, 'Kate, Emma, dead? Oh God.' Tears ran down his face and Hannah put her arms around him. Will looked over Hannah's shoulder. 'Jesus, Ray Donaldson.' He walked over to Ray and Ray sneered at him. Ray had just sat upright with his left leg to the side. He was holding his shattered knee with both hands. Will booted Ray Donaldson as hard as he could between the legs and Ray rolled into a ball. Will picked up a baseball bat and started hitting Ray. He was mostly hitting arms, that were held up in defence, but the intent was for the head. Don Grabbed Will and pulled him away. Will was screaming, 'It's his fault, all this, his fault. As if it's not hard enough living out there, he lets his fucking rapist, murdering son go out stalking children. His fucking fault!' He tried again and again to get at Ray, but he was pulled back and he eventually sat on the ground, exhausted and cried bitterly, 'Not Kate and Emma, not them. You fucking monster, Donaldson.'

Don took a knife out of his pocket, as Ray began to sit back up. He walked over and stood on Ray's left arm. Ray tried to pull his foot away with his other hand, but his efforts were futile. Don knelt on the back of Ray's hand and cut his left thumb clean off. Ray was screaming. Hannah stepped forward, 'Don?' Ray was holding his hand and screaming in horror and Don stepped forward again. Ray screamed, 'I'll tell you; I'll tell you where they'll go, Mason. No more, I'll tell you.' Don grabbed Rays arm and knelt on Ray's right hand, 'I said I'd tell you, Mason.' Don looked him in the eye, 'Oh you're going to tell me Ray.' He cut off Ray's right thumb and pushed him onto his back.

Ray was screaming, 'Somebody help me, you can't let him do this.' Dawn Todd walked out of her front garden. And took Don's knife. Did you have mercy for any of your victims, Donaldson? I think not. Well, did you?' Ray looked up, 'Fuck you whore!'

Dawn took the knife and sliced off Ray Donaldson's left ear. He screamed with shock and agony. She threw the ear in his face and stepped back. 'Fuck you, you fucking arsehole! fucking rapist!' Hannah grabbed Dawn and pulled her away, 'Dawn! Jesus, Dawn, what are you doing?' 'He knows, don't you, Donaldson? He fucking knows.' Hannah put her arm around Dawn and led her away. Dawn started to cry, 'I was just a kid, Hannah, I was just thirteen when he did it, just thirteen.'

Don took the knife and held it against Ray's nose, 'One chance to talk, Ray. Where is he going? Tell me or the nose comes off.'

Ray looked up. 'New Hartley.' 'Where in New Hartley?' 'Kylie's brothers' place. She has four brothers. Maple Court, number seven.'

Clarky walked forward with the handgun. 'My turn now?' Don took Clarky's arm. 'Keep him alive. I want him and the son together. I'm going after the fucker. Keep Ray in one of the empty houses. Don't let him die. I mean it, Clarky, I want this cunt alive.'

Don walked over to the group of enemies on the road. He took Colin Markem and led him through the square and to the outer gate. Hannah went with them. Don undid Will's belt and opened the gate. He pushed Colin into the street. 'My arm's broken, Don, I need medical help.' Don closed the gate and fitted the chain and padlock. He looked through the gate at Colin. Colin was pleading to come back inside. Don looked coldly into Colin's eyes. 'I'm going for some more of your people. If you're here when I come back, I will shoot you. If I ever see you again, I will kill you. Am I clear?' Colin nodded and shuffled away along the street, holding his broken arm.

Don went back to the group and then led Cynthia, Amanda and Sharon, back to the gate. Hannah brought Zac and Moira. 'None of you can stay and I warn you against returning to Millfield, I haven't finished there. If I see any of you again, I'll kill you.' Cynthia was pleading for Don to let them stay. She knew they wouldn't last long out there. Dead were appearing from up the front street and from the entrance to Millfield. A lot of dead. Will was right, the shooting had attracted their attention.

When Don returned to the gates with Mark and Amy Nesworth the others had left. He opened the gates. Mark was head down. 'I'm sorry for this, Don. I made a wrong call. I thought they would kill us if I didn't join them. I just wish we hadn't.' 'So do I son, so do I. If I see you again, I'll kill you, go now, the dead are getting very near. I suggest you take the alley into Hollymount Avenue and take your chance that way. Find somewhere safe, we marked an x on the doors of safe houses. A key will be under a pot. Keep quiet. When the dead disperse leave Bedlington.' Mark put his arm around Aimee. She was sobbing. He looked at Don. Don just looked through him, 'I said go Mark.'

Don locked up and returned to the square, as Mark and Aimee ran along the pavement towards the alley Don had suggested.

When Don returned to the Square, the others had tied Ray's hands and put him on the settee of an empty house.

Don walked over to the group that had saved the square. 'I can't thank you enough for what you have done today. The threat of these monsters isn't over until I catch Alec Donaldson, though. He's heading for New Hartley, but he'll be slowed up by his mother and what's on the Horton Road.'

Don looked around the square. The rest of the residents had come out and were gathering around him. Don addressed them all, 'My friend, Ian Clarke, here brought help to us. The new people here are my friends, as a lot of you know. May I request we give them homes here?' Colleen stepped forward, holding Amelia. 'It's the least we can do, Don.' Don smiled, 'Thanks, Colleen.' No one spoke against the proposal. Don continued, 'Dawn, can you show them the empty properties?' 'No problem, Don.' Don put his hand on Will's shoulder, 'I asked if any of you want to move to the farm. Has any of you given this any thought?' 'I have.' Geordie Wells stepped forward. 'I've done farm work in the past, Don. I'd like to take the farm on. Heather, Lee and Simon are all with me.' Heather and his two sons joined him. Will spoke up, 'Don, I'd like to move our people to the farm. They're all hiding over by the fields, now waiting. They're not far from there' Geordie walked over and stood by Will. 'Let's get them all into there safe then, son. You and I will work out accommodation together.' 'You have the farmhouse, Geordie, with your family, we'll take the residential, it's just right that way and the houses have far more space than we're living in now. Maybe the youngest kids can move in with you, in time. We've got two four year - olds.' Hannah stepped forward, 'I'll come with you, make sure you all get there safe.'

Don took the keys and gave them to Hannah. See you get them safe and settled. Stay there tonight, Hannah, head back in the morning.' Hannah spoke, 'Don, I'm coming after Alec Donaldson with you.' 'I'm sorry, Hannah, it's too dangerous. I need to move on my own to get past the crowd of dead by Connor's place. That's where Alec Donaldson will become unstuck, for sure. I'm not going until first thing tomorrow. Donaldson will not move at night. He'll hole up in a house and head for New Hartley when it gets light.'

Hannah reluctantly agreed and walked off with Will towards her house. Geordie and his family followed. Hannah spoke to Will on the way, 'I need to see Colleen and Marty before we go, Will. We found Marty's sister this morning and laid her to rest. Will put his head down, 'go see your wife and baby, Hannah, I'll tell Marty.' Hannah took the necklace out of her pocket, 'give him this Will.'

The residents returned to their homes.

In the square among the bodies, Geordie stepped forward. 'Lets' put these fuckers to rest before any of them turn. If we can get them to one of the un - used gardens we'll just do a mass grave. Neil and Ronnie offered to help. Paul Dawson came over. 'I'm Paul, I can use a spade as well. The least I can do is help, when you're giving me a free house' Neil, grinned, 'nobody said it was free, mate, I didn't hear Don say it was free, did you, Geordie,' 'No, don't worry, son we'll work out a rent arrangement, leave it with me and Neil.' They set off to work. Ronnie put his fork through the heads of all the bodies that didn't already have head injury and the others set about digging a large, wide hole.

An hour later Ronnie and the others turned up in the street with wheelbarrows and started moving the bodies.

While they were covering up the bodies, Don walked into the garden. He passed Geordie the twelve bore shotgun and a large canvass shopping 'bag for life,' that was full with boxes of cartridges. 'No Farmer should be without one, but make sure it's only used when necessary. Firing this was how the farmer met his maker.' Geordie held the gun out and took aim towards the bottom of the garden, 'nice, thanks, Don.'

The friends met around 9.00pm in Don's house and he served drinks. They caught up with stories of what had happened to them, over the course of the outbreak, how they had survived and who, unfortunately hadn't.

As it got towards midnight, the exhausted friends headed for home and Clarky stood with Don. 'I hope you're right about not killing the bastard, Mace.' 'Well, Clarky, it's not like he's going to run away. If I'm not back in two days kill him. If Kylie Donaldsons brothers arrive here, kill him and kill them. The Browning is in my wardrobe upstairs. There're boxes of ammunition. He doesn't get to live in any outcome here, all I'm asking is you let me catch the son first.' 'Alright, Mace. I'm going over to Millfield tomorrow. I've had a thought about these two. I'll discuss it with you when you get back.' 'About Millfield, Clarky. Will you take a group over with all the barrows and back packs? Donaldson had a huge stock of food in there. I would imagine the other two houses are the same. We don't need the valuables, but young Honour and her friends will take all the flour and baking stuff. They make bread, cakes, all sorts. We can stock the store house to the roof with tinned stuff. We might even have the luxury of a few days off scavenging.' 'I'll ask Neill, tomorrow, Mace. He seems to have the respect of the community. He can do the recruiting and we'll have all Donaldson's food over here by the time you get back. And, yes, I know, Glenmorangie is your favorite, I'm sure the bastard has a bottle. Shit, they had everything else, there. We'll bring all the drink and make one of the empty houses into a pub. Everyone will need to let their hair down at the end of this.'

Don walked to the door with Clarky, 'I'm leaving first light, Clarky, so get some rest, I'll see you in a day or so.'

Clarky headed across to the house Dawn had allocated him and Don went upstairs. Jaimie was staying over at Dawn's. She had left early with him.

The house was quiet. Don Mason sat in his armchair. He looked around the room and saw a family photo, stood on a bureau. He got up and took the photo and stood it on the coffee table in front of him. He took a drink of scotch and sat back looking at the photo. He was with Lesley, Maria, Frank and the children at a table at Gianni's, Morpeth. The waiter had taken the photo. It was just over a year since the photo was taken.

Don cried himself to sleep.

In a house a few doors away, Ray Donaldson was also sobbing. His stump thumbs knee and wound where his ear had been cut off had stopped bleeding, but he was in agony. No one had checked on him. He lay on his side on the settee, hands tied behind his back. He still had pain in his groin, where that little bastard had kicked him.

All Ray Donaldson could think of was the world of pain he would inflict on these people when his son returns with help, especially Detective Ian Clarke.

At the same time, Alec Donaldson was looking out of the bedroom window of the large house, that was just over the bridge, beside the Picnic Field. He could see the house had been cleared for a safe house by someone else, so people had been along here. It was pitch black outside. He looked back at his mother, who was asleep on the bed. He wasn't going to sleep, though. His ear and cheek were burning and the toothache in the back of his mouth was unbearable.

Alec could see that cars had been moved, freeing up a lane on the road. People had been along here, so there must be access along the Horton Road, and on towards Seaton Deleval and New Hartley. He imagined they'd walk along to the Horton Road tomorrow and if the clear road continues, he'd take an abandoned car. Mam's brothers would help dad, he was sure of this. Uncle Ken was one of the toughest guys Alec knew and he had a lot of friends. Even Dad was reluctant to mess with him. Uncle Ken would have survived, no doubt and when Uncle Ken comes back for Dad, Mason and the others will pay. Mason will pay for what he did to his Dad. Mason will pay for what they did to his uncles and their friends.

He took out his hunting knife and held it in front of him, remembering what Mason had said, 'It's the first time I've seen all your family together Alec, you don't half look like your uncle Jimmy.'

Alec looked over his shoulder at his mother, then back into the darkness outside, repeatedly stabbed the knife into the wooden windowsill and saying over and over again, 'he mine, when we get him, mine.'

15

The Pursuit

Ray Donaldson heard the door open and looked up as Neil Hipsburn called out from the hallway, 'still alive, Donaldson?' 'Yes.' Neil opened the door and entered the room. He bent over the back of the settee and cut Ray Donaldson's hands free with a pair of secateurs. He threw a small bottle of water onto the settee beside Ray, then passed him a cereal bar. 'I'm leaving the ties off. You can't go anywhere with that leg and if you do something stupid, Don Mason will make you pay with fingers.'

He sat on the armchair opposite Ray. 'They asked me to come in here, because I'm the only one they can trust not to cut your throat, but having heard some of the things you've done, it's tempting.'

Ray fumbled with the lid of the bottle eventually loosening it with his teeth and took a drink. His injuries had all stopped bleeding, but he was in agony and he didn't feel well. He looked at Neil as he tried to unwrap the bar without thumbs. 'Get me out of here and I'll spare you, when my brother – in - laws get here.' Neil shook his head, 'you've got a fucking nerve, haven't you? Help you escape, for what? More rapes, more murders, fuck you! I didn't even want to fucking feed you. Don Mason told us to keep you alive, or you'd be dead now. You really want to hope Don gets back safe, as well, because if your brother - in - laws turn up here, you're the first fucker who dies.'

Ray sneered at Neil, 'what about my injuries? you can't leave me like this.' Neil smiled, 'Don told us not to kill you, he didn't say anything about treating your injuries. Maybe if I open a window you can call out and ask the people you were going to rape and murder if they can come and fix you up? What about the woman who has adopted the baby you left for dead? Do you think she might come in and help?' He opened a window. 'There you go, you call them in, Donaldson.'

Neil left the house and walked over towards the inner gardens. Ray heard someone outside ask if he was still alive and Neil answered, 'yes, the fucker's still with us, worst luck.'

* * *

Don Mason was awake early. It was still dark outside and he wanted to be away first light.

Don stood his spike against the wall and attached a hunting knife and sheath to his right side. He took a backpack and slid a crowbar inside. He went into the garden and found a pack of heavy-duty cable ties and dropped them into the bag. He took a litre bottle of water that he had mixed with some orange cordial and a packet of Penguin biscuits.

Don took Ray Donaldson's Baseball bat into the workshop and attached a leather strap to it, then swung it over his shoulder. He took a clothes line down in the garden, bundled it together and put it in the bag.

Don went back into the kitchen and made tea. He poured Crunchy Nut Cornflakes into a bowl and covered them with evaporated milk.

As he finished his breakfast Don looked out of the window. It was getting light. He took all the items he'd prepared and made his way to the gates.

A lot of dead had been past, attracted by the sound of gunfire, but they had dispersed through the night.

Don locked the outer gate behind him as he left the square. He made his way towards the Picnic Field bank. As he neared the bank, he saw an old man stumbling across the road from Millfield. It was Zac Walker. He hadn't got far. Don looked past Zac and saw Moira coming out of Millfield Court. Don walked over to Zac, then over to the long grass on the overgrown field. Zac had bites on his face and neck and his shoes were covered in blood, from bites to his legs, that were visible through tears in his trouser legs. Zac followed Don onto the field and Don put the spike through his head and lowered him to the ground. Don then walked across to Moira. Moira had bites all over. There was a huge chunk of flesh missing from her neck. Don stood still as she approached and walked back towards Zac. As she hobbled alongside Zac's body, Don spiked her through the temple. He held her upright with the spike and turned her towards her husband. Don lowered the spike and she slid off to the ground, laid at rest, by her husband's side.

Don crossed the road and made for the Picnic Field.

* * *

Alec Donaldson never slept. He was in agony all night. His face and ear were burning, where he'd been shot by the air rifle and he had excruciating toothache, where his teeth had been smashed.

He stood looking out of the window. In the distance he could see light sky appearing, so it would be daylight soon. He knew he had to leave first light to have any chance of reaching his uncles.

Alec searched the kitchen and found some tins. He opened a tin of beans and a tin of macaroni cheese and took them upstairs with forks and two cans of coke he had found in the, now warm fridge.

He woke his mother up. She was coughing and spluttering and fumbled in her bag for cigarettes. She lit one and sat on the bed. Alec held out both tins and she took the macaroni.

Kylie lit a cigarette and ate some of the food. she took a half bottle of vodka out of the bag and took a drink. Alec looked away in disgust. 'Mam, we have to set off in a few minutes. They could be coming after us.'

Kylie finished the rest of the tin and took another drink of vodka. She'd drank half the small bottle. She stood up and went into the bathroom and closed the door behind her.

Alec took her handbag and put the rest of the cans of coke in it. He found some chocolate bars and an unopened jar of peanut butter and took those as well. Kylie came into the sitting room and shouted across at him, 'I can't fucking carry all that, I'm not a fucking carthorse.'

Alec passed her the bag, 'if we run into trouble, I need my hands free, take this.' He passed her a large kitchen knife, 'stab them through the side of the head if they get near you, mam.' Kylie took the knife and nodded apprehensively. She'd never been out of the house, during the outbreak, other than last night.

They went to the back door of the house. Alec held out his hand. 'Wait here, I'll check it's clear.' He walked onto the road outside and looked all ways. There were no dead in sight so he beckoned Kylie to join him.

They set off up the bank, to the corner that leads to the Horton Road. Alec rounded the corner. The lane was clear of traffic up to just before the Bebside turn off, then the whole road was blocked.

Alec took his mother's arm, 'Watch out for dead coming out of the driveways, Mam.' She stayed close as they made their way along the road.

As they neared the Bebside turn off, Alec stopped. He'd seen Connor on his balcony. Connor was looking their way. Alec walked on, with his mother close by and stood under Connor's balcony.

Connor stood up and lent on the balcony front, 'Can I help you two in any way?' Alec looked at the binoculars, hanging from Connor's neck. He took out his hunting knife and pointed it towards Connor, 'Yes, you can give me those binoculars, I need to look along this road, see if we can get through, pass them down, don't make me come up there.' Connor smiled, 'don't make you come up here, young feller? Tell you what, I'm giving you nothing, on your way now.'

Kylie was stood, arms folded, 'Alec, how are you going to get anyone to help us if all you do is threated them. If you'd asked properly, he'd have looked along there for you, he's got a better view anyway.' 'I don't ask for anything, I take.' Alec stepped forward and jumped onto the bonnet of one of the cars that were parked in front of Connor's hedge and boundary fence. He jumped on to the top of the car and took a step back. Alec was just about to take a run and leap for Connor's fence when the air rifle spat a .22 pellet, which hit him in the groin an inch or so just above his penis. The pellet had gone through Alec's jeans and deep into the skin. He screamed and jumped back, rolling off the car and to the ground beside Kylie's feet.

Alec was squirming on the ground and Kylie knelt beside him, completely lost, as to what to do.

Alec eventually gingerly got to his feet and looked up to the balcony. Connor was looking through the scope into Alec's left eye. 'You look like trouble, son, now you and the lady fuck off. Either direction, but fuck off. Look at the bodies around you with an eye missing or a hole in the temple. I shot them all. You'll join them if I see you again, now I repeat for the last time, fuck off.'

Alec shuffled away; his mother close behind. He was crying, but he didn't look to his mother for comfort. He'd known a long time, she was incapable of that.

* * *

Don crossed the stone bridge opposite the Picnic Field and made his way the large house on the other side. He'd checked the houses situated along the bank leading down, but there were no signs of entry. The gate was open and Don entered the yard and made for the back door. It was slightly open.

Don carefully pushed the door open with the spike and made his way inside. He saw the macaroni and baked beans cans. The food sauces were still seeping onto the floor. He knew this was the place.

One by one, Don checked the rooms of the house, but they had gone. He made his way onto the road. The route forward was clear, so he made his way up to the bend towards the Horton Road. As he neared the Bebside turn off, Don saw Connor on the balcony. He waved and made his way over.

'Don, how you doing, my friend?' 'Not good, Connor, we've had trouble last night. We've overcome a gang of living of that attacked us. Most of them are dead, now, but two got away and are making for New Hartley.' 'Let me guess, Don, a teenage boy with half an ear missing and wounds to his face and his knackers and a pug ugly woman?'
'Sounds like them, Connor, but I don't know about the knacker wound.' Connor picked up the rifle, 'oh he has, Don and it's one of your pellets. He was going to climb up here and off me with a fucking hunting knife, he was.'

Don lent against one of the cars, 'He's the boy that's been stalking and murdering children in Bedlington, Connor. How long ago did they pass?' 'About half an hour, Don, but the dead will be nearing the end of the road along that way. There's about four hundred, now. I think there must be a gap between the cars that are blocking the way and there's so many trying to get through there's no way out when these ones reach it. When they turn and come back, you'll all be walking into them. It's likely the two you're after will have to stop and take refuge in one of the two houses on the roadside, or the church. You will too, if you go after them. There're so many dead, it will take them half an hour to pass between all the cars. Don, if you see the dead coming and you can't get to the houses, make for the fields. Go a few fields over, towards the Heathery Lonnen, you know, that long footpath between the Shoes pub and Bebside Road, then double back to here. They aren't attracted to open space, unless they detect potential food.'

Don set off and made for the first house, which was about half a mile along the road.

* * *

Alec and Kylie made their way between cars. The road was covered in patches of dark, slime like residue, which stank and they constantly stepped side to side, trying to avoid stepping in it. As they neared the first house, they walked past a group of twelve dead, who had wandered off the road and through a gap in the hedge, into a field. They hadn't spotted Alec and Kylie, nor had Alec or Kylie spotted the dead, but Kylie's bag caught the wing mirror of a car. All together the dead swung their heads and looked their way. They lifted their heads, as if listening and smelling the air. Alec turned towards Kylie, 'Try to be quiet, will you? These things are attracted to sound.' He looked past her.

The group of dead had started to pass through the gap in the hedge onto the road about a hundred yards behind them. Kylie looked back, 'Alec, Alec.' 'Don't panic, Mam. Just walk. They walk slower than us. We only run if we need to. The dead don't tire. If you tire yourself out, they'll catch you, just walk.' They walked quickly along the road. They were leaving the dead behind and nearing the first house. The house was large and there was a derelict out - house building in its grounds. There was a fence all the way around and Alec could see the downstairs was all boarded up. There was an entrance that was blocked by cars and Alec helped Kylie over and they walked up the drive.

Alec tried the front door and it was really secure. There was no way in, there. He didn't have time to find something to force it. He went around the back. The door was secure there, too. There was a long coat hanging from a hook. It was covered in wet filth, just like the slime on the road. There was a bucket half full beside it with a wide paintbrush standing in the slime.

Kylie was getting anxious, 'what will we do, Alec?' 'I can climb up the drainpipe and break a window. If there's anyone in there I'll kill them and let you in.' He stepped towards a metal waste pipe and took hold with both hands.

'I was going to come down and let you in until you mentioned the word 'kill' and now I think I've changed my mind.'

Alec looked up. A dark-haired man, about forty years old was pointing a shotgun out of the window at him. 'I watched you walk along here in front of those dead. I reckon you've got a couple of minutes before they get here, then you're stuck there. Unfortunately, I'm going to shoot you in about one minute, but I'll give you the chance to leave. They're about a hundred yards down the road, don't waste any time, now.' Alec grabbed Kylie's arm and they left over the barrier. He held his knife and pointed it at the man, 'I'll fucking kill you when I come back.' He looked along the road. The group of dead were about forty yards from them. The two set off walking quickly towards the church.

As they neared the church Alec saw more dead, this time between cars. They were near the cemetery, which makes up the grounds of the church and Alec pulled Kylie along to the stone wall, alongside. Two dead were making their way towards them, so he helped his mother onto the wall and leapt over. She was screaming as he dragged her into the cemetery, 'One of them was touching me, one of them had hold!' Alec slapped her face. 'For fuck's sake shut up. They can't climb a wall. You'll attract them from in here. Stay close or I'll fucking leave you here.' Alec made his way around the church and ran up to the door. There was a long, iron hasp and staple with a large padlock across the door.

Alec looked ahead. There were dozens of dead up past the next house, but walking away from them, towards the Shoes pub. He grabbed Kylie's arm, 'This way.'

They made their way along towards the next house. Alec knew it was now their only chance. The group of dead they had got away from, were following again and the dead that had been in the cemetery were following as well. There were around forty dead following them. 'We have to run now, mam, to buy me time to get in this house.'

There was no sign of people, as they scrambled into the drive of the last house. They could see hundreds of dead heading for the top of the road. Alec's heart sank when he saw the black metal security shutters on the window. He ran to the front door, but it was locked. Kylie followed as he ran around the back. The dead were closing in and entering the drive behind them. He tried the back door and it swung open. They quickly got inside and Alec closed and locked the hardwood door.

Kylie slumped into a chair and took the bottle of vodka out of the bag. She could hear bumping against the back door, as she took the rest of the bottle in one drink.

Alec made his way around the house, knife in hand. There was no one there. He stood at the bedroom window looking out at the horde of dead. They were going to be here a while.

Alec went into the bathroom and undid his trousers. He pulled them down over his boxer shorts. The shorts were stuck to the wound underneath and he carefully peeled them away from it. He took a flannel and soaked it with cold water.

The wound stung really bad when he pressed on the injury. He got it clean and looked down. There was a half centimeter sized round hole just above his penis. There was no sign of the pellet. It was in too deep. He tore a towel that was hanging from a rail and laid a strip over the wound, then fastened up his trousers.

Alec came back downstairs. Kylie had been through cupboards and found a bottle of brandy. She'd filled a tumbler half full. Alec looked at the drink, then her, 'It's not the time to drink,

Mam. I'm going to look for food in the kitchen. Drink that but no more. You need to be ready to leave when we get the chance.'

Alec found two tins of soup in a cupboard, opened them and brought them through with two spoons. As he handed a tin to Kylie, he saw blood on the laminate floor by her feet. 'Mam.!' He knelt beside her and pulled up the leg of her joggers. Kylie had been bitten on her left calf.

* * *

Don made his way along Horton Road. There were no dead in his path and he made good ground towards the first house. He moved around the outside, but it was secure. No one could have entered this place. He quickly got back on the road and made his way towards the Church.

He saw a large group of about forty dead, walking down the road towards the church, from beside the next house. He climbed over the wall and entered the cemetery.

Don made his way around the Church. It was all locked up. More dead were converging on him from inside the cemetery. He ran out onto the road. Some of the large group had passed the church entrance, heading for where he entered over the wall, the others were approaching from the church entrance gate.

Don was surrounded. He held up the spike as around fifty dead approached from all sides. One of the dead, wearing a long coat walked ahead of the group entering the gate, it was carrying a bucket in one hand and a blanket in the other. It threw the blanket, then lifted the hood of the coat and whispered, 'put this over you or die.'

Don wrapped the blanket around him and the man threw the contents of the bucket over him. As the man passed, he whispered, 'stand totally still.' Don felt bodies brush against him, one after the other. He stood still, terrified to lift the blanket. The smell was unbearable and

he was retching. He stood for around two minutes, then heard a voice whisper. 'Walk slowly

with me. Trust me. Stay under the blanket.'

Don walked with the man, blindly. The man led Don by the arm along the road and then

helped him over the bonnet of a car. They walked a short distance more. Don could hear

gravel under his feet. He heard a door unlock and the man removed the blanket and threw it

into the yard. Don looked around, as the man pushed him into the house and shut the door.

He was sure he must be back in the first house.

'My name is Vic, Vic Hind.' 'Don, Don Mason.' 'Well, Don Mason, why the fuck would

you be doing heading along a road, towards four hundred dead?'

'I'll not lie, Vic, I'm after a young lad, who has been murdering survivors in Bedlington. A

very dangerous boy. He's been raping and murdering children, Vic. I have to stop him. He's

heading for New Hartley to seek a group of brothers and whoever they may have with them. I

have his father locked in a house. We've made safe Hollymount Square and the farm at the

end of Church lane, but they tried to take it over. The boy and his mother got away, though.'

'Yes, I encountered the boy not long ago. Said he was going to kill me so I warned him off

with my shotgun. He headed off towards a massive crowd of dead. His only chance would be

if he made the house along there. When I saw you earlier should have opened the window,

but I thought you may be with him. I changed my mind and came out after you. I knew you

had no chance. So, I brought the stuff.' 'Stuff?' 'Shit, Don. It's zombie shit. The dead have

acute hearing and smell, that's how they locate things. If you interfere with these senses, for

example, smell like them, they just don't see you as food.' 'How the fucking hell did you find

this out, Vic?'

'This isn't my house, Don. It was like this when I got here, but the people had gone. I found

a ladder and got in through an upstairs window. I'd been in the traffic jams on the spine road for over a day. It was broadcast on the radio not to leave the cars, but people were leaving cars all over, because dead were walking around and trying to get into the vehicles. People were being bitten everywhere you looked. I ran for the field behind here, not the slip roads, like others were. It was carnage, I could see I had no chance among people and nearly got to the field, but I ran into a girl who had turned. She was cold and grey skinned and there was dried blood all over her face, so she had been dead for some time. When she grabbed me, we fell to the ground. She was wearing a short skirt and her legs were covered in that slime. I wrestled and wrestled with her to stop her from biting me and she just stopped all of a sudden. She stood up and wandered off. At first, I couldn't understand why I had been spared, but when I looked around, dead were walking past me. I realised I was covered in the slime off her legs and put two and two together. I came across the fields and found this place and I've just stayed here. I go across the fields to Hartford Colliery over there and get food. I can wander round the shops among the dead and get tinned food and stuff they can't reach. I just take my time, walk like them, you know. I carry the bucket all over. The dead walk up and down this road. There's a really tight gap in the cars at the end of the road and there's hundreds wandering around the roundabout, that try to get through. Every now and again one gets in, but none get out. The ones our side can't get through the other way. They stand a while and then turn around and go back. When they pass, I take a shovel and scrape up the slime. I put a bit of water in with it and paint it on the long coat and hood. I'll do a coat for you when they pass. I'm not going out there now, though.'

Don stood up and saw marks of the slime on his clothing and hands, 'can I wash, Vic?' 'There's still running water, not hot, though but you can have a good wash, I've got plenty shower gel and, Don, there're clothes in the bedroom on the left. By the look of the clothing, the owner was around your size, so you can change any clothes that got shit on, oh and chuck your dirty stuff out the window, it fucking stinks.'

Don stood up, 'Thanks, Vic, I'll not stay long. I'm going after Alec Donaldson when the dead pass.' 'Don, I'm coming with you. Take me into one of your safe places and I'll help you get this boy. I can't stand it anymore on my own. I gave up looking for people some time back.'

Don went upstairs and washed. He found a black tee shirt and clean socks in the bedroom and he went into a drawer and found Levi jeans his size.

Vic was in the front bedroom, when Don had dressed. Don stood by the window with him. They had the chocolate biscuits and juice, that Don had brought with him. Vic looked along the road, 'They're coming, Don.'

Don watched as the dead approached. He could hear the slapping of hundreds of feet against the ground as they walked, clumsily and slowly past. 'It takes about half an hour for them to clear, Don then we'll head for the end house. If the boy tries to go beyond the roundabout he'll not survive, especially with the woman slowing him down. I've had an idea, though Don.'

* * *

Alec Donaldson watched the dead pass, from the upstairs window. He would need to scout the best way across the Spine Road, so he wouldn't be leaving right away. He went into the kitchen and poured some orange juice he'd found un opened in a cupboard. There was a jar of extra-large hot dog sausages in one of the kitchen units and he ate them one at a time. He looked across at his mother. He'd have to leave her, until he came back with his uncles. He could blame Don Mason for the condition she was now in.

Alec returned back upstairs and looked up the road from the top bedroom. The last of the dead had passed twenty minutes ago, so it would be a good time to take a look at the roundabout area. He looked down and saw Vic standing in the road. He was waving. Alec put a hand on his hunting knife, then opened the window.

Vick looked up at him, 'Son, I've come to apologise, I want no trouble. You look like you can handle that knife and I said a few things that may have offended you. I'm sorry, I don't want to lose my life because of something daft I said. Are we good, son?' Alec grinned.

'We're good, I'm coming down let's shake on it.' He took his hunting knife out of the sheath and held it behind his back, as he made his way down the stairs. Vic stood inside the gateway as Alec opened the door. He held his hand out, 'Vic, I'm Vic Hind.' Alec pulled the knife from behind his back, 'soon to be fucking dead Vic Hind,' Vic's smile disappeared and Alec walked out through the front door.

Don stepped from the side and smashed Ray Donaldson's baseball bat into Alec's face. His back and head hit the ground and he lay unconscious. Don quickly knelt down and took away the knife. Alec's nose was clearly broken and blood was pouring out of it.

Don rolled Alec over and attached cable ties around his wrists tightly, behind his back. Don took the washing line rope out of the bag and tied the hands together again, then led the rope up Alec's back and tied it around his neck, leaving a long length hanging.

Don looked up at Vic, 'let's get him inside, we can't go anywhere until the dead pass the other way. Hopefully he'll be awake by then. His mother's probably inside. Stay here I'll see to her.' Don picked up the spike and entered the house.

He didn't even go into the sitting room. Vic watched him turn and come back. 'She's dead Vic. He's cut her throat.' 'What?'

They carried Alec inside and laid him on the settee. Vic looked over Kylie's body. 'She's been bit, here Don.' Don looked at the marks on Kylie's leg. 'He killed her because she'd have slowed him down. His own fucking mother.' Vic shook his head.

Don went through Alec's pockets and found the gate and store house keys. He had nothing else on him, other than a lock knife. There was some food and drinks in Kylie's bag. Don put the lock knife into his bag. It was blood stained.

Alec Donaldson started to come round a half hour later. He started struggling and pulling against the ties on his hands. Don had tied his feet with cable ties, so he was unable to move. Alec looked up at Don and Vic.

Don stood over Alec and took out a lock knife. He held in front of Alec's face. 'I'll tell you only once. You're coming with Vic and me back to Bedlington. If I have any concerns whatsoever about you, I will cut off a finger or ear. If I feel you will put us in danger, I will cut your throat and leave you where you drop, understand? Alec started to cry, 'yes, yes, don't hurt me anymore, I'll behave.'

An hour and a half passed. Don sat in the kitchen with Vic, chatting, as the dead passed. They knew they had about half an hour or so before the horde turned and headed back. Vic went outside and looked along the road. 'They're away, Don.'

Don led Alec out. He was holding onto the rope, 'if you take one wrong step, I'll fucking hang you with this.'

They made their way along the road. As they got to Vic's place, Vic ran into the yard and took his bucket and donned the coat, 'I like to be invisible, Don. I'll walk on ahead.'

Vic spotted a couple of stray dead on route towards Connor's place, pointed them out and Don took them down, one handed with the spike as they neared. He never let go of the rope.

As they got within sight of Connor's place Alec swung round and took a kick at Don's hands. Don dropped the rope and Alec ran towards Bebside Road, rope trailing behind him. As he rounded the corner, he hit the ground hard. Connor stood up and grabbed the rope. He dragged Alec back towards Don and threw him to the ground, 'For fuck's sake, Don, did you think this fucker would come back with you and not try anything?'

Don took the lock knife out of his pocket and cut off Alec's injured ear. Alec screamed with pain and horror. 'He won't anymore, will you?'

Don put his hand out and shook Connor's hand. He noticed the air rifle and a large backpack at the side of the road. 'You've decided to join us after all, then, Connor?' 'There's nothing for me here, Don. I'm ready to move on.'

They all headed down towards the Picnic Field, Vic walking ahead, then up the steep bank into Bedlington. One dead man was slowly hobbling towards them, as they reached the top of the bank. Vic stepped aside of it and Connor shot it through the right eye. It fell dead to the floor.

Vic took off his coat and dropped it to the ground, inside the perimeter of Hollymount Square, as Don locked the gates. He put the bucket down alongside it and they all walked down the Square, Don leading Alec Donaldson by the rope.

Geordie and Neil ran over and Don passed them the rope. 'Put him in a different house to his dad, if the bastard's still alive. Make sure the fucker's feet are tied as well.' He slapped Alec across the wound where his ear had been and Alec cried out in agony. Don gave Geordie a bunch of cable ties and Geordie took the rope and replied to Don, 'oh Ray's alive alright.' 'Where's Clarky?' 'He's been over Millfield since you left, Don.'

Don took Connor and Vic around to Dawn's house and knocked on her door. Dawn answered, 'two more for accommodation?' Don nodded, 'if you don't mind, Dawn. These men are friends, good friends.'

Jamie ran out and nearly knocked Don off his feet. He was crying with joy. 'Grandad, Grandad.' Don picked him up and hugged him tightly. 'I need you to stay with Dawn just a little longer, Jamie.' 'Ok Grandad.' He ran after Dawn.

Dawn led the two men around towards the empty houses, 'plenty to choose from,' Don stood in his doorway and watched Neil and Geordie lead Alec Donaldson into a house along from where Ray was being held.

Don went inside and walked over to the kitchen sink. He washed his face with cold water and ran his fingers through his hair. He'd caught the monster that had caused the death of his Granddaughter and so many other people, but what now? People like these cannot be warned off. Don knew the two had to die.

He looked at his watch. It was 2.00pm. Don heated some water on the stove and made a pot of tea.

Hannah came to the door and Don let her in. He poured her a cup of tea and she sat with him. 'You did it, Don. You stopped him from bringing more trouble to us.' 'The problem now is what to do with them.' 'I hate to say it Don but they have to die.' 'I know, Hannah, I've known all along, but I wanted the two bastards together for it.'

Everything is alright in the square, Don. Clarky's been away since yesterday.' 'I know. I'm going over to see him after I finish my tea.'

Hannah hugged Don, 'thank God you got back alright, Don.' 'Yes, and with two friends. Connor's here and another guy I found, Vic Hind. Hannah, Vic walks among the dead. This could be major for us. I'll tell you all about it when I get back.' 'Everyone got into the farm safely, Don. The animals are alright. Let's get together tonight, we'll bring Amelia and Marty. He's back on his feet. We emptied the Donaldson place. I'll bring a few bottles of wine. Clarky gave me a bottle of malt whiskey for you as well. He said it's a good one. I'll bring it along 7.00.'

Hannah left for home and Don made his way towards the gates. Half way there he caught up with Dot Smith. She was heading for the gates pulling a two - wheeled shopping cart, you know, one of those with long handle and the tartan pattern on them. 'Where you off to, Dot?'

She turned around and looked at Don. 'Oh, Jack, I was just going to pick up some groceries.' 'It's Don, Dot, Jack was my dad. Where's Lance, Dot?' 'Lance? he's in the garden, Jack. I'm just going to the shops to pick up some odds and ends.' 'I'll tell you what, Dot, they've opened a shop in the square, just yesterday, it's a good one, as well. Everything's free, Dot, come with me and I'll show you.' She took Don's arm. 'Alright Jack, let's have a look at this new thing you're going on about.' She stopped, looked at Don and tutted, 'you need a shave, Jack and a haircut as well.'

Don led Dot down the square and round towards the storehouse. Hannah saw them through the window and went to the central garden and got Lance. Lance caught them up and stood back as Don let Dot into the store house. She walked around the downstairs rooms, picking odd tins off the benches and out of full cupboards and walked out. 'It's a nice shop, Jack. I got what we need. I might come back here.' She saw Lance in the street, 'Lance, where have you been, I had to do the shopping on my own.' Lance looked over at Don and smiled. 'Howey Dot, you can put the kettle on and make us a cuppa. I'll put the shopping away.' Don put the store key in Lance's hand. 'Just bring her any time she wants to come, Lance.' Dot linked her husband's arm as they walked off, Don smiled and shook his head, as she spoke to Lance, along the way, 'That Jack Mason could do with a shave and a haircut mind, Lance. I wouldn't allow you let yourself go like that.'

Harsh Democracy.

Don made his way to Millfield to see Clarky. He didn't need to access from Church lane and Millfield North any more, the threat of the Donaldsons was gone. He had a clear path and headed into Millfield.

As Don followed the road in, he saw the pallet wagon parked outside the Donaldson houses. On the field, Clarky was standing half way up a twenty-foot-tall sack of pallets. Dowser and Paul were holding a pallet in place and Clarky was tying it into the stack.

The stack was built with a layer of pallets on their sides, then a layer laid flat and Clarky was tying the pallet up at the fourth layer. There were all sorts of things stuffed between the gaps in the pallets, papers, cardboard, broken furniture, the fire was packed full. Don looked along the stack and saw a gap, like a small corridor inside.

Clarky jumped down. 'Good to see you Mace. Did you catch him, fucker who killed Maeve?' 'Yes, he's tied up in one of the spare houses.' Don looked at the stack of wood. It reminded him of the bonfire at the top of the woods, they had lit, all those years ago to spoil the Donaldsons' Guy Fawkes night.

Don stepped over and looked at the construction with Clarky, 'look Clarky, we have to talk about what we do with these two.' 'Nothing to talk about, Mace. I knew when you got the boy back there would be apprehensions or second thoughts about killing them. No one will want their deaths on their conscience, so it's my guess that it's up to the people most affected by them, to put them down. I mean, what the boy did to Emma, her friend and all those children and what the monsters did to my wife and all the vulnerable people along Millbank and Dene View West.

I'm preparing for their end Don, so you can leave this with me. I'll take responsibility for the two of them.'

Don shook his head, 'What the fuck is this, Clarky? We're not like them. We can't fucking burn people at the stake.' 'So, what do you want to do, Mace? Let them go?' Don put his head down, 'no.'

'So, what is it then, Mace?' Don was silent. 'Listen, Mace neither of these fucks can be allowed to live. Remember what Ray said outside your door when he thought he had you? There's no law now, but that works both ways, Mace. These people killed our loved ones.'

Don raised his voice, 'Clarky, you can't do this to someone, man.' Clarky stood face to face with Don, 'Listen Mace, if you haven't got the stomach for what's going to happen, what these two cunts have coming, then step aside and leave this with me.' 'And what about all the dead this will attract? Have you given any thought to this?' 'Yes, I have. The dead will be delivered back to the Hartlands. That whole area is lost. They'll return the following night, I guarantee it. Don, you kept Ray Donaldson alive so you had these two together.' 'Not for this, Clarky.' 'In that case I should have shot the bastard in the Square, like I was going to, until you stopped me.'

Don turned and headed back to the square. Clarky called after him, 'so I get to bring them here? Finish it my way?' Don stopped and turned. 'We've got around 70 residents in the square, Clarky. They need to have a say in what happens to them, as well. I'm going to call a meeting outside my house at 4.00pm. Please be there.' Don walked away.

At 4.00pm Don went outside. Jamie had earlier gone around all the occupied houses and most of the residents had come along.

Don greeted everyone, 'Thanks for coming out. I just want to update you all on events of the last couple of days. As most of you know, we were betrayed by Colin Markem and the Mcevoy brothers. The people who had joined with the Donaldsons are now dead or gone.

I went after Alec Donaldson this morning. He was making for New Hartley, to seek help. I couldn't allow further threat to the Square. I caught him and brought him back. Alec Donaldson had murdered his own mother, because she had been bitten and would have slowed him down. He is tied up in an empty house at the moment.'

Don held up and arm towards the two new arrivals, 'two men returned with me today, Connor and Vic. Connor supported us to get to and from the tip safely, enabling us to secure the fence and Vic saved my life this morning. Vic is able to walk among the dead. His means of doing so is quite unpleasant, but it means we are going to be able to access places we couldn't before, like shops and chemists. Dawn allocated the two men houses last night, but I'd like to officially confirm with you the residents, they can stay.' Geordie spoke up, 'welcome friends and thanks for all you've done for us. Of course, we'd like them to stay.'

There were pats on the back and handshakes for Connor and Vic, as everyone agreed.

Don spoke again. 'We do have the problem of what to do with Ray and Alec Donaldson.'

Hannah stepped forward, 'Don, they've shown the threat they are. They have to die. They are too dangerous.' 'Yes, Hannah, but how?'

Clarky spoke up, 'Don they murdered my wife. They've murdered vulnerable people all around Bedlington. The boy raped Emma. He murdered her friend. I'll take them. Leave them with me. I'll take them back to Millfield. You'll never see them again.'

Don shook his head, 'Clarky, you're my best friend, but you're planning to burn these two men. We're not like them, Clarky.' 'You're not like them, Don and that's to your credit and it's why you're so well respected here, but a bullet in the head is too easy for these two. It will not help me in any way, after the suffering they caused me.'

Don stood quiet for a moment, 'What about the residents, what do you all want to do with the Donaldsons?'

Geordie replied, 'Don, no one here wants to walk in those houses and put two men down. Clarky lost his wife. You lost Emma, then there's the Ashfords and what about the old lady and little girl we had to lay to rest at Dene View? These two are monsters, Don. Far more threatening than the dead. I say we let Clarky take them.' There were words of agreement running through the group of residents.

Dawn stepped forward, 'Ray Donaldson sexually assaulted me when I was thirteen, just like his son is doing to children, now. My dad was terrified of Fred Donaldson and nothing was done. I've never recovered. I've had to endure Ray Donaldson grinning at me every time I've seen him since that day. Now these two know they don't even have to let their victims live and we're standing here talking about burning being too bad a death for them. Give me the matches and I'll light the fire. Get rid of them once and for all. Life is dangerous enough these days. Don, haven't you noticed, people aren't even coming outside into the square today, because they know these two are here. They're scaring people, even when they're tied and locked up. We can't live with this threat.'

Head down, Don looked around the group. 'Alright, we'll put it to a vote. All in favour of Clarky taking the Donaldsons raise a hand.' Nearly everyone raised their hand. 'So be it.'

Don continued, 'My final thing is about seeking survivors. It's taken time to secure our safety, but when this is over with the Donaldsons I intend to keep my word about trying to locate friends and family. Please put a note through my door with names and addresses. I'll put them in a hat and draw them in turn and try to find out if they are still with us. I'll bring any survivor back I find.

Midgy stepped forward, 'you've all been good enough to give us safe homes, here, so the least I can do is join Don and help him with this.' Dowser and Clarky also volunteered.

Don went back inside the house and the group dispersed. Hannah followed him.

Hannah sat on the armchair opposite Don, 'You've done everything you could to make us safe, Don. You shouldn't lose sleep about how two monsters are going to die.' 'Clarky's going to burn them alive, Hannah.'

'I'm only burning Ray alive, Don.' Clarky was in the doorway. 'I've got plans for Maeve's murderer. I want you there, Don. I want you with me. We both need closure for what these bastards have done. You can't see it now, but I can. Please take my word for this.'

Don took three glasses and put them on the coffee table. He took the lid off a bottle of 18 years old Glenmorangie and poured three drinks, 'I didn't get a chance to thank you for the Whiskey, Clarky.' He took a drink and passed a glass to Clarky, 'alright Clarky, we do it your way, tomorrow. I'll not go against the residents' majority.'

Clarky finished the drink and put the glass down on the table, 'I'm going back over to Millfield for another couple of hours, Don, can I borrow the Machete?' Don passed it over, gave Clarky a gate key and Clarky left.

Vic was having a cup of tea when he heard a knock on the door. He opened it and Clarky was standing. 'Ian Clarke and you're Vic?' 'Yes.' 'Vic, can I ask a favour?' 'yes, anything, Ian,' 'I get called Clarky. The walking among the dead thing. Can I have a try?' 'Well, I don't see why not, Clarky, as long as you stay calm. You don't look like the sort of guy who would panic. Do you want me to come with you?' 'No, No. I just need to pop somewhere. Somewhere that may be a bit overrun.'

They walked towards the gates. Clarky looked at Vic, 'so you were with Don when he caught up with the Donaldson boy?' 'Yes, he'd got surrounded and I helped him back to my house.' 'Where were you living, Vic?' 'First house along the Horton Road, Don came to the door, but I was worried he may be a threat. I let him walk off towards all those dead, but something told me he wasn't a bad man, so I went after him. He'd never have made it to where the boy was.' 'So where was the boy?' 'The end house, that's where Don got him. The one with the metal security shutters, just before the Shoes pub.'

The two arrived at the gates and Vic helped Clarky on with the coat and he left, locking the gates behind him.

Don and Hannah checked on Ray Donaldson. He was still alive. He lay on his side and looked down as Don put a bottle of water on the coffee table beside him. 'Can you take the top off, Mason?' Don walked out the door and Hannah took the lid off the water and left behind him.

They checked on Alec. He was lying in the same position he'd been left. Hands behind his back and feet still tied. Hannah opened a bottle and helped him take a drink. She fed him half the bottle and Don said 'that's enough.' As Don walked out Alec looked up at him, 'My Dad? Is he alive?' Don looked through him and walked out. Hannah followed.

17

The Fire

Don and Geordie entered the sitting room where Ray Donaldson was being held. Geordie had found a wheelchair in one of the abandoned houses. Clarky had been around to Don's, first thing and they had agreed to take the two prisoners over to Millfield. Ray was screaming as they bundled him into the wheelchair. Blood started oozing from the gunshot wound to his knee.

Don pushed the wheelchair into the square, then headed to the house where Alec was held. In a couple of minutes, Don appeared, dragging Alec by the rope, he'd re - tied around his neck. Hannah looked at Alec as he was led out. His nose was distorted and he had two very dark black eyes. Hannah was holding Marty's hand. Neil and Dawn joined them and they set off for Millfield, to get there for 11.00, as agreed.

They arrived on time and Clarky was waiting with Midgy Dowser and Paul. Clarky took the wheelchair over to the pile. Ray was panicking, 'What's this, what the fuck is this, Mason!'. Clarky got Ray to the pile, then dragged him off the wheelchair and through the space between the pallets. The inside of the stack was like a small room. Ray screamed with terror and pain as Clarky dragged him through and sat him up. He was sat between the bodies of Albert and Brenda Ashford. Clarky punched Ray in the face and started removing his clothing. He soon had Ray stripped to his underpants. He looked down at the scar tissue where Ray had been burned all those years ago, then looked him in the eye. 'That was me, that was.' Ray tried to swing his right hand at Clarky, but Clarky just caught it and forced it against the timber wall. He took out a long cable tie and secured Ray's right hand. Soon he'd secured the other. He smiled at Ray, 'don't go away, I'll be back soon.'

Outside, Alec Donaldson was on his knees begging, 'please, please don't let him hurt me, don't let him.'

Clarky came out and Don handed the rope to him, head down. Clarky dragged Alec so hard, he fell to the ground. Clarky pulled the rope around and kicked Alec in the groin, right where he'd been shot. He was screaming, as Clarky dragged him towards his dad.

Ray screamed at Clarky, as he dragged Alec in, 'don't harm my son, don't harm him, I've got money, lots of money, let us go and you can have it all.'

Clarky tied both of Alec's hands tightly to the walls. Alec was standing beside the body of Lisa Ashford. He screamed for help, 'Dad, Dad, don't let him hurt me.'

Clarky picked up a large cardboard box and tipped thousands of pounds in notes over Ray Donaldson, 'Is this the money you're offering me, Ray? The money from your house? We fucking emptied the place. Your stuff is ours now. One thing we don't need is money.'

Ray put his head down. 'What are you going to do with us?' 'Well it's like this Ray. I enjoyed watching the fire with Don Mason, all those years back, from the Picnic Field. Fucking hilarious watching you fucks desperately trying to put it out. You getting burned, you know? I enjoyed it so much I thought we'd have another one, but with a twist. Oh, I nearly forgot our other guest.'

Clarky picked up a back pack from the corner of the room and opened the top. He rolled Kylie Donaldson's head out, between Ray's legs. 'There you go Ray, I brought Spit Roast along.'

Ray screamed, 'Kylie, Kylie, what did you do to her you fucking murderer?' 'Murderer? I didn't murder Spit Roast, your fucking psychopath rapist son did that and guess what, Ray? you're going to be his last victim.'

Clarky turned to Alec Donaldson. He pulled Alec's hunting knife out of his bag. 'Is this the one, Alec? The one you killed all those kids with? And my wife?' Alec was crying hysterically. Clarky held up the knife. 'Where did you stab my wife, Alec Donaldson.' 'It wasn't me; it wasn't me.' 'Oh, it was you, you fucking murdering bastard.' He cut off Alec's other ear. Alec was screaming. Clarky held up the knife. 'I've got all day, son, where did you stab my wife?' 'The chest.'

Clarky looked back at Ray and smiled, 'Chest it is, Marty.' Marty entered the room and took the knife out of Clarky's hand. He stood looking into Alec Donaldson's eyes. Alec was pleading with him not to hurt him. Marty stood quiet, then said 'this is for Ellie, you horrible bastard.' Alec glanced down and saw the gold, 'Ellie' necklace around Marty's neck, as Marty lunged the knife deep into his chest. Alec gasped and slumped forward, pulling at the ropes, in a vain attempt to free his hands.

Marty turned and walked out onto the field and stood by Hannah.

Inside, Clarky grabbed Alec's chin and lifted his head and looked in his eyes as he pulled out the knife. Alec Donaldson was spluttering, but couldn't make words. Blood spurted out of his mouth instead. He quickly bled out and was dead within minutes.

Clarky stepped back, let Alec's head drop and turned and faced Ray. 'Well Ray, I guess it's goodbye, then.' 'Lec! Lec! Clarke, you! you bastard, bastard! I'll kill you!'

Kylie's head was still lying between Ray's legs, as Clarky turned and cut Alec down. Alec fell to the floor, dead in front of his dad and his mother's head.

Clarky left the stack of pallets and joined the others. Midgy, Paul and Dowser took cans of paraffin and poured them all over the stack.

Inside Ray began to panic, 'you, you can't do this! You can't leave me here! He'll turn!'

Don looked at Clarky as he emptied a paraffin bottle over the debris, then threw it inside. He said nothing.

Clarky stepped away from the stack. 'Well, does anyone want a drink?' Don stepped forward, 'What are you doing, Clarky?' 'You'll see.'

The group went through the pallet barricade and inside into the Donaldson house. Clarky had wine and spirits, salted peanuts, out of date crisps, chocolate and various tinned foods on the table. He took everyone upstairs with drinks and they sat in the bedroom, overlooking the grassed oval shaped field and the massive pyre. Clarky had the window wide open.

Occasionally they could hear Ray Donaldson screaming for help and Clarky ran outside with Midgy on one occasion, when it had attracted a couple of dead. They quickly put them to rest and laid them against the pyre.

At 7.15pm Clarky stood up and looked out of the window. He'd heard Ray shouting again. Everyone in the room went quiet and looked out of the window. It was starting to get dark and Ray called again, 'Help! someone come over, help! he's moving, his fingers are moving! Help!' Clarky looked over to Don, 'this is it, Mace.'

They stood silent, then heard Ray again calling, 'Lec, son, Lec, it's dad, Lec, it's.' then there were screams. Lots of screams. Clarky, Dawn and Marty went outside and Dawn took the matches and struck one. She lit some newspaper that had earlier been soaked with paraffin and the paper went up in flames, that quickly spread. Marty did the same at the opposite side of the pyre.

Clarky summoned the group outside and they watched on as the fire quickly burned through and into the centre. Ray Donaldson was screaming inside, as they left and they headed back towards the Square.

Clarky took a right turn, in the direction of Millfield South and Don called after him, 'where are you going, Clarky,' 'I arranged to stay at the farm tonight, Don. I'll be back in a couple of days. Get the kids to watch the sky over towards the Hartlands at nine o'clock tomorrow night. I'm putting on a fireworks display.'

The group got back inside the gates and Don looked across the road over Millfield Court in the direction of Millfield. The sky was glowing orange. He made sure the gates were secure and went back home and joined Jamie.

Jamie was overjoyed to see Grandad. Don pulled a packet salted peanuts and some crisps and chocolate out of his coat pocket.

Jamie went outside and into the workshop and came back in with two oak crosses.

'Grandad, I know you asked me to do one of these for Ben and the farm lady, but it turned out Ben and Colin were with the Donaldsons. I don't think it's right he should have one of these. I carved 'Emma Jones and Kate Ashford' on this one.' The cross was really well made and Don had tears in his eyes. 'Let's go down the garden, now Jamie. It belongs there. We'll put the other one where I buried Marion and her family at the farm. It's the least we can do after what she has given us.'

They set the cross over the grave in the garden, then went back in and sat together until bed time.

Don put Jamie to bed at 11.00pm. Don was exhausted. So much had happened in so short a time. He undressed and got into bed. He'd carried the bottle of whiskey upstairs with him. He poured a drink and sat back.

Don was still sat in the same position at 10.00am the following morning. Jamie came into the room and woke him up, Grandad, are you alright? you're always up first. Don went downstairs and ate with Jamie.

They chatted all morning, then Don went into the workshop.

Don had made a bespoke silencer for a member of the gun club some time back and he had found the spec. He'd decided to make a silencer for the Browning, in case he ever needed to use it in emergency. He commenced working. Time flew, that afternoon.

At five o'clock, Don remembered what Clarky had said. He walked across to Dawn's place.

Dawn came to the door, 'are you alright, Dawn.' 'Yes, Don, best I've slept for years.' 'Me too, you know. Dawn, Clarky said to have the kids outside at nine tonight. Would you go around and let them all know?' 'Yes, Don. Vic asked me over for a coffee. We'll do it together. I think word's already out, though, the college girls have been baking all morning.'

At 8.55pm the families of Hollymount square stood outside looking at the black, starlit clear sky.

At the same time, Ian Clarke stood on the overgrown football pitches behind the Hartlands. He'd earlier entered Punter and Hope's house, laid them together on their bed, then set light to the house and to a whole row of adjoining houses at the Hartlands. He looked at his watch and, as it turned 9.00 Clarky lit the fuse wire. He climbed the fence and entered the farmers' fields disappearing into the darkness.

For the next hour, the sky was ablaze with fireworks. Clarky had taken the four large display quality fireworks from the farm, set them up and lit the first fuse right on 9.00pm. The farmer had ordered an hour-long display, so they were connected by fuse wire to engage one after the other, each one carrying a fifteen-minute display. It was spectacular and could be seen clearly from the square. As the display ended, the house fires blazed strongly. Roofs were caving in and flames were spitting high into the air.

At the Square, Honour and the student girls were handing out hot dogs, cakes and biscuits and the kids were having a whale of a time, like a street party. Adults had drinks, that had been confiscated from the Donaldson house and there were fizzy drinks for the kids and sweets, lots of sweets.

Will and Geordie stood together in the back bedroom of the farmhouse and watched the fireworks. Geordie looked down into the yard. All the kids had come outside and were pointing to the sky, as the display went on.

Heather had spent the day baking and there was a large table, in the yard, covered in scones, cakes and biscuits. There was a large bucket of non - alcoholic punch, the kids were helping themselves to.

Geordie patted Will on the back, 'Clarky did it then?' 'aye, Geordie, the Donaldsons are gone for good. Just the dead to worry about, now. He was right about the fireworks, when he came, last night. I can already see dead heading across the twenty Acre field. I hope he takes my advice and moves through the fields, though. There're a lot of bodies out there.'

Geordie looked at Will. He was just a kid, but he'd done so much, taken so many risks to his own life, to make so many people safe. 'You're some kid, Will. All these people are safe because of you.' 'I still have some of my friends to visit, yet, Geordie, but after what Clarky told us about walking among them, I think I can do it much safer, now. I'm going to carry on looking, until I find every one of them. That's my job, now. Bring them home, or put them to rest.'

They both went down, took plates and helped themselves from the buffet. For once they could have a good night, fear free.

More importantly, though, by around 11.00pm thousands of dead were returning to the Hartlands from Millfield and Bedlington Front Street heading towards the fires, that had caught their attention.

18

Two Outings One Discovery

* * *

Hannah was violently sick on the ground, beside the inner gate. She was stood bent over, hands on knees and Vic stood alongside, patting her back. 'Jesus, this stinks, Vic, God almighty.'

Colleen was watching from a distance, holding the baby. She shook her head and walked back into the house.

'Let's try again.' Vic took the slime covered coat and wrapped it over Hannah's shoulders and she slipped her arms into the sleeves. Hannah quickly pulled a snood over her mouth and nose. Vic stood for a moment, 'ok?' Hannah nodded and pulled up the slime covered hood.

Vic looked Hannah up and down. She had found a long coat that went down to under her knees and she wore leather boots, that Vic had painted with the slime.

Hannah opened the gate and stepped out.

Vic and Hannah took hold of rails, front and back, that had been attached to a small trailer, which had been on Neil's drive. They had used plywood to raise the sides.

Vic turned and looked back. 'Don't forget, Hannah, they can't detect you. Only you can give yourself away, so no matter what happens, just stay still, calm and quiet.' 'Ok, Vic.'

The two set off on their journey along the road, up Bedlington Front Street.

* * *

Don, Clarky, Midgy and Dowser were standing at Don's dining table. It was around ten in the morning and the group were getting ready for the next search for survivors.

Midgy put his hand into a cardboard box that contained folded up names and addresses. 'Please be a survivor. Yesterday was an absolute downer. I need to pass on some good news.'

He handed the folded paper to Don. 'Damon Andrews. My son Mark and his wife and two sons, 4 River View Close.' Don looked up at the group, 'Damon's on his own. He's been helping Ronnie in the gardens.' Clarky stood, head down. Don glanced over. He knew why.

Clarky looked up and took the address, 'I know these houses.' Dowser nodded, 'aye, they're the bungalows beside the Bank Top pub.'

Don emptied the box. 'Ok, let's find any addresses in that area and we can plan a route.'

They all unfolded the rest of the papers. Clarky put one on the table, 'Cambo Avenue, Don. If we head down past where the Terrier pub used to be, Cambo's just alongside Poplar Grove.' Dowser put another address forward, 'this one's Hirst Head, the bungalows beside the cricket ground, that's on the way as well.'

After checking the rest of the addresses, Don put the three notes in his pocket and the group folded the rest and put them back in the box. 'Ok, Bob Reece is Jacob's dad, Bob's at Cambo, Avril Hudson is Vera's sister, she's at Hirst Head and the Andrews are Damon's family at River View Close.'

They got to the gate, then took four long coats that were hanging on hooks. Don took a bucket and painted down the other three and Clarky took the brush and did the same to him.

Faces covered with scarves, they left the Square, locking up behind them. They travelled light, Don carried the spike, the others the Donaldsons' baseball bats and they had three bags with long coats inside, in case they found survivors. Midgy carried the bucket of slime. They all had water and some chocolate bars in their pockets. The group made their way to the Northumberland Arms corner then headed down towards Beech Grove. There were a few dead ambling around, but none of them took any notice of the group. They were stumbling around, aimlessly.

* * *

Hannah and Vic slowly made their way up to the Red Lion roundabout. There were a lot of dead wandering around and Vic steered the trailer through them, stopping every time one got too close.

Hannah could feel her heart in her mouth as dead walked up to the trailer and the two of them, then turned and walked away. Vic just stopped and moved when there was a path through.

Hannah could see Vic had done this before. He had immense patience and poise. They made their way towards Morrison's supermarket. Vic stopped at the mini roundabout. He slowly walked alongside Hannah. There were no dead nearby, but he could see a large group walking in and out of the supermarket. He whispered to Hannah, 'No matter what happens in here, just remain still and quiet. They can't see you as food. If you fall, lay still. Wait till they have seen what made the noise. Then get up. Just don't panic. I'm going to go in first. You just stand outside and, oh, if you have something in your hand one recognizes as food, just let it take it. Once you get stuff into the trailer, it will be out of sight to them' 'Ok Vic.'

They slowly steered the cart into Morrisons car park and Vic left Hannah and walked inside.

A number of dead walked over to Hannah and she closed her eyes tight shut as they bumped against her and the trailer, then turned and wandered off.

It seemed like an eternity before Vic came out the supermarket, but he walked straight past Hannah. Lots of dead were following him. Hannah watched as Vic turned and pulled four large bags of dried pasta from inside his coat. He split open the packets and spread all the pasta over the ground at the back of the car park.

Hannah was astonished as the packets tore open and every one of the dead in the vicinity turned their heads simultaneously, then made for the food. Vic stood still as they brushed past him and went to ground. As last of the dead walked out of the supermarket, Vic and Hannah walked in with the trailer.

*　*　*

As the men headed towards Beech Grove, Don held up his hand. They had caught up with a dead man, who was rounding the corner into Beech Grove. His right forearm was clearly broken and swung back and forth, by his side.

Don stepped forward, 'It's Colin Markem.'

Don walked up behind Colin and Colin turned around. His face and neck had been bitten. There was no cheek on the left side of Colin's face and both sets of teeth were clearly visible. There was a lot of dried blood down his front, from the deep neck wound.

Don put the spike through Colin's head and he dropped to the ground dead.

The group slowly made their way down through Beech Grove and stopped beside the entrance to Hirst Head. The entrance was blocked with cars, but this had only kept the dead out from the outside. There was a substantial housing estate further in and a lot of dead were wandering around back and forth from there.

'This is the one.' Don walked through a gate and down a garden path. The house was boarded up.

Don tried the side door and it was locked. Around ten dead were attracted to the sound of the gate and the noise of Don trying the door, so the group all stood still. The Dead stood outside the garden and all held up their heads, as if listening and smelling the air. Then they turned and walked off. Don waited until they were away, then took a crowbar and popped open the front door.

Clarky stepped inside and opened the living room door. An elderly lady sat, terrified on the settee. Clarky turned to Don, 'A survivor.'

Clarky quickly threw the coat outside and the others quickly did the same and entered the house.

'Do you have any food?' the lady looked desperate. Don passed her a chocolate bar and she quickly took off the wrapper and started eating.

Don passed her a bottle of water, 'I'm Don, I was sent by Vera, Vera Sharpe.' 'Vera? She's still alive?' The woman started to cry. 'Are you Avril Hudson?' 'Yes.' I've been trapped here for weeks, now. I stayed inside, like they said, but no one came. Tom from next door was bringing me food until three days ago. He went out and never came back. I ran out of food yesterday.'

Don sat beside Avril. 'Listen, Avril. We have to go down to River View Close. We're checking two more houses. Can you stay here and we'll come back for you? It's too far to walk down and back for you after what you've been through.'

Avril started crying. 'Please don't leave me here.' Midgy took a coat out of one of the bags. 'Don, I'll take her back, now. She's desperate, here.'

Don explained the process of the coat to Avril and she covered her face with a scarf and put it on. Midgy painted the coat over with the slime and she pulled up the hood.

Outside the estate Midgy took Avril's hand and they slowly walked back towards Beech Grove. He looked back at Don, 'I'll be back with the key for you, Don.'

* * *

Hannah and Vic slowly made their way around the supermarket. There was cardboard, plastic, all kinds of wrapping, spread across the floor. And slime. There was lots of stinking, wet slime. Hanna slipped a few times, but soon learned to keep her feet close together and take short steps

Everything that could be opened and consumed easily, was gone. Lower shelves were all empty. Vic stopped the trailer, 'They can't open cans, Hannah.'

They took lots of canned food and carefully and quietly placed it into the trailer, then headed for the baby foods. Hannah quickly loaded everything from the shelves into the cart. Meanwhile Vic had taken a basket and started filling it with batteries, lighters, chewing gum, paracetamol tablets and anything of use from the front counters. Vic put the whole basket into the trailer, then made for the rice and dried foods. Most had been eaten, but there was pasta and rice on the top shelves and Vic quickly cleared them into the trailer.

The two made down the baking aisle and took all ingredients, again which had been out of reach to the dead. They took cleaning products, kitchen and toilet roll, wines and spirits, something of everything.

The two continued their way around until the trailer started to feel heavy. Vic stopped pushing. 'That's all, Hannah, we've got to get out of here safe. He stepped over towards the doorway and came back in. 'Some are coming back, Hannah.' Vic walked out, again with four packs of dried pasta. He tore open the packets at the left side of the car park and the dead diverted towards it.

In a few minutes Vic and Hannah were leaving the car park and slowly moving down the road. The trailer was full to the top.

* * *

Don made his way to the front door of the address in Cambo Avenue. He tapped on the door and there was no reply. He went to the front window and a dead man smashed a hand through the glass of the side opener window. Don jumped back as the arm reached to try and grab him. His heart was pounding, with the fright, but he took the spike and smashed the main front window, then put the spike through the head of an old man. Dowser walked forward. 'Must be Bob Reece.'

Some dead had been attracted to the noise, so the three slowly wandered off, towards River View Close.

The Close was wide open, but one house had cars right across the front of the long, wide garden outside. The men climbed over the bonnet of one of the cars and Don tapped on the door. A young boy, around sixteen years old came to the front window. He had a long, pink scar down the right side of his face. Don pulled down the scarf. 'We're here for the Andrews family. Damon sent us.'

The door opened. A young boy stood in front of them. 'Come in, but don't open that door. He pointed to the bedroom door on the left. There was bumping against the door. Don looked at Clarky. 'I'm Kelvin and this is my brother, Robbie.' 'Don, Don Mason. Damon Andrews sent us to look for his son and family.' 'Mum and dad are dead.' He pointed at the bedroom door. 'They were bit last week, out looking for food. They locked themselves in there and told us to keep out. I'm sorry, Don but you stink.' Don handed Kelvin a coat, 'you need to as well, Kelvin, if we're going to get you and your brother to your grandad safe. Does Robbie have a long coat?'

'He's got overalls, he was given for a school recycling project, go put them on, Robbie and a hoody.'

Robbie ran to his room. Don took Kelvin outside and started painting him down with the slime. 'Grandad lives at Hollymount. That's near Millfield. Alec Donladson lives near there.' Don finished covering Kelvin and passed the brush to Clarky. 'Alec Donaldson is dead, son.'

As Clarky painted Robbie down Don took Kelvin's hand. 'Listen, son. No matter what happens stay calm. Let the dead walk up to you. They cannot see you. Stay quiet, do you hear Robbie?' 'Yes Don.'

Kelvin looked back at the house. 'Mam and dad?' Don walked back into the house and closed the door. He carefully opened the bedroom door and stepped back. One after the other he pierced the heads of Mark and Phillipa Andrews.

The group set off back towards Bedlington.

* * *

Hannah and Vic made their way along Schalchsmule Road, towards what used to be the Barrington Arms pub, better known as the Monkey. There were no dead, walking nearby, but Hannah pointed out to Vic there were a lot of dead at rest on the road.

Vic walked over to a middle-aged woman, lying face down and rolled her over. She moved and reached out with her hand. Vic stepped back. He looked carefully around him and there was slight movement in all of the apparent laid to rest dead. Some reached out arms, some turned heads to look at the movement and noises around them, but none got up.

Vic returned to Hannah. 'Hannah, the woman was still able to move, but didn't have the strength to get up. She's got no head injury. Her face isn't covered in blood. Hannah, I think she's starving to death. We need to get back and talk to the others. This is a massive thing, massive. Look at the amount of dead that have collapsed here and can't get back up'

As Vic and Hannah made their way to the junction, that leads up to the Northumberland Arms Midgy was rounding the corner off Beech Grove. He caught them up. 'This is Avril, Avril, Vic and Hannah.' Midgy took the trailer handle and Hannah supported Avril and they made their way back to the Square.

Midgy got the gates and they all got inside and took off their coats. Hannah proudly pushed the trailer into the Square and Colleen came running over, 'you did it, you did it.'

Midgy held Avril's hand. 'Your safe now, flower. Let's get you to your family. Avril walked into Midgy's arms and held him close. 'Thank you so much for this, son.'

Midgy was crying. 'After all we've been through, here Avril, I needed this as much as you.' He headed back to the gates, as Vera Sharp and Maisy came running out of their house.

* * *

Don, Clarky and Dowser had the two boys with them as they walked towards Algood Terrace.

A large group of dead were up ahead and Don quickly spoke with the boys. 'No sound, no sound at all. We're going to all stand still and let them pass. Robbie. Pull the scarf over your eyes. If they bump you just stand still. They will kill you if you attract them.' Kelvin pulled Robbie close as around forty dead walked past. They held as a group, shielding the boy, as the dead bumped against them. Robbie was being so quiet he was even holding his breath and he had his eyes tightly shut.

Don patted Robbie on the back. 'Good boy, they're heading away, wait.'

Don walked out of the group. The dead were about fifty yards down the road, but two had collapsed and lay face down. Clarky stepped forward, 'maybe they haven't been hit hard enough?' He walked over with the bat. Don followed him, 'wait, Clarky. They stood over the two dead. They both reached for Don and Clarky. One tried to get to its feet, but its legs collapsed away from it. 'Look at them, Clarky, no blood on their face. Their clothing is dry, no slime. They haven't eaten. They're starving to death. Just like we would. The others were staggering, much more than I've seen before. They're running out of food. Look around, there're lots of them lying on the ground.'

Don and the group headed back past the Northumberland Arms and ran into Midgy. 'Here's the key, Don. We got Avril back safe.'

They all headed down the Front Street to the gates. They got inside, hung up all the coats and entered the Square. Colleen, Hannah and Marty were carrying bags of baby stuff from an over filled trailer into the house and other residents were taking the rest of the goods down to the store house on wheelbarrows.

Don caught Hannah's eye, 'successful mission, then?' 'Yes, and we've got something really important to tell you about the dead.' 'About them collapsing?' 'Yes, you've seen it too?' 'I have. Look at all the baby stuff. Well done Hannah, Vic. Meet at mine for a drink later, 7.00?' Hannah smiled, 'sounds good to me.'

Don made his way with the kids to Damon Andrews' house and the three stood outside. Don prodded Robbie, 'go on then.' Robbie knocked on the door. Damon was overjoyed when he answered the door and hugged the two boys. Don told Damon about his son and wife and Damon cried, as he hugged the two boys again.

Don hardly heard Damon's thanks for rescuing the boys.. He was watching along the road, where Clarky was speaking to Jacob and Amanda Reece. They were both sobbing in Clarky's arms.

The friends all met at Don's. Hannah and Colleen had brought the baby and Marty. Hannah was carrying two bottles of wine. Dawn was there with Vic and Geordie and Neil had brought their families, including Will.

Neil teased Vic, 'mind Vic, you haven't wasted any time with Dawn, mate.' Vic smiled and

held Dawn's hand, 'Mate, after some of the places I've been and some of the scrapes I've

been in, you're happy with the little time you have.' Don held up a glass, 'I'll drink to that.'

When everyone was settled, Hannah stood up. 'I was out today with Vic, seeking provisions

and baby stuff and we found dead that had collapsed and lay helpless on the ground.' Don

stood up and put his whiskey on the coffee table. 'It looks like food is running out for them.

We saw it too. I'm going to propose we go quiet for a fortnight. If the theory is right most of

them will go down with starvation and the only real threat will be newly dead. It may be

getting safer outside. Maybe we'll hear from the authorities, soon?'

Clarky stood up, 'you all need to know, the military abandoned the people, when we were at

Newcastle. Our job was to safely evacuate as many people as possible, but as the place was

getting overrun, their superiors got a communication and they withdrew to the Town Moor.

Chinook helicopters shuttled the troops away to the countryside for redeployment and we

were left. The superintendent pulled us all together and sent us home to defend ourselves and

our families, rather than be overrun and killed. He said the military had been pulled out to

defend politicians and the rich establishment, at locations all over the country. The

Superintendent was spitting fucking nails about it, screaming down the radio, when he got

the orders. The Chinooks made so much noise it drew thousands of dead out of Newcastle

and towards Gosforth and the surrounding towns. It was them who instructed people to stay

in their cars in traffic jams, rather than escape on foot, the worst thing they could have

advised. People were waiting to be eaten, not to be rescued, but it was buying time for

evacuation of the selected people. Fucking nobility, fucking filthy rich, fucking MP's. All of

us, we were abandoned by the people who should have protected us.

And what will they spend their billions on, when this is over? They haven't even saved

people who can get the country back up and running, just themselves. Just a few weeks, that's all it took to nearly wipe most people out in this country. Just one bite and you're one of them. I wonder how many survivors there are out there? Only one person in Dene View took mine and Maeve's advice about staying indoors. Poor soul was murdered doing the right thing. The rest of the people in the street are dead or missing. I stood in the fields watching the dead return to the Hartlands. The crowd was bigger than a football crowd. Thousands and thousands. I recognized some of them. The twenty-acre field was covered. You're right, Don. If they starve, like we do, we need to lay low. Let them fall with hunger. They've clearly ran out of sources of food, so they'll either die or try to migrate elsewhere. Time's running out for them.'

Midgy spoke up, 'well we found three survivors today in Bedlington and that's a good start.' Midgy held up his glass and toasted the survivors. He reached over to the cd player.

Don had set up the generator in the shed outside and he'd brought an extension cable through. Midgy skipped through the tracks of a cd he'd put into the drive. REM came on. It was the song 'it's the end of the world.' He sat back with his hands behind his neck and a huge grin on his face.

Dowser took a cushion and threw it across the room. It bounced off Midgy's head, 'For fuck's sake, Midgy, how corny is that?'

A few minutes later Connor knocked on the door and entered the doorway, 'am I missing anything? I heard the racket. You lot could wake the dead.' He put up his arms up as three cushions flew across the room and bounced off him, 'what? did I say something wrong, here? I'm new here, I certainly don't want to offend anybody.'

'Connor!' Midgy was patting the seat next to him. 'The only person here who understands my humour, take a seat here mate, let's get to know each other.' Connor nodded at Don as he headed for the settee and Don passed him a large Glenfiddich.

Connor looked around the room, as he sat beside Midgy. He looked around the people who had gone through so much to make life safe for their friends and neighbours. He knew he was finally in the right place to start anew, after his own loss.

The group of friends decided to lock down on everything, except the search for family members and they would spend tomorrow informing the residents about the situation with the dead and resume the searches the following day. The advice would be to stay out of sight of the gates and fences and keep as quiet as possible, when outside.

At five o'clock the following morning, Don locked the gate behind him, as he left the Square, He was covered in a slime - covered coat, hood up and carrying his spike and a back – pack. He made his way up the street and turned down, past the Northumberland Arms. There were more dead on the ground than the previous day, some crawling, or lying still and looking around and the ones walking, appeared slow and off balance. He knew they were still very dangerous, though, so kept a wide berth, as he passed.

Don entered the Beaufront park Estate and took a piece of paper out of his pocket, then made his way down towards Fountain Close.

As he arrived at the address on the paper, Don stood still. There were twenty or more dead walking towards him. Some brushed past, but two stood still. They stood, heads to the side sniffing the air, then simultaneously looking at him again. Don stood perfectly still, but he was becoming concerned they had detected something. He tightened his grip on the spike. One of the dead took hold of his bag and Don let the bag slip off his back.

Across the street, two Blackbirds noisily flew across the road. They were jostling for territory and all the dead turned towards them and headed in their direction.

Don picked up his bag and waited until they all reached the far side of the road, then tapped on the door. He waited a while. The downstairs of the house was boarded up and he couldn't see in.

The dead had wandered away, after the Blackbirds flew off, so Don took a crowbar out of the bag. There was a chocolate bar in the bottom of the bag, that had a torn wrapper. It must have been what had attracted the interest. He threw the bar across the street.

Don turned to Lever open the front door, just as the bedroom window opened.

A few moments later, the front door opened and Don stepped inside.

Don arrived home at eight o'clock. Jamie was in the kitchen and ran through, 'Grandad, did you find her? Was she alive?' Don sat down, 'yes, son, I found her, she's fine. How about we see if we can get the big telly connected to the Play station and do some two - player shoot – em - up's, all day? What do you say?' We can use the play station to play DVD's as well can't we?' 'Yes we can. Grandad, I'll bring it all down from my room, you sort the generator and leads.'

Clarky made his way down the stairs, after being rudely awoken by the knock on the door. He'd had far too many whiskeys, last night and hadn't planned to get out of bed until far later than this. Who the hell would want him at this time in the morning?

Clarky got to the bottom of the stairs and opened the door. Eileen Moorehouse smiled and handed him a piece of paper. It had her name and address on it and was in Clarky's handwriting.

Clarky stood looking in disbelief, as Eileen caught his eye, 'are you going to invite me in or what?' 'Well, you stink a bit.' 'Well, Ian, you can blame that on your friend, Don Mason. He insisted on painting me with Zombie shit.' 'No, no, you've stunk for a long time, Eileen, but before all this I didn't have the heart to tell you.' She stepped inside and took Clarky in her arms.' Clarky cried, 'Eileen, Maeve.' 'I know, Ian, I know. Don told me everything.'

They closed the door and went inside.

The following morning the four friends stood in Don Mason's kitchen. Midgy put his hand into the cardboard box and pulled out a folded piece of paper.

Printed in Great Britain
by Amazon

50351390R00123